One Through the Heart

The explosive new Ben Raveneau thriller.

Bones in a backyard bomb shelter reactivate a San Francisco cold case and a painful connection for Raveneau after missing Ann Coryell's desperate call for help a decade ago. But he sees something much darker in threats made by online followers of historian Coryell's writings on genocide. Nothing pieces together, but all the pieces fit … Raveneau edges closer to a core group who are certain the time for retribution is now, but will he be able to stop them in time?

Further Titles from Kirk Russell

The John Marquez series

SHELL GAMES
NIGHT GAME
DEADGAME
REDBACK *

The Ben Raveneau series

A KILLING IN CHINA BASIN *
COUNTERFEIT ROAD*
ONE THROUGH THE HEART *

**available from Severn House*

One Through The Heart

Kirk Russell

Severn House Large Print
London & New York

This first large print edition published 2014
in Great Britain and the USA by
SEVERN HOUSE PUBLISHERS LTD of
19 Cedar Road, Sutton, Surrey, England, SM2 5DA.
First world regular print edition published 2012 by
Severn House Publishers Ltd., London and New York.

British Library Cataloguing in Publication Data

Russell, Kirk, 1954- author.
One through the heart. -- (The Ben Raveneau series)
1. Raveneau, Ben (Fictitious character)--Fiction.
2. Police--California--San Francisco--Fiction. 3. Cold
cases (Criminal investigation)--California--San
Francisco--Fiction. 4. Serial murder investigation--
California--San Francisco--Fiction. 5. Detective and
mystery stories. 6. Large type books.
I. Title II. Series
813.6-dc23

ISBN-13: 9780727897374

Printed and bound in Great Britain by
T J International, Padstow, Cornwall.

One

A demolition crew found the bomb shelter. They cut the lock, opened the hatch cover, and the foreman climbed down. Then he waited a day to report what he found to San Francisco Police. His name was Matt Baylor. He was twenty-nine with a face that looked ten years older and a tattoo of vertebrae running up the left side of his neck that he kept touching as he talked with Raveneau.

'I figured one more day wasn't going to matter to those bones and we put a big beam on the hatch cover last night. No one got in there, Inspector.'

'What did you do when you were down there?'

'Looked around with a flashlight and counted the skulls like I told the dispatcher.'

'Did you touch or move anything?'

'Didn't touch anything.'

Raveneau crossed through the gutted main floor of the house with Baylor and out through an opening where French doors once opened on to the patio and terraced back gardens. The house had new owners, but for Ben Raveneau, a San Francisco Homicide inspector, it would always be Albert Lash's house. It was stucco, white-painted, two stories and big, on a slope overlooking the Presidio and San Francisco Bay.

From this patio off the kitchen or from any of the windows on this side, Lash was able to look down at the cottage he rented to Ann Coryell, a UC grad student living here and working on her PhD in nineteenth-century American history when she disappeared in 2002. Raveneau looked at the cottage below. It was stripped to its wood frame, bare studs standing in gold fall light. He looked through the roof rafters to a eucalyptus grove below in the Presidio, and then out to the bay again. He checked out the changes in the rest of the garden before following Baylor down the stone steps.

Bird bath and fountain were gone. The big camellia at the north-west corner of the house was healthy and larger. Lash was gone or gone from here, a victim himself now, confined to a wheelchair, diagnosed with ALS – Lou Gehrig's disease, amyotrophic lateral sclerosis – and living Raveneau wasn't sure where, but in an assisted living facility somewhere in the Bay Area. He was going to have to find him.

The steps ended at the patio outside the cottage, and from the chairs grouped together and paper wrappers blown up against a stone retaining wall this was where the demo crew ate lunch. A white gravel path led from the left corner of the cottage to all that was left of the garden shed, a small concrete foundation bright in sunlight, and the galvanized steel hatch cover of the bomb shelter. Fifteen feet underground were two partial skeletons and fourteen skulls, or that's what Baylor told the 911 dispatcher. Raveneau had talked to her on the drive here. He'd also run Matt Baylor's name, though he didn't know yet what had come back on that.

The two uniform officers who responded after Baylor's 911 call were out in front of the house right now. They had strung crime tape, and Raveneau took that in, the yellow tape making a ragged transit across rock roses and rosemary before falling back to the path. He stepped over it on to the concrete slab.

Raveneau's partner, Elizabeth la Rosa, his partner in the Cold Case Unit, was on her way. So was a photographer and a pair from CSI. The Medical Examiner was standing by, interested and curious and waiting on a call from Raveneau. The ME had given the forensic anthropologist a heads-up. She was a subcontractor to SFPD and lived north of here an hour and a half away, but with multiple skulls they might well need her.

Nothing said Ann Coryell's skull was among them and nothing said this was a cold case, and yet Raveneau prevailed at Homicide. He had pulled the Coryell file from the Cold Case closet and argued he should be the one to go evaluate, though now as he looked down at the galvanized steel cover he couldn't get his head around how they missed finding this ten years ago when Lash opened his house and gardens to the homicide inspectors. Raveneau had been here then. He turned to Baylor looking for an answer.

'How was it hidden?'

'See those wooden slats over there?'

Raveneau saw rectangular wooden frames

stacked on top of each other crushing plants on the lowest terrace.

'I had two hombres tearing down the shed. They found the cover when they pulled those up. They were put together like one of those puzzles that has to go together just right. They pulled them up and came and got me.'

'What time was that?'

'Eight, maybe eight thirty in the morning yesterday.'

'They came and got you and then what?'

'I got some bolt cutters and a flashlight and we cut the lock and I climbed down.'

'What did you think it was?'

'I thought it might be where they hid stuff.'

'What stuff?'

'I don't know, maybe like a wine cellar, but I didn't touch anything. My uncle is a San Francisco cop. He's got this demolition business going because he's going to be retiring soon, but he's been a cop like forever and he's taught me what not to do.'

And just like that Raveneau knew who Baylor was. Just as quickly, he decided to leave that alone for now.

'My uncle will probably chew my ass for not calling the police sooner.'

Raveneau went back to his car for a flashlight. He opened the hatch cover and laid the heavy-hinged lid down on the concrete. There was a metal pole alongside the steel rung ladder leading down that at first he mistook for a flagpole. But after studying the pulley system attached, he realized the pole was for hoisting or lowering things into the shelter.

When he grasped the steel ladder and stepped on to a rung he saw Ann Coryell's face again, the angles of her cheeks sharp, dark hair and coat wet with rain. She had already walked the eucalyptus grove just over the low stone inside the Presidio with the police officers who'd answered her call. She walked it again with Raveneau and rain had pattered on the dry strips of eucalyptus bark and made the slope slippery as they listened for a woman screaming. They didn't hear anything but he gave her his cell number in case there was anything more that night.

He told her to call at any hour and she did. She called at 3:14 a.m. and he slept through it, the ringer accidentally or clumsily off on his cell. That message was the last known moment she was alive. Raveneau had never forgiven himself, probably never would. He stared at Baylor a moment then climbed on to the rungs of the ladder and descended into darkness.

Two

The air was cool and musty with mold. Raveneau didn't smell decomposition. He smelled concrete dust and rotting canvas and an earthiness that might be the bones. A faint faraway whistling came from a ventilation shaft that he located now with the flashlight beam. Boot tracks marked the dust, and following those he spotted small pieces of mud and figured the prints were Baylor's. He shined the light on the concrete wall to his left, worked the perimeter, touching on folding chairs leaned against a wall, a metal card table of a type he hadn't seen in decades, and then a steel cot with a stained mattress.

He took several steps toward it. Straps attached to the frame looked like old auto seat-belts. He held the light on the mattress and then the floor under the cot. As he brought it back to the straps, he exhaled slowly and stepped closer, the light steady now on dark stains on the mattress. He moved the light back to the concrete floor beneath the cot, the stains there, and then squatted and held the beam on the underside of the mattress before standing and stepping back.

He took in what surrounded the cot, a chair with a rattan seat, a metal stand with a stethoscope and blood pressure cuff, both coated in dust. He guessed neither had been moved in a long while. He swept the domed concrete ceiling and brought the light back to the stethoscope before continuing on. He got the parameters of the space. It was bigger than any fallout or bomb shelter he remembered, a Cadillac of a backyard shelter. Along the ceiling were several cracks moist and lined with gray-green mold.

Now he rested the light on the first of the skeletons. Half or more of the ribs were missing. The other skeleton was without pelvic bones or the bones of the feet. Both lay on rotting gray blankets and each blanket had folded clothes, shoes, one pair that looked like a woman's sandals and the other ancient black boots, hardened and twisted.

'Baylor lied to me,' he said to no one, but the tracks were there. He moved the light off the skeletons and on to thick white candles that sat on the concrete floor, wax puddled in front of them, the candles worm-like. Beyond the candles, stacked against the concrete wall, were three rows of yellowed skulls, the skulls tipped back against the concrete wall one on top of the other. He counted fourteen, same as Baylor. Each row up was shorter than the one underneath, six along the bottom then five then three. He moved the flashlight beam along the upper three and on the teeth looking for gold caps along the back molars. Was one of these Ann Coryell's?

The first two were missing most of their teeth and he moved closer, surprised how much it affected him, the rise of emotion, sorrow, and the recurring sense of having failed her. Several skulls had desiccated skin, hair hanging. He couldn't remember seeing any reports in recent years of grave robbing but skulls were also trafficked online. He knelt and with the light checked the teeth of three. Their ground down molars made him think they were elderly and he abandoned an idea this was a trophy display of a serial murderer. This was something different, a gathering, a statement of some kind.

When he returned the light again to the upper skulls he saw a flash of reflection as the light bounced off something shiny. He stepped closer and was fairly sure it was glass but decided to wait on the CSI team and moved back toward the steel ladder and stopped. He took several photos and scanned the space once more, two bunk beds, the set-up around the cot with the bloodstained mattress. He moved as close as he felt he could to the cot and stood a long moment looking at it. Then he turned to the other things in the shelter, canned food, a contraption below the ventilation duct that appeared to be something you sat on and pedaled. He saw more stored goods, leaking batteries, and Korean War vintage water storage containers.

Fallout was like pumice in consistency. Gamma rays coming off it all traveled straight. You needed to get where the gamma rays couldn't get to you and wait for the radiation level to die down, so you could then climb to the surface and start civilization from scratch. He was young when these shelters were getting built and judging from the contents he guessed this one dated to the 1960s.

He moved the light beam up to the airshaft again and remembered Coryell's dark eyes as she described faint screams lost to the rain. She was sure enough to call 911. He remembered Albert Lash inviting him back to the house for a drink after the homicide investigation stalled, Lash a likeable storyteller and tenured history professor at UC Berkeley best known for writing pop culture history. His books sold well and very well. Raveneau read several after Coryell disappeared. Lash made the characters interesting enough and you got a story and a hook in the present. He wrote a history of San Francisco through the eyes of the San Francisco Police Department; he started researching that one before she disappeared and picked it up again after remains and clothing found on a western slope of Mt. Tamalpais were identified and DNA confirmed in the spring of 2004 the remains belonged to Ann Coryell. Her skull was never found.

When Lash was forced to take a leave of absence from UC he taunted SFPD by deepening his research for the police viewpoint book. He interviewed homicide inspectors, including Raveneau, and they couldn't have been more cooperative with him. It was a dance. Raveneau drank gimlets with Lash. He sat in Lash's library, Lash the literary squire in those conversations, the professor confident in his grasp of the elements of truth. Lash praised Ann Coryell for brilliance and pitied her instability, calling it the price of genius. Before her remains were found he held that she fled the pressure of her thesis and grad school.

Lash said, 'I write books for people who watch TV. I'm as ordinary as them, but Ann saw history. It blew through her like a wind. She understood the core of us more than I ever will.'

A minor Coryell cult formed after her death. That had to do with her blog, her writings, and after her death, a book. He brought the flashlight beam to the cot one last time and then to the skulls. Raveneau had seen three satanic murder sites in twenty years and a few other cult killings, but he didn't see cult here. The candles and cot and meticulous arranging of the skeletal bones and belongings on the rotted Army blankets gave him the feeling the skulls were arranged to communicate something distinct and possibly far worse.

He lingered at the base of the ladder until it came to him. This was Cambodia and the killing fields, or Rwanda and the inside of a church. He was looking at homage to genocide, a nod to the ninety thousand stacked skulls Genghis Khan left at the gates of Delhi. The cold air settled around him and he held the light to the skulls one last time then climbed the rungs.

Three

Hugh Neilley was one of the two SF homicide inspectors who worked the Coryell killing. He was also the uncle Baylor mentioned and an old friend of Raveneau's, which was a lot of coincidence if Raveneau believed in coincidence. Hugh was still with SFPD though not with the Homicide Detail. His homicide career ended in 2004 when he volunteered to leave after his drinking became an open problem. Friends arranged for a transfer to the Southern Precinct, and he had been there ever since though was due to retire at the end of this year. That was less than three months away.

Hugh sounded as if he'd just been laughing at something as he picked up the phone and asked Raveneau, 'Where the hell have you been? I thought I'd be back at Homicide trying to figure out what happened to you. I've left you two messages in the last two weeks. Don't I rate at all anymore?'

'I've been swamped. We cleared another old one with a DNA match and I was in New Mexico finding our guy when you left the first message.'

'What about the second?'

'I'm calling you right now. I'm out at Albert

Lash's house. I just met your nephew. His crew demolished a garden shed yesterday morning and found an old bomb shelter with skulls and two partial skeletons in it. Stop me if you already know this. Did your nephew tell you this last night? He didn't call us until this morning.'

'No, he didn't tell me, but we've been arguing. Is her skull in there?'

'I don't know yet. There are fourteen skulls.'

'What?'

'Yeah, that's the count, and we've got everybody on their way here. The hatch cover was under a lattice of deck boards inside the garden shed.'

'And we missed that when we searched Lash's place?'

'Yes.'

'I can't believe that. I'm driving out there right now. I need to see this.'

'Don't come out yet. It's going to be a zoo here the rest of today and into tonight. I just want to know if your nephew told anybody yesterday what he found. The demo crew here, these four young Hispanic guys, claim he didn't say anything to them.'

'Those guys are all scared of police. They're all going to say they don't know anything.'

'We separated them. We talked to them. La Rosa is very fluent and she doesn't think he said a word to them. I'm not reading anything into it, but it's odd. Why don't you ask him about it?'

'You know I will. I'll let you know.'

Raveneau was willing to leave it at that. He knew plenty about Hugh's saga with his nephew. He knew Hugh would question him hard.

'I've got to come out there, Ben. I can't take this. I was in that garden shed when we searched his place. Well, you know that, you were there, but I was in that garden shed. I stood on those boards. I remember that, and I was there last Saturday. It's not on the plans. The architect missed it. That garden shed was full of old pesticide bottles. The contractor got a hazardous waste company out there to clean it out.'

Raveneau wasn't close enough to Hugh anymore or, more to the point, Hugh wasn't close enough to the homicide office anymore for Raveneau to say much more, yet Hugh was one of the two original homicide inspectors, so he would be briefed. He was going to be in on the investigation and Raveneau decided to tell him about the cellphone.

'We've found an iPhone with the skulls that wasn't even manufactured until after Lash was in a wheelchair. Someone else has been in there. The phone number is an active account.'

'I'll see you there. I'm coming out now.'

'No, you're not.'

Raveneau listened to Hugh a little longer then broke off the call. He spent the next two hours with the coroner, the Chief Medical Examiner, and a forensic anthropologist. The ME, Hayes, decided to tag the skulls with numbers and then bring them out individually in body bags after the CSI crew finished. The fire station over on Grove Street brought in more lights for the CSI pair. The iPhone, the glass face of which Raveneau's flashlight beam had caught, went into a clear plastic bag and then into Raveneau's trunk. The phone was going with him.

A sheet was slid under each partial skeleton to lift them away from the floor. The rotted blankets, the clothing, shoes, all the personal effects came out, then the cot and mattress. The leaking batteries were left and the swollen cans of food, as well as the rest of the furniture and kitchen utensils and supplies. The candles were bagged individually with the hope there might be touch DNA.

The iPhone was on a trajectory of its own now. It got checked first for trace DNA and turned out to be wiped clean. Raveneau plugged it in and charged it and la Rosa started chasing down the Verizon account. It was registered to a corporation with a Belmont apartment building address though the phone had a New York prefix. A single phone number was in Contacts and before calling it they talked it through.

'Someone knew the construction was coming,' Raveneau said, 'and the phone is there for us. Let's call it. It's what we're expected to do.'

They moved into an interview room and put the iPhone on speakerphone so they could tape the conversation. La Rosa went quickly through it once more. No apps, photos, email accounts, nothing but a single name under Contacts. The name input was Call Me.

'Ready?' she asked and without waiting tapped the phone number. The phone rang four times, followed by a click followed by a humming, and they heard static and a recording started to play.

'Old school,' la Rosa whispered, meaning the outdated answering machine, and Raveneau nodded. The voice was male, disguised but not muffled, the tone matter of fact.

'Money borrowed is repaid with money. Lives taken must be repaid with lives. America owes for the genocide of the western expansion. A first payment will be made very soon in San Francisco.'

It ended there, clicked off, and the connection broke. They listened to it twice more and then la Rosa looked up with puzzlement, asking, 'Why do we get all the freaks? Why don't they stay on the east coast or Texas or wherever they're from? The genocide of the western expansion, I have no clue what that means. Did he mean the Western Addition? Is this a racial deal?'

'I get it.'

'You know what he's talking about?'

'Yeah, it's how we dealt with the Native American tribes. It's about the Indian Wars. Ann Coryell, the woman who lived in Lash's guest house, wrote about unreconciled genocide and what it does to our collective psyche.'

'Excuse me?'

'She wrote about what genocide does to a society.'

La Rosa sat on that for a little bit then asked, 'We're supposed to pay now for something that happened in the nineteenth century?'

'That's what he's saying, that's what I hear. Ann Coryell's thesis was that if genocide isn't acknowledged and answered it never goes away.

A society carries it and its culture is stunted.'

'What are we getting into here?'

'Right now we need to get a search warrant to get into an apartment in Belmont.'

Four

The apartment building was soot-colored and four stories. The property manager, Lisa Berge of Berge Properties, was parked out front along the curb in a shiny black Lexus, and after a polite exchange of cards Raveneau handed her the search warrant. She read it with a look of disdain but didn't comment until they were upstairs and she was unlocking the door of 4F.

'I resent the search warrant but I'm not surprised and I called our lawyer yesterday after I got off the phone with you. Police are very heavy-handed nowadays. My grandfather started this business and we've survived three generations by keeping our word and protecting our reputation.'

'We don't want to hurt your reputation,' la Rosa said. 'We're responding to a phone threat.'

Raveneau didn't hear what came after that. On a counter in the kitchen was a cordless phone cradled in a vintage black plastic answering machine. He pulled on latex gloves and used a pencil eraser to push the button to replay the recording. Nothing played. He rewound. He pressed play again then checked the connections. The answering machine was simple and familiar. He used to have one just like it and didn't miss it at all. He turned to Lisa Berge.

'What happened to the tape? Has the renter been here?'

'No, and we cancelled his lease. He won't be back.'

Raveneau checked the machine again before disconnecting it. He paused as he realized the tape was missing. Then he slid it into an evidence bag and searched the rest of the apartment as la Rosa talked with Berge in the corridor. The apartment was a one-bedroom and nearly empty. A flat screen TV faced a couch and coffee table. It could have been a hotel room, except for one thing. On a nightstand was a black plastic iPhone case. Like a scavenger hunt he thought, geo-caching. They were being led along, and he stared at it knowing that he was going to slip it carefully into a bag and they would take it with them and there wasn't going to be any DNA or prints. It would be as clean as the iPhone.

None of this fit with the investigation he imagined. He shouldn't have imagined anything but so many times over the decade since Coryell disappeared he had turned different ideas in his head.

On the drive here la Rosa asked, 'Why did you give Ann Coryell your cell number if the officers were already there and writing a report?'

'Because I knew she wasn't going to call 911 again. It was her third call in a week and the responding officers were pretty close to believing Lash. They were on his porch when I got there. I could hear him. Lash was selling that she was brilliant but fragile, and he invited all three officers to come over for a drink when they were off duty. He wanted their stories. He told them about the book he was writing. Coryell was scared but determined, and I don't think she knew what to do next.'

'And you slept through her call?'

'I don't really know what happened. I was tired. It was late. I ate a little and drank a couple of glasses of wine before I went to bed. The phone was on the nightstand next to the bed, but I may have accidentally turned off the ringer. I've thought about it over and over, and I still think about it.'

'Why didn't you work the case after her remains were found?'

'They were found on Mount Tamalpais thirteen months later in November 2003 and it was a Marin County case until fingerprints and clothing suggested it was her and DNA testing was done. Those results didn't come back until April the following year. I went to the lieutenant and tried to get the case assigned to me, but he knew about the phone call I missed and was worried a defense attorney could make something of that later. That might have been true then though not now.'

He glanced over at her and said, 'Hugh Neilley and Ray Alcott caught the case. Did you ever know Ray Alcott?'

'No.'

'Hugh and Ray Alcott worked it for six or

seven months but it got stranded when Hugh left his homicide desk and transferred to the Southern Precinct. Hugh was going through a divorce and drinking hard and I don't know how much work he put into it. He wouldn't talk to me about it. Neither would Alcott after Hugh told him not to. Alcott got a new partner and the Coryell investigation went into the Cold Case closet.'

'When did you first hear about followers of Coryell, this cult thing?'

'I'm not sure it's a cult. It's definitely a following and it was academic at first and over the years I think it has grown into something else. But I wouldn't really know any more, though now that we're working this you should read her. It's all still online. She had a blog and published a few papers. A small press put out a book with her writings and for awhile I think her disappearance made her more mysterious. Do you remember the media storm when Lash became a person of interest?'

'Sure, but I've never read anything she wrote.'

'She was against violence but wrote about a spiritual cleansing and acknowledging what we did to the Indian tribes as something we had to do. Her take was we were always going to defeat the tribes. Our force and numbers were far superior. We reneged on treaties and she believed there was genocide, though it wasn't called that then. The word genocide didn't come along until the twentieth century. Plenty of people in the nineteenth century knew that the reservation system was soul-destroying and amoral. She didn't believe the truth was in

America's history books.'

'I'm getting that. So where do we go with this now?'

'We go back to the beginning of the case. We start with Hugh Neilley and Alcott. I'm going to call Hugh now.'

When Hugh answered, Raveneau said, 'Ray Alcott says he doesn't remember anything and you never forget anything, so it starts with you. We need at least a couple of hours to go through everything. We'd like to do that this afternoon. Are you good with coming upstairs?'

'How long have we known each other? Almost thirty years, right? Does that mean anything to you?'

'Sure, but this is the place to go through the files.'

'I don't ever want to set foot in the homicide office ever again. I'd rather sit down with you somewhere. Bring the files and you can brief your partner later.'

'It needs to be here. Call me back with a time that works for you.'

Hugh hung up and Raveneau laid his phone down.

'Did you just try to make him angry?' la Rosa asked.

'Yeah, I did. I know him. We need to get him talking. I think he knows things that aren't in the files. He and Alcott didn't do her justice and he knows I feel that way. It's going to get ugly.'

'Great.'

Five

Hugh Neilley was at his desk in the Southern Precinct on the first floor of the Hall of Justice and very aware of the time. His heart raced and he was dizzy with a tinny ringing in his ears. He tried the deep slow breathing that was supposed to lower his blood pressure. He didn't expect this from Raveneau. Neither did he want to sit and dredge through the Coryell files. He delayed another fifteen minutes before crossing to the elevators and riding up.

Raveneau and la Rosa were waiting for him in their little Cold Case Unit office. Ben suggested they use the kitchen with its long table as a place to talk and Neilley shook his head. He started to point a finger and fought the impulse. He rested a hand on Raveneau's desk.

'No, if we're going to do this, let's do it right. Let's talk in an interview room with the tape running and I want a copy of the tape afterwards. I want your word on that and I don't want to get broadsided with questions about a case that's eight or nine years old. Ben, I know what it was to you, but for me it was just another murder investigation. I don't remember all the details of every case I worked and I don't have anything on this one that's not already in the files.'

'No problem, Hugh, we'll videotape you. We'll do it in an interview room.'

Neilley glared at him but thought, *just calm down. You're making too much of this*. He followed them to the interview box and Raveneau made a show of turning on the tape before they went in.

'Coffee, Hugh?'

'Nothing for me but let me ask you a question before we get started.'

'Go ahead.'

'Is it right for you to be on this investigation, Ben? You talked for years about how you let her down by missing that phone call. You were very affected and I can say that as your friend. I think you still are. If you ask me, you're too close to the case. Why don't you give it to somebody else? You've got a couple of other inspectors on your Cold Case Unit, right? What do you think about that?'

'Time has gone by, Hugh.'

'Not for you.'

But he was never going to rattle Raveneau, though Raveneau wouldn't like that comment sitting there right at the start of the videotape, and Neilley stayed with it until Raveneau cut him off.

'How did you get the demolition work at Lash's house?'

'Are you kidding, we're going to talk about my side business?'

'We're not here for that but I'm curious.'

Neilley took a deep breath. 'I bid for the work, Ben. That's how it works out in the big world.

You're not that far away from retirement and you're going to need something yourself because it's guaranteed they'll cut our pensions. Otherwise you'll end up working part time as a bank security guard or worse. Do you want to greet people when they come in to make their deposits and chase away assholes parking in the bank lot while they do their other shopping?'

'I want to know if you had any reservations about taking the job.'

'None.'

'Nothing?'

'Don't get sanctimonious with me. I got a call from the contractor. We've done other work for him and I wasn't going to turn him down. If I do that, someone else gets the job. I recognized the address – of course I recognized the address – but it's just a house now. I met him on-site and we walked the project on a Saturday when I wasn't at Southern. I looked in the guest cottage and there was nothing in it but an old bed and some furniture. It's just another remodeling project. There was nothing to say she ever lived there and obviously I didn't know about the bomb shelter.'

'Did you talk with your nephew?'

'About what?'

'About why he waited to report what he found in the bomb shelter.'

'I talked to him and I'm going to talk to him more about it. He made a bad decision and I apologize for it. We're behind on the job and the contractor is pressuring us. He's threatening to backcharge us because his contract with the client has got a tight time frame. Matt didn't want the guys getting distracted by a police investigation. He wanted to get done in that area and then call the police. That's what he did. He finished with the garden shed and cottage and moved the crew back up to the house.'

'He told me he didn't touch anything when he was inside the bomb shelter.'

'He's got his issues but he doesn't lie.'

'He lied to me.'

'How do you know that?'

'I saw his tracks. One of your crew was spraying water to keep down the dust and he tracked some mud.'

'But he didn't try to hide his tracks, did he? So he knew you'd see where he walked. I think he was curious and he walked around and when you questioned him he exaggerated a little. He wanted to please you and he was trying to tell you he didn't take anything or touch any evidence. He knows better. But what did you expect him to do when he got down there and saw what was there? Anyone would have taken a closer look. I would have.' Hugh sighed. 'He's not as bad as I make him out to be sometimes. You've heard me talk about the problems with trying to get him straightened out, and that's probably colored your thinking. But what's the big deal here? Do you think Matt took something?'

Hugh Neilley stared at Raveneau trying to figure out what this was really about. He couldn't read anything in Raveneau's eyes. Raveneau could be a cold sonofabitch when he wanted to be.

Raveneau slid the case files toward the center of the table. 'OK, let's move to yours and Alcott's investigation. Why did you move off of Albert Lash? What cleared him?'

'The answer is we didn't have anything that connected him to her disappearance and he had a pretty good alibi – not airtight, but better than most. He liked to work in the early morning. He'd get up, make coffee, and his housekeeper would let herself in at six thirty and make his breakfast. We interviewed the housekeeper several times and she said Lash lived by that pattern. She said he was like a clock and we used her testimony and the cook and the gardeners and all the other little people who made the great man's house work. We mapped out his days using them and decided it was very unlikely he abducted her, took her over to Mount Tamalpais and killed her in the time frame we were looking at. For a variety of reasons we came to that conclusion, but a lot of it was verifying his statements to us through the people who worked for him.

'The housekeeper got off by two thirty in the afternoon and had a son in elementary school that she was able to pick up after school every day, so she liked the early hours. She could always tell how long he'd been up by the coffee pot, how much coffee was left, how dried out the grounds were. He told us he was up a little before five that morning and working. She guessed about the same time when we asked her, and his editor in New York got an email at five fifty-seven Pacific Time.'

He looked from Raveneau to la Rosa. He didn't know much about her, knew she was at Vice before she came here. He didn't particularly like the way she watched him and sat silent.

'Of course, we didn't know about a bomb shelter with a bloody cot in it back then. We were imagining her being incapacitated and then moved. The Marin coroner thought she was shot on the mountain and that's where our ME came down too. We couldn't see little leprechaun Lash carrying her very far so we ruled him out of moving her on the mountain. He wasn't big enough.

'We also had other reasons to believe the killing happened on the mountain. Remember, the dogs scented on a spot where the soil had residue that may have been her blood and that was after thirteen months and a winter. It wasn't conclusive but it was corroborative from the angle we were looking at. And Lash was cooperative. You were at the house for the search, Ben. You remember the garden shed. You looked in there too, didn't you? Did you see a hatch cover to a bomb shelter? You missed it too and you were looking for anything that would tie him in. She may have been alive on that cot underneath you when you missed a three-foot wide metal hatch covered by boards. How do you feel about that now?'

Now Neilley felt more confident. He thought Raveneau didn't really know what he was doing here. He obviously didn't have any real questions about his and Alcott's investigation.

'At the time we concluded it wasn't possible

that he stored her body and moved it later. Some of that's in the file but in notes that might be hard to read, but you'll interview Alcott also, right?'

'If we can get him in here. He doesn't seem interested.'

'That's because we already went the extra mile. There's nothing more to say and he knows you've been going over these files for years. You probably know them better than me. I don't have the Coryell murder hanging over me like you.'

'That's true, and you don't seem to care much about solving it now.'

'Fuck you.' Neilley felt anger surge, heat rise in his face. He flipped open the top file and found his summary notes and shoved them at Raveneau. 'Where do you get off saying that?' he asked. 'Who are you to say what I feel or care about? I mean, you of all people.' He turned to la Rosa. 'If you want to go through the timeline and how we got to where we did, that's fine. We can do that. But I'm not here to take shit because Alcott and I didn't solve this one or all of us missed a bomb shelter.'

La Rosa didn't say anything and he was close to asking her if she spoke English. But he didn't do it. He went somewhere else instead.

'I'll tell you what's really not in the file, and Alcott will back me up on this. When we didn't get anywhere, Alcott wanted to question you. He didn't understand why you took so much interest in her. He wanted to pull you in and really grill you. That's no bullshit. He'll say the same thing and that's probably why he doesn't want to come in now. I've never told you that before have I, Ben? That's out of respect for our friendship, but now you have it on tape. You were pretty close to becoming a suspect. Probably wouldn't have helped your career here, and I kept that from happening.'

Raveneau looked at him wondering if that was true, then asked, 'Did the Marin detectives make that same connection to me?'

'They didn't make any connections. That pair couldn't connect their car keys to their car.'

'How did you get a warrant to get into Lash's house if you had nothing on him?'

'You already know that answer.'

'It's not in the file.'

'Lash gave us access. We didn't need a warrant and, for that matter, he wanted to be our friend. You know that too and you know the answers to everything you've asked so far and all I'm getting out of this meeting is a waste of time. Lash was working on a book where he wanted interviews with SFPD officers. Not only did he not want to alienate us, he wanted to charm us. He wanted to get to know us. Of course, once we got in there we went through everything. But you were there too. You know all that. You did the same thing with him. Lash's big mistake was he slept with her. If he hadn't we still would have looked at him in the same way. And the press fueled that too. They liked the love affair gone bad angle. The media really got on him yet he still cooperated with us in every way.'

'And became a friend of yours.'

'Easy there, Ben, and I wasn't any different

than anyone else. I did get to know him and I did like him and the more I looked at the case the more confident I became he wasn't who we were looking for. Also, his book thing was legit. Those interviews with us showed up in his book. If I remember correctly you've got a copy on your shelf.'

'When is the last time you saw Albert Lash?'

'I don't remember exactly when; several years ago, I guess, before he sold the house, before he got sick. I couldn't tell you where he is today. But why don't we just call it like it was? He figured out fairly fast that I had a drinking problem and he fed that so he could get what he needed from me. He never got any information about the investigation from me but that was the game, trying to get it. Or that was the tease. He kept trying and as long as he asked I stayed curious about him.

'That's part of why I accepted his invitations. Good food and free booze and in the back of my head the Coryell case. He used me until he didn't need me for his research anymore and he asked the occasional question about the investigation to keep my interest.'

'What sort of questions did he ask?'

'I don't remember.'

'So give us the date you last saw him.'

'I can't remember when.'

'What year?'

'I don't know. When did his book come out? A year before that, I think, but I could be wrong. I went by his house about once a week for awhile, but so did a lot of cops.'

'So when was the last time you saw him? Was it one year after the investigation ended or later?'

'Is there some reason you're asking? I feel like this is a fishing expedition on a boat without a skipper. Who cares when I last saw Albert Lash? When did *you* last see him?'

'We'll interview Lash soon and I want to know before I ask him. I want some hard facts on our last contacts with him, since he knew about the bomb shelter and even if he didn't know about the skulls he knew about the cot. He kept that secret safe and now we're going to have another run at him. I believe you were his last police contact. That's why I'm asking. You say he used you. I want to know how long he used you and who else was there at the poker games and the barbecues and all of it.'

That was Raveneau starting to light up and Hugh stared hard at him deciding how he wanted to deal with that.

'The answer is after his book came out the invitations stopped. So I guess it was the year after the book came out.'

'The book came out in 2008.'

'There you go, 2009, and if that's different than what I told you a minute ago, then go with 2009, and that's it, Ben. I'm done here.'

Neilley stood and his chair scraped the floor behind him. He waited to see if they'd stop him and no one said anything until he was halfway to the door. He knew he was overreacting but he didn't like the tone and couldn't stand being in the homicide office. All of his best days on the force were here. Now he was just pushing paper and marking time. He thought about his long friendship with Raveneau. Well, that could go too. Raveneau had better figure that out and fast. He'd never had that thought before, but it was true. If Raveneau kept this up, he was done with him. I'll call him later today and tell him that, he thought. I'm not revisiting those times or all that led up to his getting kicked off the Detail. It all ended with the Coryell case and not Raveneau, not anyone was going to drag him back through that again.

Six

Raveneau stepped on to the porch and knocked lightly on Marion Coryell's door. The cedar-shingled walls of the house were stained the same dark brown, the wisteria wrapping a corner porch post with a trunk now as thick as his forearm. He heard her footsteps and when the door opened he was looking into eyes a piercing black, the planes of her cheekbones more gaunt and flint-like a decade later, though her long black hair was now streaked with gray. Blue jay feathers were tied in the last few inches of her hair. She caught Raveneau looking at those.

'I haven't lost my mind, Inspector. I'm just remembering things I left behind a long time ago. Come in, and I have to tell you I'm not surprised it's you.'

The immediate feeling he got was that Ann Coryell's mother wasn't any more at peace now than then. She led him to her living room and after they sat she removed the bird feathers as if they now embarrassed her or Raveneau judged her for wearing them.

Raveneau had jeans, shoes, and a watch he wanted her to look at. Nothing said they were Ann's, but they were in the shelter. High on the left front pocket of the jeans was an octagonal embroidery design. The shoes were plain flats and a nondescript faded dark blue color and the watch had a light chain link of some alloy and a distinct face she might recognize. He took a breath and then explained finding the bomb shelter though not everything in it. He didn't say anything about the stained mattress but the media had the story now of the skulls. She would learn about those soon enough just from watching TV.

'Are you saying it was always there that close to the cottage where Ann was?'

'Yes.'

'Please, no, please don't say she was there.'

'We don't know yet.'

Her fingers freed the last feather and she rocked back and forth very slowly, almost imperceptibly in her chair. For a minute or more he wasn't sure she was aware of his presence.

'Didn't I say it was him? It was him after all, wasn't it? The one inspector was a drunk and the other let himself be told what to do. I grew up around alcoholism. It's what part of my family became. I have Oglala Sioux blood and the Oglala went to the reservations. The reservation system destroyed the tribe. The reservation system was a trick to destroy all of the tribes. And I'm not saying that as a Sioux. I don't have enough blood to do that. It's just the truth.

'Down the street one of our neighbors built a bomb shelter and warned all the neighbors to do the same. He built it himself with the help of his sons. He was certain nuclear war was inevitable but the Vietnam War came instead and both of his boys died there. He didn't live but another few years himself. How does a group of police officers searching miss a bomb shelter?'

'We've been asking ourselves that.'

'I think it's a lack of competence. Please forgive me, Inspector, I just seem to say what I think now. Where are the things you brought?'

'In my car, and they're in clear plastic bags so we don't contaminate them with our DNA. They'll get tested but I'd like you to look at them first, though you don't have to.'

'You hope to find who killed her so you feel better about yourself.'

'That's certainly there, Marion.'

'Forgive me if I am becoming old and bitter. There were so many lies I believed when I was younger and I don't believe in any of them now, any more than I believe in the lie that knowing who killed her will free my heart.'

Marion Coryell was originally from North Platte, Nebraska, and met her husband after moving to California. He remembered Hugh telling him what she told the inspectors, that becoming pregnant with Ann was a miracle that happened the year she turned forty. Her husband was dead; his photo and a watercolor portrait of Ann were on either end of the fireplace mantel. The room held the same furniture, older but not more used. The lamp by the armchair, the book and magazines, her place seemed to be the same as when he was last here.

'Promises were made before and nothing came of them. Things were said to me that did not come true. I always knew that it was him. I told the police then. I told them and they said they were looking closely at him, but they did nothing. I'm not sure any good will come of what you are doing now, but I will help you if I can. I don't believe what you're doing will change anything, but I will help you.'

She lifted her right hand and pointed for a moment toward a hallway.

'In her bedroom are all the things she left behind. Sometimes they make me sad and sometimes they help. In the first year I slept in that room. It was what I had to do, and someday I will let go of all of her things. If these clothes you've found are hers what will it prove other than like those things in her room they are things she left behind? Does he know you've found these bones?'

'Albert Lash?'

'Yes.'

'Not yet, but he will soon. He's in an assisted living facility now, Marion. He has ALS and is unable to move his limbs. He isn't going anywhere and we'll question him there.'

'I'm glad he is sick. I know that's not accepted, but that's how I feel and I hope the emptiness ahead is frightening to him. I'll look at the things you brought now. I'll do what I can to help you.'

Raveneau returned in a few minutes. She lifted each bag and held it as if the weight of it told her something. When she put the jeans down she said, 'Ann was at college and had been for awhile. She bought her own clothes and I just don't remember whether I've seen these or not.'

After studying the watch, she shook her head. She picked up the bag with the shoes and turned the shoes over so she could study their soles.

'I do not remember these shoes but this is the way that her shoes wore down. Do you see this here on the heel?' She picked up the watch again. 'This was hers. Yes, this was hers.'

'Are you certain?'

'Yes.'

Raveneau watched the fierceness die from her eyes after she recognized the watch. She told him the story of where it came from and rose slowly to her feet afterwards. She reached for a cane, explaining that she had fallen nine months ago and broken a hip that bothered her still.

'I'll walk out with you,' she said, and Raveneau read that as a signal she couldn't take this any farther today. But as they got out to her porch she surprised him, asking him to sit with her on the porch bench a few minutes.

'Ann had a problem when she was fourteen which at first we thought was adolescence and the changes, but her doctor said no. He advised a psychological evaluation because she said she was hearing voices and told the doctor that dead people were talking to her. They wanted to diagnose her as schizophrenic and to stop that we pulled her out of public school and put her in a private school. She wouldn't have had any chance in life if she'd been diagnosed as a schizophrenic. But then she wouldn't have gone to college and met Professor Lash.

'Every day I am so sad. I still think about her all the time. She found a way to get around her problems and she would have done so many things. I am so sorry he took that from her. He seduced her and when she refused to sleep with him anymore he became aggressive. I told her to move out but she was complicated and proud to have this famous professor mentoring her. She found me pessimistic and negative, but I could see him for what he was. When he offered her that guest cottage she called me and was so excited and I ruined it for her by arguing with her, telling her she shouldn't move there. Think of what he did. The mentoring was all a game for him.'

'Marion, there's something else I want to talk with you about. I'm wondering about people who may have approached you about Ann. I'm particularly interested in anyone who has repeatedly contacted you about Ann's life or writings.'

'Many have.'

'Has anyone come here? Have any come to visit you?'

'Over the years several have.'

'Anything you can remember about anyone who has visited about Ann, I'd like to know about. Will you call me if someone comes to mind?'

'I'm a good judge of character, Inspector, and I haven't talked with anyone who disturbed me.'

'Can you give me any names of anyone who has visited you more than once?'

'I'd rather not, right now.'

'Why not?'

'Ann is gone and her ideas are carried by some small group of people and maybe in time they will give those ideas to others and her ideas will spread. The people who carry her ideas are like seeds that may grow into trees and if so her ideas will live. That is how I see it now.'

Raveneau thought she had someone in mind but she shook her head and took his card saying she would think it over. He felt her watching him walk to his car and then heard the front door close just as he got in.

Seven

Rather than catch the 101 southbound and return to San Francisco he drove through San Anselmo and on up to Fairfax and the road that ran out through watershed and skirted the shoreline of Alpine Lake before climbing steeply through trees to the spine of Mount Tamalpais. From there you could go left and follow the ridge to the summit or over and down to Highway 1 and the coast. Raveneau did neither. He eased off the road and parked between two redwoods near the start of a trailhead sign.

Both Marin detectives were dead, one of a heart attack, the other drowning in rough surf on a long-awaited vacation to Antigua. That left Hugh Neilley and Ray Alcott. Alcott was happy to talk about the RV he was restoring and equipping with rooftop solar panels. He and his wife planned an extensive tour of the national parks next spring and summer, starting with the desert parks, Zion, Bryce, the Grand Canyon, places where the summer heat would be too much for his wife later. Raveneau learned about the new tires going on the RV, but nothing about the Coryell investigation, and Alcott's explicit message was that he was retired.

Raveneau started south on the trail and was

soon on the open flank of the mountain where the rye grass was pale brown, knee high and rustled as he walked across and down. At the horizon a thin fog colored gold as the sun lowered. He found the offshoot trail he was looking for and soon was well down the slope, hesitating now, stopping as he looked for the Y-shaped oak he remembered.

He spotted the oak, the crooked Y a third of the way up, the tree taller and fuller. When he reached the tree he reoriented himself again with two steep ravines, and then worked his way down to where the clearing had been and where brush grew now. Last night he watched the video made of the kill site and knew he was in the right spot now. He also reviewed tape of an Albert Lash interview done in the old homicide office. Lash's left hand had a faint tremor and he wondered if that was nervousness, as it was read as then, or whether it was a precursor of the disease that left him crippled now.

But Lash didn't make the phone threat. Lash didn't burn the candles or leave an iPhone and in part Raveneau made the trip up here to try to get his head around the difference between now and then. He ticked through various ideas: that she was killed here but walked down at gunpoint or under some threat by Lash, or that he had help, or that she was abducted as she went once again back into the eucalyptus grove trying to locate where the screams came from. The unnamed, unknown, random abduction was where Alcott and Hugh finally settled. But they had no evidence of that. What they had was a lack of evidence of anything else.

Raveneau looked down to the coast highway below. A car came into view and disappeared again. Twilight wasn't far away, the light softening on the ocean and the water turning from blue to gray. He didn't have any new insights about why she was brought here. It was likely just that it was relatively remote, a gunshot wouldn't be heard and animals would find the body first. They had.

Was she murdered because of her writings? Was it someone who read her blog and became enraged? Sure, that was possible. They were out there. Coryell wrote that genocide is a cancer in our collective psyche. She drew from the Holocaust and cited the French dispute now with Turkey over acknowledging the slaughter of Armenians nearly a hundred years ago, her point being that it doesn't go away. It doesn't leave us until we face and acknowledge the wrong.

Raveneau took a last look at the ocean and then turned. He thought of her, youthful, frightened and rain-soaked, yet vibrant, standing in the doorway of Lash's guest cottage. He began to climb the slope. He spoke to her. I have not forgotten you. He climbed toward the Y-shaped oak and was startled to see a man standing there.

As he got close, he saw the man was waiting for him. He saw a white guy in his mid thirties, tall, thin, long-legged and slightly stooped at the shoulders. He wore glasses with the popular black frames of the moment. Narrow blonde sideburns crept down a long head and he sported a little bit of a goatee, also trimmed narrow. He wore a black T-shirt, and despite his pale arms and stoop, Raveneau saw strength at the shoulders, a stark contrast to the rest. His eyes were bright as if anticipating something in this encounter, and that he was there at all made Raveneau wary. This wasn't a trail and he didn't see anybody earlier and the guy was clearly watching him approach, waiting.

'Brandon Lindsley,' he said. 'I was a grad student in history at the same time as Ann Coryell. I knew her fairly well. I talked to her all the time. I remember when she first raised the idea of our collective unconscious as a living thing. I always come here in the early fall around the time of year she disappeared, but I'm not some freak, Inspector. Don't worry. I don't have a hidden gun, but I do know who you are. I know the case is open again. I was hugely influenced by her and I liked her a lot and I care that her killer is caught.

'There was a TV report last night on the skulls in the fallout shelter. They said you and your partner were investigating the case, so I googled you both and found photos. That's how I recognized you, but I came out here this afternoon because I was thinking about her. I still miss her. I miss the way she saw the world. She was special.'

'I'm a little slow here. You were at Cal with her?'

'Yes.'

'And your name is Brandon Lindsley?'

'Yes. I was in grad school at the same time and we both were writing dissertations on aspects of nineteenth-century American history. But I wasn't in her league and I didn't last in grad school. I couldn't really find my place. I didn't fit and fumbled around and wasted years. I had the money to pay for it, so I didn't have to get things figured out. Sorry, I know that's too much information.

'I got to know her much better when she was living in Lash's guest cottage. I knew Lash pretty well. He was my professor also and if I had a role model it was him. I'm still trying to imitate him. I've written a couple of pop history books, though I haven't sold any yet. One of them is up on Amazon if you want to check that out, but I'm still looking for a publisher. I can name the characters in every book Professor Lash wrote. I know he was a suspect but you've got to admit he's a pretty clever guy. I'm working on a new one now, a book about a miner living in San Francisco during the Gold Rush, Mark Twain meets Grizzly Adams.'

'Do you want to walk up with me?'

'Sure.'

'Are you still in contact with Professor Lash?'

'I saw him a month ago but he's pretty sick now. I never believed he killed her. SFPD didn't either.' He turned and smiled. 'What do you think now?'

'I think it's going to get dark soon.'

They climbed back to where Raveneau had parked and, as it turned out, Lindsley as well. Raveneau gave him a card and got Lindsley's cell number as he asked again how Lindsley happened to be out here this afternoon. He checked out Lindsley's car and got the plates and ran them on the drive back to San Francisco.

Eight

Raveneau heard her scream though it was faint and masked by wind rattling through the dry eucalyptus trees. The trees shed long tinder-dry strips of bark which broke underfoot as he worked left through the grove, turning once back upslope, using the stick frame of the cottage to tell where he was. He needed to hurry. La Rosa was impatient with the idea to start with and wouldn't remain in the bomb shelter long.

A surveyor's map showed an easement for underground power lines that slashed across part of Lash's former property and then angled down through the eucalyptus. His guess was the builder of the bomb shelter quietly reopened the trench and added the air intake duct after the power went in and the utility crew left in 1962. If that was true he should be able to find the other end of the vent feeding air into the bomb shelter. Somewhere it surfaced.

He crossed a shallow gulley and started up the other side when he heard her voice from behind him. He turned and yelled, 'Elizabeth!'

He couldn't make out the words but she called

back to him and the sound came from somewhere close by, and after staring a long moment he put a hand on a fallen tree and then ran his hand along it in disbelief. It was concrete, colored concrete, a cast of a eucalyptus log. He squatted down. He looked behind it and found concrete rocks in the shadow, then made out a steel grate. Some sort of mesh was in front of it though torn. He yelled into it to la Rosa and when she didn't answer he stacked rocks so he could find it again.

When he got back up the slope la Rosa stood with her hands on her hips waiting for him. She let her hands fall. She was hoarse and not all that happy.

'We could have gotten a smoke stick and an electric fan and blown smoke out the vent. We could have used a boom box or anything that made enough noise. You're walking around with a map in your hand. Maybe they were all writing about the nineteenth century, but we're not living in it. This is a halfass way to do this and I still don't see the point, and aren't we too late now?'

'It was worth it. Coryell heard screams and it's worth knowing if a woman's voice could carry from in there. Yours was faint but I could hear you.'

'You could hear me, OK, fine, but what good does this really do us? The trip here to do this chips three hours out of today. I just don't see it helps. But all right we proved a woman's voice will carry out the air vent. Now what?'

'Now we go see Lash.'

The Gordon G. Wright Senior Living Centre was a new building. As Raveneau signed the guest register he had his chance to ask who Gordon Wright was but missed it. They followed the manager, a petite and earnest woman who seemed to want to tour them through the building before taking them to Lash. She used the walk to probe and try to find out what their goal was today. She was protective, wanted them to understand Lash could handle questioning but not interrogation.

'He's far along,' she said. 'He's quite fragile.'

Most lived three years after a diagnosis of ALS. Fourteen percent made it past five years. Five percent beat the six year mark and a remarkable few lived decades. It's a cruel disease, attacking the motor neurons but leaving the mind intact and trapped inside a frozen body. For Lash, as with most, it started with his legs. All that he could move now was his head. He had reached the beginning of pulmonary issues and that's where it would end.

On the third floor, the top floor of the Gordon C. Wright Senior Living Center, they saw the movie theater and dining area and the room where residents worked on projects and did crafts. La Rosa rolled her eyes. She was agitated today. But Raveneau figured that if it was important to the manager to walk and talk with them they could spare the additional ten minutes.

Carpets and bathrooms were spotless. They looked at the dining room where the residents ordered off the menu and were waited on. After a meal they could return to their apartments or gather in the common area adjacent to the dining room, or perhaps go out on one of the excursion busses.

'We work at making it a happy place,' the manager said.

'Is Albert on this floor?' la Rosa asked.

'No, he's on the first floor. All of those who need twenty-four-hour care are on the first floor. We'll go there now.'

The once thick head of dark hair was snow white. The bones of his shoulders propped up his coat, the skin of his face papery and splotched, right cheek twitching, yet his eyes were the same and his recognition instant and apparent. Raveneau didn't doubt that he'd watched the TV reports. He studied la Rosa longer and when he spoke the words were very labored and slurred and directed at Raveneau.

'What – do – you – think of – meee – now?'

'You're still the brightest guy in the room.'

'Very ... diffi–cult.'

'Albert, this is my partner, Elizabeth la Rosa. The investigation is active again and you may be able to help us.'

'By ... con–fesssssing?'

Raveneau saw the light in Lash's eyes and smiled.

'I didn't kill errrr.'

Lash had a mouse he could move with his head and tap Y for yes and N for no. He used that and used speech. The mouse was painstakingly slow, but he answered every question, the same co-operative guy he always had been. He acknowledged he knew about the bomb shelter and said he hadn't been in it since his father was alive, thirty-six years ago or more. He didn't mention it when the property was searched because it was locked and hidden, staring at Raveneau as he said this, both of them aware of how many years he'd had to get ready for the day it was found.

'You're saying you haven't been inside since your father died in 1984. Is that correct?'

Lash tapped Y. He tapped N when asked again if he had it built. It was his father's project in 1962. He typed out 1962. He didn't know of anyone who'd been in the bomb shelter. He tapped N to knowing anything about two partial skeletons and the skulls. He waited for the next question and Raveneau didn't ask it. He didn't ask anything about the cot. He wanted to take this in small pieces with Lash.

'We're going to come back and see you again soon.'

'If – I'm – still – here.'

Lash watched him pick up the new file with the photos showing what was inside the bomb shelter.

'One final question, Albert, and I almost forgot this one. When did you meet Brandon Lindsley and how well did he know you and Ann?'

Nine

They were back in the car when Raveneau said, 'Let's stop by Berge Properties and see if Lisa is there. We're only ten minutes away.'

'Confronting her will only make her more stubborn.'

'Let's find out.'

'I'd rather not.'

'I can go in alone. All I want to do is let her know it's not going away. We're not going away.'

This was a thing about Raveneau she didn't like and she hoped now that Berge wasn't there, but as soon as they turned in la Rosa saw the black Lexus. Berge was sitting behind her desk staring through the glass wall into the reception area when they walked in. She flinched and her mouth tightened and there was no need to talk to the receptionist. Berge was already on her feet coming at them.

'Why are you here? I've given you everything you've asked for.'

'You gave us a copy of a lease and just about nothing else,' Raveneau said. 'My partner doesn't think so but I think we ought to arrest you and question you about your role in this plot. You covered up for them by removing the tape and you're blocking us from finding out who wrote the rental checks. It's not going to stand.'

Berge got red in the face. She was angry, and la Rosa stood back and watched. She didn't believe in this cowboy approach and refused to join in, in fact, enjoyed it as Berge closed on Raveneau and jabbed a finger at his chest. For a moment she thought Berge was going to punch him. She looked capable.

'I'm going to sue you personally, Inspector. I'm going to get you fired. Berge Properties has been around a lot longer than you.'

'Blow smoke somewhere else. You've until four this afternoon.'

'You won't have a job next week. You're an embarrassment to San Francisco.'

'I asked you not to go into the apartment or touch anything. I told you it was a murder investigation and the tape recording was a link we needed. You broke that link and were in a hurry to do it, so for now you're on the other side of the wall. You're a possible suspect. You can change that.' He laid a card on her desk. 'Four o'clock.'

When they got back to the car, la Rosa said, 'That doesn't work for me and I don't like being part of it. She's prickly but I could have gotten everything from her without getting in a screaming match. Sometimes you make it harder than it has to be and that's about as nice as I can say that.'

'It would take weeks for you to get that from her.'

Raveneau was still agitated from arguing with

Berge so la Rosa chose her words.

'It might take more time but in the end we'd still be able to talk to her. Instead, she's going to call and complain about us and we'll still have to pull teeth to get information from her.'

'I'm going to get to her.'

'Yeah, well, I don't like being dragged along. It doesn't work for me and this threat is almost certainly bogus. Only a nut would cite something out of the nineteenth century.'

'I won't drag you along.'

'So now your answer is you're going to go off on your own. You want to know a truth, Ben? You like to work alone.'

'I like working with you.'

'But you do it your own way almost every time. I'll have to answer for the complaint she makes just the same as you and I'm not staring retirement in the face. I can't just quit if I get angry enough, and I am angry because I didn't get any say in this. That sucks.'

'She's not going to file any complaint and she'll think it through and decide to cooperate.'

'You aren't listening to a single thing I'm saying. I stood in that bomb shelter this morning and screamed because we had to do it your way. Now you're picking a fight with her. I don't get it.'

They hit traffic driving back and Raveneau got a text that absorbed him. He was quiet then turned to her.

'I just got a text from Brandon Lindsley. That's the guy that appeared on the mountain. He's offering to set up a meeting with some people he knows who are completely into Ann Coryell's writings. He says there's a chat room they go to.'

'So what?'

Raveneau glanced at her and then started to text Lindsley back. It angered her that he was not listening, not willing to have any real conversation about how they worked together. For a moment she considered asking for a transfer, asking for a new partner today.

Instead, she said, 'Give me his name again.'

'Brandon Lindsley.'

'What do we know about him?'

'So far, I haven't found much. No criminal record, valid California driver's license, lives in Mill Valley.'

'Tell me again how he just appeared.'

'I was down where Coryell's remains were found and that's a pretty good distance down the slope and away from any trails. When I started back he was waiting by a tree. He followed me down there.'

'Maybe he's telling the truth and you've got it wrong. What were you doing there anyway? Why would a homicide inspector be out at a site that's a decade old? There's nothing to see.'

Raveneau ignored that and said, 'I think it's as you said when we found the iPhone case. It's game on. We're dealing with people who want to engage us. Now he's setting up this meeting.'

'That's a lot strung together.'

'It is.'

'Sometimes you suspect everybody.'

'This is one of those times.'

'I think you're being paranoid.'

Raveneau went quiet now, went dark, went back to being the man alone.

'When is this meeting he's setting up?'

'I don't know yet. Look, let's not go back to the Hall yet. Let's go get a coffee and talk. I hear you, I know what you're saying, and I know how I can be. Let's go sit somewhere and talk.'

Ten

The next morning Raveneau called a county sheriff in Missouri named Jennie Crawford. She put him on speakerphone and sounded skeptical that he was a San Francisco homicide inspector. Raveneau heard a low murmur, a male voice in the background.

'Who all is in the room, Sheriff?'

'Deputy Carlson is here with us. Say hello, Jim.'

He did and Raveneau asked, 'Why are we on speakerphone?'

'Deputy Carlson has worked on our investigation and I want him to hear this.'

'He's not working mine and some of what I'm going to tell you isn't public information yet.'

'There's no issue with things leaking out of our office. They don't leak, they pour out. I gave up ten years ago on trying to keep anything secret around here.'

'OK, but how about taking me off speakerphone and letting me talk to you first?'

She did that and now her voice was more immediate and rich and warm. He put her at forty-five or fifty and hardened, but with a real sense of humor.

'We have two partial skeletons and fourteen unidentified skulls primarily from elderly individuals. We've gone out to NamUs with this, but our forensic anthropologists guesses they came out of a graveyard.' NamUs was the National Missing and Unidentified Persons System and he assumed the sheriff was familiar with it, but maybe she had no reason to be. He paused a moment as he thought about how to communicate with her without saying too much about the homicide investigation. 'Sheriff, I read about the graveyard that flooded and I understand you're looking for some missing skulls. How many are you looking for?'

'Fourteen, and eleven are from older individuals, all relatives of local families. This wasn't some forgotten graveyard the river turned up. A levee broke.'

'Must have been a nightmare.'

'It was.'

'Sheriff, these skulls are part of a murder investigation, a victim killed here about a decade ago.'

'What's the name of your victim?'

'Ann Coryell.'

'Spell that for me.'

He did, and as she repeated the letters he guessed Deputy Jim was searching the Net for Ann Coryell articles. Computer keys tapped. He heard the squeak of an old monitor being turned, probably so the sheriff could read what he was finding.

Sheriff Jennie Crawford was in Lewis County in the town of Cagdill on a bluff above the Mississippi River in the northern part of the state. Raveneau checked out the town before calling her. He drove down Main Street on Google Earth and found the red-brick building she was probably in right now. But more importantly he found the road along the river and the story of the levee break and the cemetery washout. She was too quiet, conferring with her deputy he guessed.

'These could be yours,' he said. 'If they are I'll FedEx them home to you, but I'll need a credit card and I should tell you we have a no-return policy.' He gave her a moment before asking, 'Do you want all fourteen, and will that be Visa or MasterCard?'

She didn't miss a beat, said, 'Visa,' and then laughed a good laugh, the right kind.

'What is it you and the deputy are looking at while I sit here holding the phone?'

'We were looking you up.'

'Did you find me?'

'Yes.'

'So can we talk more now and can you tell me how you lost the skulls?'

'The levee breached, and then it broke and flooded part of the town and the graveyard. We evacuated people as the water came in. The caskets washed out in a sea of mud. It was awful. It made me think of the End Times they like to talk about around here. Sometimes I think they hope for it, but I won't go there right now. Caskets ended up on both sides of the highway. We marked them with red flags and we couldn't get our vehicles up there, so we had to tromp through the mud in waders to put flags on them. A grave robber opened half of those caskets that same night. He took skulls, jewelry, and some bones. We figured it was skinheads.'

'I didn't know there were any left.'

'They all moved here.'

'Any arrests?'

'None.'

'Any leads?'

'None that have been worth a damn.'

'I'm going to get both our medical examiner and our forensic anthropologist to call you.'

'What are their names?' He listened as she wrote the names down. 'I would love to get this solved, but if they're ours how did they get all the way to California?'

'They probably got a ride with whoever opened up the caskets. That's if they're yours.'

She was quiet a moment then said, 'Well, I'm really interested. There's an old farmer named Jacobs who saw the grave robber and is sure it was a man, but that was before dawn and he wasn't all that close.'

'I'd like to hear all about that. I'd like to get a telephone number on him if this starts to look real. Do you have any dental records?'

'A few.'

'Have you reburied them without their skulls?'

'We had to rebury them. We were paying an

undertaker for storage and it just wasn't working out. It was costing too much and people were getting upset about Grandma Millie in storage without her head, so I gave them the option of reburial or waiting. No one wanted to wait and we ran into a wall with the investigation. But we've got castings of tires tracks and boot prints. The castings are good but a boot print in that river mud isn't worth much.'

'Did you keep anything with DNA?'

'We did but don't tell the families.'

'I won't. How many did you keep DNA from?'

'All of them.'

'How many have dental records?'

'Nine, and the records are scanned. We can get them to you today, and I'll tell you this, if there's a case I'd like to solve it's this one. Some of the relatives cross the street to avoid me and high school kids show up at my door on Halloween in skeleton suits. I know an older widow whose husband's skull was taken and whenever she sees me she makes the sign of the cross. I hear about it every day.'

'Let's do it this way – I'll get our ME to call and he'll coordinate the forensic anthropologist. He'll email you photos of all of the skulls. There'll be frontal and side shots and someone should be able to work with the photos and the dental records. If it looks like there are any matches you can send us your DNA samples and we'll get them run. How does that sound?'

'Sounds fine, but you haven't told me where you found them. Where were these?'

'In a bomb shelter. Go to sfgate.com. It's local

news now. If you're old enough to remember the Khmer Rouge and the killing fields and the photos of skulls taken there, that's what comes to mind.'

'I do remember. I was a little girl, and I remember looking at *Time Magazine* and getting the feeling they weren't people anymore. There were too many bones. They became things.'

'That's what these look like.'

Raveneau gave her his cellphone number before they traded emails. A few minutes after they hung up he sent her a photo he took inside the bomb shelter before anything was moved. That wasn't like Raveneau, especially with someone he didn't know. But he wanted her to know something about who they were looking for, and how she spoke of the skulls the Khmer Rouge left behind had reached him. He probably shouldn't have let a case photo go out, but he had. In the photo the candles were still there, the skulls stacked and leaning back against the dank wall.

Eleven

'Inspector Raveneau, my name is Cecelia Nance. I've known Marion Coryell since we were girls in Nebraska, and that's quite a while. I turned seventy-one last week. If Marion knew I was making this call I don't know if she would ever speak to me again.'

Raveneau reached and shut the door to the Cold Case office. Now he could hear her better. Her voice was quiet but firm. He pictured a woman who was careful about her dress and appearance and whose weeks were checkered with appointments and routines. That conjured the image of Marion Coryell with blue jay feathers tied into her hair and how unlikely that had seemed.

'Marion is one-eighth Oglala Sioux. She still has family at the Pine Ridge Reservation, mostly second and third cousins, and I don't know how much you know about the Oglala, but they are a very proud people, even in their current condition. Red Cloud and Crazy Horse, do you know those names, Inspector?'

'Sure.'

'People know their names but they don't know who they were anymore. I heard on TV the code name for bin Laden was Geronimo. Geronimo wouldn't give up the Apache land. He was a terror to the settlers but he was fierce and brave. I don't understand giving his name to a bin Laden, but maybe that's just me.

'Marion couldn't stand the drinking, not the members of the tribe who drank or those in Whiteclay who were there only to sell them liquor, so she left. That's the real reason she came to California. She moved in with me and found a job and married the man I was going out with at the time. We used to laugh about that. I'm telling you this so you understand that she's strong-willed when she wants something. She wanted Ann to be different than she was. Ann had characteristics Marion wanted to change. Ann was different than her mother and Marion was at times very hard with her. That's what happened that night. Ann was frightened and Marion wouldn't let her come home. I think you know she called her.'

'Yes.'

'You may not know everything.'

'I know of three calls.'

'Yes, but I don't think you know that Ann told her mother she was coming home anyway and Marion said no. Marion told her to stay and be stronger than her fear, and then Ann said she was going to call you. She used your name and Marion remembered it. Ann was going to call you and if she couldn't get you she was going to walk to her car and drive home. When she wasn't able to reach you, she may have left the cottage on her own. Marion should have told that to the police then, but I guess she just couldn't do it. I didn't know until yesterday. I don't think she'll ever forgive herself and I'm worried about her. She talks about moving away from here, going back to Nebraska or somewhere else, but there's nowhere else for her to go.'

Ann Coryell's car was found four blocks away though the keys to it never turned up. In the cottage there were no signs of struggle and it could be that there in the night she was hurrying to her car. It was so possible it turned his gut.

'There's more. Ann told her mother that if she wasn't home in an hour she should call the police, and Marion told her no. She told her stay where she was and not to leave that cottage. I believe Marion thought she would stay.'

'She told you this yesterday.'

'She did. That was after you visited her. Your visit upset her. She asked me to come over and sit with her. Marion was never the same after Ann disappeared and I always knew there was something else that she blamed herself for. I think she and Annie had a very bad argument that night and Marion said things she wishes she could take back. She couldn't have known it was the last time she would ever talk to her. Even when the Missing Person Report got filed I don't think she believed Annie was gone. That's why she didn't do anything for days. She may have thought Ann was angry and hiding to make her feel guilty. I know she kept waiting for her to call, even a month, two, three months later.'

Raveneau remembered. Marion Coryell insisting that her daughter was staying with friends and working on her thesis. She couldn't say where or why she would hide, though, and the police view was the mother was unable to face the other possibilities. It wouldn't become a homicide case for more than a year, and he guessed Marion was thinking now what he was, that Ann may have been alive in those first days after she vanished. Alive in the bomb shelter and alive in a way he would never let her mother know.

'That's what I wanted to tell you, Inspector. Now if you tell Marion I said this it'll end a long friendship. But you do what's best for Ann, that's what's important. The truth is bigger than us.'

'What was Ann like?'

'What was Annie like?'

'Yes.'

'She was adorable as a young girl, troubled as a teenager, and then remarkable as a young woman. We used to guess at what she would grow up to be.'

'Did you guess history professor?'

She had a low laugh with a little rasp to it. 'No, I sure didn't. Marion thought she would make a good lawyer. She was never argumentative but even when she was little she was quite incisive with her questioning. Annie needed answers the way the rest of us need food and drink. She had a tremendous imagination. She might have made a great scientist. I'll be frank, I've read what she wrote and I don't think there's anything earth-shattering there, but I believe Annie had a quality of empathy that's rare and that history came alive for her.

'The things that happened generations ago she could visualize as having happened today. I remember her describing the battle at Little Bighorn when Custer attacked the Indian camps thinking he would overrun them and burn and shoot and kill, and then discovered there were many, many more braves than his scouts thought. Annie told the story of how Custer fell back and the desperation of his men as the warriors trapped them. Annie couldn't have been more than twelve, and it was at dinner with Marion, Annie, and me, and Frank who is dead now.

'I could smell the greasy grass and hear the ponies and the Sioux on their horses racing up the river bank and Custer's men marching in even as at his flank soldiers fled into the woods. Annie took us there. Like a movie you get completely into, but it was just her voice and the way that she spoke you just believed she was there and had seen Custer with his long gold hair and buckskin. It was eerie.'

'Did she think she was there?'

Cecelia coughed. She cleared her throat. 'What an odd question, but in a way I think she did. And really, though, that's true. When she described Custer on his hands and knees, shot through the side, and bleeding from his mouth with his hair falling alongside his face, watching as they closed in and did to him what he swore he would do to them ... It was as I said, frightening, as if she was standing there when it happened. It frightened Marion too. She got up and left the room. She didn't want Annie studying history or anything to do with the history of the tribes. Marion wanted nothing to do with that. There was nothing good in it, but Annie was after something that was back there. If she thought there was something to find, she wouldn't quit. I don't know if that answers your question. It probably doesn't. Please don't tell Marion I called you.'

Raveneau wouldn't. He laid the phone down and thought about what she had said.

Twelve

Celeste sounded out of breath and the cell connection was poor, but she was happy to be home. Raveneau heard airport noises and guessed she was just off the plane and walking toward baggage.

'I'm back. Where are you?'

'Leaving the Hall.'

'Do you want to meet me at M33?'

Raveneau shook his head at that. He still didn't get the name change. She had a name that fit her bar/restaurant and after an up and down start it looked like Toasts was making it in San Francisco, a bar that served crostinis and small pizzas and artful salads, but was earning its rep with mixed drinks. A month ago she told him she was changing it to M33, which to Raveneau sounded like a new combat gun or possibly a rock group. He didn't get it.

He and Celeste had an unusual relationship but a good one, or mostly good, and it had been a couple of years now. They lived separately with no talk about changing that. She slept over. He slept over. Mostly it was Celeste coming to his place, but both with keys to each.

But for the last week she had been with her sister in Michigan who insisted she should break off the relationship because it hadn't progressed to marriage. The sister flew out last year to assess him and then put a timetable on things for Celeste.

At Toasts Celeste started from zero, and now the place was busy midweek in early October. But it was also a warm night and people were out. A hot offshore wind blew from the north-east. They sat outside in the wind and he looked at her face and the warmth there as she reached across the table for his hand.

'What's up, big guy? I'm home but you're quiet.'

'I'm thinking about Albert Lash.'

'I wish he'd write more books.'

'I don't think that's going to happen.'

They talked about Lash's books and he skirted around the Coryell investigation. They ate salad and two small pizzas and drank and talked and would have left together if not for a text from Brandon Lindsley.

'Can I call u now?'

Raveneau texted back and his phone rang.

'Do you want to meet them tonight?'

Raveneau glanced through the glass to the bar where Celeste was talking with her chef. He was looking at her as he answered, 'Yes.'

'There's a bar called Grate's Place. It's south of Mission, I'll text the address. I didn't fake anything. They know who you are.'

'Why shouldn't they?'

'There's no reason, I just didn't know how you wanted to do it. They're taking my word about you being into Ann's writings and that's really why they agreed to meet. You'll need to know your stuff. Two of them are super serious about everything she wrote. Have you read any of *Death Cathartic: Spiritually Reconciling the Genocide of the US Western Expansion*? That's their bible.'

'It's my favorite book.'

'I'm not kidding.'

'What time are we meeting?'

'Ten o'clock.'

'See you there.'

Thirteen

Raveneau arrived at Grate's early. When he was last here it was a deli serving office buildings that ringed three sides of the courtyard. He liked it more as a bar though it wasn't his kind of bar. It was trying too hard. He ordered a Pilsner – a Trumer – and then waited for Lindsley, who came in a few minutes later. Lindsley threaded through people, made his way over.

'That wood table through the window there is where we usually sit. Let me get a drink and then let's go out there.' He adjusted his glasses. 'We can talk out there.'

'How often do you meet these guys?'

'Used to be once a week.'

'What is it now?'

'Lately, I've been missing the meetings.'

'Why is that?'

'Can I get a drink before we do this?'

'I'll see you outside.'

Raveneau walked out to the table but didn't sit down yet. The hot valley wind was still blowing and it was more sheltered in here, but the wind reached around the corners. It shook dry leaves from a tree in a metal planter. He had looked forward to being with Celeste tonight, but needed to do this and didn't see any reason for subtlety with the three men who were supposed to meet them. He still didn't know what to make of Lindsley.

The table was a heavy wooden picnic table painted a dark green and now he and Lindsley sat with their backs to the still warm stucco wall of the bar and watched the other three arrive. The one leading was a wiry man of average height and younger than Lindsley. His name was Attis Martin and his handshake was moist and soft, but his eyes were focused and hard as he sized up Raveneau.

The second man seemed to be a woman, although this was one of the few times Raveneau wasn't sure. His or her name was Ike Latkos, and she sat to the left of Attis and close to him. She didn't give her name and let Attis introduce her as did the third man, whose name at least for tonight was apparently an inside joke that the rest got, including Lindsley. Attis introduced him as John the Baptist, and Lindsley giggled. He was dark-haired, square-shouldered, and in his mid-thirties with the look of a former soldier who had seen too many things.

When no one volunteered it, Raveneau asked, 'Why do they call you John the Baptist?'

John stared, didn't answer. Neither did anyone else, and Raveneau leaned back against the wall and waited for Attis. He was clearly the leader. When Attis was silent, Raveneau said, 'Her murder is an active case again and I need your help. I'd like to get phone numbers and email addresses from each of you. I need a way to get in touch with you.'

'You already have our names,' Attis said and reached and put an arm around Ike's shoulders. 'Have to warn you, Ike likes to change names and John doesn't use his last name anymore. John has stripped out the things in his life he doesn't need.'

'What about you? Have you stripped out the things you don't need?'

'Soon.'

'How soon?'

Attis didn't answer, and Raveneau turned to John. 'Whose idea was it to call you John the Baptist?'

'Mine,' Attis said.

'Is that because he recognized you?'

Attis didn't like that much, but that was OK with Raveneau. This meeting wasn't what he had hoped for and felt contrived and staged and as he got a text from la Rosa now he stopped to read it. Attis Martin didn't like that either.

He wrote back: *'With them now.'* He typed the address of Grate's Place and dropped the phone back in his pocket after sending it.

'Sorry,' he said to Attis. 'Where were we?'

Attis sent John the Baptist in to get drinks, another vodka Collins for Lindsley, two vodkas on ice for Latkos, and sparkling water for him. The conversation wandered around the Coryell investigation and the bomb shelter coverage on local TV where reporters questioned Raveneau's belief that the bone find wasn't evidence of a serial murderer at work. Experts consulted also questioned SF Homicide ruling out serial murder.

John returned with the drinks and nothing for himself. He took the same seat at the end of the table and adjusted the long coat he wore over a T-shirt and black jeans. His face was pale and drawn as if fasting, his focus on Attis. It was quite a crew.

Attis asked, 'Are you one of us?'

'Is this where I show what the aliens implanted in my neck?'

'I'm asking if you believe in the Boundary.'

Raveneau nodded and regretted now letting Celeste go home alone so he could be here. He glanced at John the Baptist and knew he wouldn't be talking at all tonight, so that left these two and really only Attis, who so far spoke for all of them.

'You're talking about Ann Coryell's Boundary idea?'

'Yes.'

'I don't think she meant a boundary like a fence. She was communicating something about how memories are passed on and how a society has a personality and being that exists as our collective consciousness. We all contribute to it, and what we contribute individually outlasts our lives. She was writing about how unanswered things get passed on.' Raveneau took a drink of his beer.

'You're wrong.'

'Maybe, but here's the thing, I'm working her murder, not an interpretation of her work. Brandon says he knew her. What about you? Did you know her?'

'What if I told you I've been to the Boundary?

What would you say to that?'

'That you were a decent guy and we had a drink together but sometime before I met you you fell too hard on your head.'

Attis smiled. He lifted his right hand and reached across the table to fist bump Raveneau. 'You're right about me. I'm crazy. What do you think about page twenty-nine?'

Raveneau was ready. He'd trolled the Internet. He saw once, twice, five, a dozen times the mention of page twenty-nine in her thesis. He read the commentary. It was where she speculated how successive generations were connected. She believed history wasn't a series of events but one ongoing event and that the repetitive nature of our struggle to understand ourselves as a species, the recurrent wars, patterns repeated, was manifestation of unconsciousness awareness of our spiritual incompleteness. She called religions mythology but our spirituality our one true thing.

For her, the settling of the American west was a tragic chapter in that struggle. She acknowledged atrocities on both sides, but the defeat of the American Indian tribes included a pattern of broken treaties, a soul defiling reservation system, and knowing genocide by a far stronger force. That was the unanswered thing carried forward that she believed had to be answered.

'She left it to us to interpret how genocide gets answered,' Attis said, 'and that gets us to the Indian Wars and the American western expansion.'

'Now you've got my attention,' Raveneau

said.

'It's why we're here. I invited you to get your attention.'

'Is that right?'

'What better witness than someone who has read Coryell and better still a homicide inspector? It's perfect.'

'OK, you're communicating something important and I get that, but I'm a little slower than you, same as I can't interpret her writings as clearly, so spell it out for me. Are you preparing to do something?'

Attis stared then glanced at Lindsley who sat motionless, no more shifting of his shoulders or adjusting his glasses. Latkos picked up her second drink. She gave him a sly smile as Raveneau asked Attis if he was by any chance missing an iPhone.

'A phone threat was made,' Raveneau said. 'We get some surprising and sometimes off the wall threats from time to time, but I can't remember hearing another where the caller threatened to make the people of San Francisco pay for America's nineteenth-century western expansion. It just doesn't come up that much. Do you know what I mean?'

'It doesn't come up, but it never went away.'

'Ann Coryell shunned violence. That was one of her problems with the religions of the world. She wrote about a non-violent cleansing, talking it through, acknowledging what happened. But again, I'm not here to interpret her. I want to find her killer. I want to know why.'

'She knew she had to die.'

Attis held out his hands as if balancing weights in each. 'There's living and there's dead and each has a place and the places have a boundary between them that can be crossed and sometimes recrossed but only if our consciousness is kept in a heightened state. You have to remain very aware just at the moment you're right on the edge of dying. If you do, you can cross over with awareness, and if you have the awareness then you're free to touch both sides. She's around us right now and you're starting to frustrate me. I'm trying to help you see, but your questions are blunt and your vision narrow. You were brought here because Brandon said you understood her and now you're making Brandon look bad. You were given an opportunity and you're wasting it.'

'I saw her remains.'

'A snake molts and leaves a skin and we've come to understand that. I'm not unhinged, Inspector. I'm not insane or deluded. I studied physics. I could have gone on in theoretical physics. I believe in science and mathematics, and I also believe she was ready to be free of her body. She understood her death differently than you do. She saw our true being in that collective unconsciousness. That's how history is woven and passed forward and where change happens. Everyone at this table believes except you.'

Raveneau turned to Lindsley. 'Do you believe that?'

'I believe in aspects,' Lindsley said.

Attis cut in, saying, 'That's him, that's the way he is, which is to say he doesn't know who he is and the consequence is he's two-faced. We deal with that. You will too. I sent Brandon to find you. I called you here. You're destiny's witness and you're perfect, a man sworn to find the truth. Death is an illusion, Inspector.

'When the bird leaves the nest that first time it has its instincts and what it has seen other birds do. Coryell saw things you don't. She saw the flow of humanity through time and she knew she was in touch with that. She had the gift to see the Boundary and she went for it. I see that too. I understand it and you look at me and see a threat. That's the way you're trained. But you're also trained to observe. You're the highly skeptical observer who will record what he sees and that's why I agreed to meet you.'

'So now we're meeting,' Raveneau said. 'We're talking. We're having a drink and I'm going to ask, do you know who made the threat?'

'If I said yes, you'd have to detain me and take me down to a police station. The answer is no.'

'That's a different answer than a straight no.'

'Of course, and again, that's why we're meeting.'

'Are you using me to communicate with the San Francisco Police Department?'

'Here.' Attis pulled his wallet out and handed Raveneau his driver's license. He told Ike and John to do the same, but said nothing to Lindsley. 'You have your phone, Inspector. You can take photos of us, but what you can't do is stop the flow of history.'

'OK, then let's just get some photos.' Raveneau turned his phone on John the Baptist first. 'How about a big smile, John?'

Ike smiled. Attis stared. Raveneau wrote down driver's license numbers, addresses, phone numbers, and emails.

'What am I going to witness?'

'Inspector, can I give you anything more than I already have? Do you want to follow us out and get the license plates of the car we came here in?'

'Sure, I'll do that.'

'Then walk out with us. Brandon will stay with the table.'

'I will walk out with you, but before we do that how are you and I going to communicate after tonight?'

'With the email address I just gave you.'

He walked out with them. The car was a 2010 Malibu. Its burned out shell was found two days later out at Hunter's Point.

Fourteen

Brandon Lindsley was still at the table and had ordered himself another drink while Raveneau was out front with Attis and the other two. It was close to midnight and the bar was getting busier. The bar door was open. People spilled out into the courtyard and a techno beat vibrated into the night. Raveneau wanted more from Lindsley before they left here, but it was harder to talk now.

'He called you two-faced. How do you feel about that?'

'Really mad. I guess I'll beat him up after school.' Lindsley adjusted his glasses, offered a wry smile. 'I don't know, Inspector. How should I feel? I don't feel much of anything right now and it's not the first time someone has claimed I'm not who I say I am. The police did that when I was sixteen.'

'Let's talk about that.'

'No, we're not up to that part of the script yet and I'm ready to call it a night.'

'You sat here. You listened to him. You know him. Explain it to me. He all but said he doesn't trust you, but you're part of the group.'

That got to Lindsley. For the first time he stirred. 'I'm not part of them, and if Attis included me in their group I'd be looking in a mirror wondering what was wrong with me.'

'John jumped up when Attis told him to go get drinks. You sat and took what he said. He had an arm around Ike. He's talking like he knows more about the threat we're investigating than I do. What am I supposed to do with that?'

'I don't hang with these people. I talk to them online and we talk about Coryell. You wanted to meet people who chat online about Coryell. You want to get into that community. I set you up. This other stuff Attis was talking about I don't know what you do with that. I heard him too. It was weird. Maybe you should bring him down to the police station and interview him. You're the expert. I'm the guy who wants to write books like Professor Lash wrote. That's my whole deal, following in Professor Lash's footsteps.'

'You've told me.'

'I'm just saying I've got a goal that's apart from anything to do with these guys.'

'Is your inheritance from your parents?'

'Yes.'

'When did they die?'

'When I was sixteen.'

When he didn't volunteer more Raveneau moved the conversation to Ike Latkos.

'This is what Attis told me,' Lindsley said. 'She's a hacker and some pretty bad people are after her, but they're not law enforcement types. She has protectors in some agency in Washington that she helped out. The first time I heard about it the city was Berlin and then it was Leningrad, and after that Prague, and now it's back to Berlin. She got away with some large chunk of somebody's money. Transferred it and ran and hid and will be hiding for the rest of her life if they don't find her first. She was a he when she stole the money and had a sex change in Mexico and not because she wanted to. She needed a female body to hide in, but she doesn't live in it. She lives online and she's got about a thousand identities and supposedly secret friends in high places.'

'What's all that mean?'

'That you shouldn't waste your time with her driver's license.' Lindsley smiled a crooked smile.

'And what about John the Baptist? What church would I find him in?'

Lindsley smiled again. 'That's a good one,' he said. 'I've got another story about Ike that Attis told me. She set up a Spanish language website for doing US tax returns for almost no charge. Then she collected a bunch of names, social security numbers, everything needed, and killed the website. The following January she filed for early returns on something like a thousand names and made up numbers for everything including what they were owed as refund checks. Attis said she collected millions of dollars, and I didn't believe it, but a couple of days ago I read it's a big scam out there. The IRS has paid out something like ten billion in phoney claims. No one comes to arrest her. That's why Attis was stroking her head.'

'Where's John from?'

'Fuck if I know.'

'But you know about Ike.'

'From Attis, not from her, and John doesn't talk much, or maybe you didn't notice. He might have a job in medical engineering. I don't think Attis works and I'm pretty sure he and John met in the Coryell chat room.'

'How would you find Attis tomorrow?'

'I'd go online.'

'What about a phone number?'

'He won't give it to me. He calls me on those temporary prepaid phones. Ike got all my personal information and he's got that. He let me know by telling me I should strengthen my passwords.'

'OK, I'm back to where I started with you. Things are almost believable, but not quite, and you need to really think about that. If they're planning something, there's not going to be any gray middle ground later. Attis called me a witness. You've got to think about what kind of witness you'd want me to be later in a trial.'

'Whoa, whoa, slow down there, Inspector. You asked me to connect you and I did, and I'm telling you again, right now and here, that I don't know about anything they're planning, and if Attis knows anything about this threat the police told the media about this morning, and it sounds like he does, I don't know anything. I heard the same things you heard and that's all I know. But you don't believe me.'

As he looked at Lindsley he got a bad feeling. Lindsley's face and features seem to change and shift as he spoke again and for the briefest moment Raveneau wondered if something was slipped into his beer when he was out front.

'I'm being pretty straight with you, Inspector. I'm protecting myself, sure, but I'm not really part of their group. When Ike hacked into my computer I changed all my accounts, passwords, everything, and cut off any contact with any of them. Somehow Ike figured out how to find me again and he did this whole apology thing, but I don't trust them. I never will, and like you saw, Attis is the dude. The other two are followers. He read the tea leaves, talks to God, and makes the plans.'

'What's he planning now?'

'You're back around to that and I don't have any answers.'

Lindsley took a sip, and they both shifted fast as there was a loud pop down the wall to their left. Sounded like a shot at first to Raveneau, but was one of the floodlight bulbs bursting in a light fixture on the wall. Glass fell on to the concrete and it was darker at the table.

'I set this meeting up so you could connect with them and maybe they could help you figure out who killed Ann Coryell. It's something everyone in that chat room has obsessed over. I didn't know he was going to call you out as a witness or get coy about this threat and suggest he knows about it.'

'You didn't know?'

'Not at all.'

'You're certain?'

'I'm very certain.'

'I'm going to repeat myself. Investigations gather momentum and you don't want to be on the wrong side of one looking at a threat like this.'

'So I shouldn't have set up the meeting or said anything to you on the mountain? Is that what you're saying? You're telling me I should have just stood there and watched you walk past even though I recognized you?'

'That's not what I'm saying and I'm not the one who called you on it. Attis did. He wasn't talking to me about you. He was talking to you and letting me hear. The message was you have to pick a side and now.'

'Oh, come on, talk about reading between the lines.'

'That's what I heard.'

'But he didn't say that.'

'It's a word game only for so long, Brandon.'

'I hear you but right now all I've got are regrets that I introduced myself to you.'

'Another way you could do this is say to him you're in. Call him tonight. Tell him you heard him loud and clear and you're in. Then work with us. That way you can be two-faced and legit.'

'Two-faced and legit, did you just say that?'

'Yeah.'

'Bizarre.' Lindsley stared down at the table and then finished his drink before rising and saying, 'I'm done for the night and I might be done completely because I don't really like the way you keep turning it back at me like I'm the problem. I see Attis. I get the guy is weird as hell, and I don't want you tying me to him.'

Raveneau walked out with him and watched

Lindsley go around the corner before crossing to his car. Ten minutes later when he picked up a car following him he led the car away from where he lived, and then set the driver up and was out of his car and got a good look at the profile of Brandon Lindsley as he drove past. He thought about that for awhile before driving home.

Fifteen

The next morning Raveneau crossed the city in the clear early light. Two Ford pickups, one dark blue, one white, both with black lumber racks were parked nose to end in front of Lash's house though it was too early to start making noise on a Saturday. A plumber's truck was in the driveway, and Ferranti, the general contractor, stood drinking coffee enjoying the early cool talking with the plumber before the start of what was forecast to be record-breaking heat.

Ferranti nodded as Raveneau drove slowly past, his expression a question mark about Raveneau's presence today, though Raveneau had little doubt Ferranti would use the chance to ask about the bomb shelter. He did, intercepting Raveneau as he walked back down the street toward the house.

'One of the owners of the house called me about half an hour ago. They're tripping out on the negative energy. They think their house is going to be marked forever.'

'What do they want to do?'

'Fill it in, and they're going to sue Lash, the realtors, and the people who did the inspections. But I know why none of the inspectors went very far into the garden shed. It was full of poisons, old insecticides, and some of it must have been fifty years old. I had to have a hazardous waste company come haul it away.'

The claim the current owners made that the bomb shelter wasn't disclosed at sale by Lash was true and kind of amazing when Raveneau thought about it. What it said to Raveneau was that Lash didn't know what to do about what was down there. He may not have known about the skulls, but not disclosing the bomb shelter meant he knew something was in there. Maybe he was going to point to his father or maybe with a death sentence already he just didn't care.

'They want me to get it filled with sand and capped off with concrete right away. That's what the engineer is calling for, and then we've got to build a landscape wall over the top of it. I know you're probably tired of hearing this, but if you can give me a date that would really help. It's supposed to be hot this week but this might be my last chance before it rains.'

'I can't give you a go-ahead today.'

'Then can you give me some sort of idea, and I'm sorry to bug you, but I've got to set everybody up ahead of time.'

A new black SUV rounded the corner at the far end of the street and Raveneau knew that was

Mark Coe, the FBI agent he was here to meet. Coe was going to have the same problem finding a place to park. He nodded as he drove past and Raveneau took in the changes in Coe, his face thinner, edging toward gaunt, a streak of gray at his temple. He turned back to Ferranti. 'It should be within a week, but I can't guarantee that.'

'But everything has been cleared out, right? Is it OK if we go down there and figure out what we have to do with the other stuff down there? Aren't there leaking batteries?'

'There are.'

'So that's like another hazardous waste deal. Can I schedule that?'

'You can get someone in to look at it and give you a price but don't pull them out yet.'

'Don't you have photos and everything else?' Ferranti couldn't get his head around the continued delay. 'Inspector Raveneau, I just don't get it. How is it going to affect your investigation if I get the batteries dealt with?'

Raveneau turned to answer and then didn't have to as Coe walked up and an agitated Ferranti confronted him.

'Who are you?'

Coe smiled and Raveneau expected him to pull his ID, but he didn't. He said, 'I'm with the city historical committee and here to take a look at the fallout shelter. You must be the contractor.'

This was a thing Raveneau liked about Coe. It was a streak the FBI very definitely didn't cultivate or encourage.

'How can you do that?' Ferranti asked. 'It's on private property.'

'Of course it is, but that doesn't mean we won't preserve it if it is of historical significance.'

'A bomb shelter?'

'We call them fallout shelters, and I realize you're too young to remember the Cold War Era, but we had planes in the air twenty-four hours a day carrying nuclear weapons and ready to go. These shelters played a very significant role in thc societal dynamics of that period. I arranged with Inspector Raveneau to meet this morning so I can evaluate and determine what we're going to do about this one. The inspector has told me you're anxious to get it filled in and that's one of the reasons we're meeting on a Saturday. If we do a study we should have an answer within a year, or I should say I like to aim for a year. I always make that goal.'

'You're joking, right? You're another homicide inspector.'

'Please don't say that.'

'Tell me you're joking.' When Coe hesitated, Ferranti said, 'Do you know what this is for my clients? It's their worst nightmare. A committee on bomb shelters, that's insane—'

'It's a fallout shelter, not a bomb shelter, sir.'

'I can't fucking believe this city. I can't redo the guest cottage before I get the lowest landscape wall built. I won't be able to do anything in the back.' Ferranti stared hard at Coe. 'It's a concrete hole in the ground. There's nothing special about it.'

Raveneau knew Coe was about to let Ferranti off the hook but Ferranti spoke first.

‘One of the subcontractors here used to be on the San Francisco Homicide Detail. He says this should have been released by now.’

The comment wasn’t for Coe. It was for him, and Raveneau knew as he heard it that it was true. That was Hugh, and as Raveneau confirmed it and Coe told Ferranti he was joking Ferranti said something else under his breath that they couldn’t hear and huffed off.

Raveneau and Coe went down into the shelter, Raveneau carrying photos with him. They looked at those, and he showed Coe where the skulls were and told him the Missouri connection was looking more likely. Bone samples were on their way here to compare DNA. He talked through the drink at Grate’s Place with Attis Martin, Lindsley, Ike, and John the Baptist, and then they climbed back out into the light, and Coe, who was something like fifteen years younger than Raveneau, asked, ‘You’re old enough, aren’t you? How did all these shelters happen?’

‘I was young, but I remember. In the sixties we tried to put in an air raid warning system. If you heard the siren go off at two in the morning the idea was you’d have ten minutes to get your family inside. In the shelter you’d have food and water and a radio if the antenna was still up. Half of the people who died at Hiroshima and Nagasaki died in the first day – most of those in the blast but some for lack of protection. That’s where we were getting our information. Then the bombs got a lot bigger and it didn’t seem like there was any way to ride it out anymore, so the idea faded away.'

'Where do you want our help first?'

'Interview Lisa Berge, the property manager who took the tape. She's only partially co-operating with us and blew off a deadline I gave her. I could make another run at her but I think you'll have more success. I'm going to talk to my commander about possible surveillance of the Attis Martin crew if we learn more. Anything you learn about them will help.'

'Send me what you've got and we'll see what we come up with.'

'You'll get it this morning,' Raveneau said.

'Are you that worried?'

'Not really, but I'm also not sure what I'm dealing with here. I'd like to know.'

'We'll get in touch with Berge today. Are you still bringing this Brandon Lindsley character out here?' Coe asked.

'I am.'

'Maybe you should wait.'

Raveneau understood Coe's message. The Bureau would assign a few agents and find out what they could about Lindsley and the three-some last night, and Coe thought SFPD should keep it quiet until the Bureau checked into these people.

Raveneau shook his head. 'Lindsley is my key to this case. I'm going to keep working on him.'

'Other than talk to her, what can we do to help you with Berge?'

'Track the money the rent got paid with. We've got it as far as a shell corporation. Find out who was paying the rent and then find them. I don't

know if this little band has the ability to do anything, but let's find out. Let's talk later today.'
'Call me.'

Sixteen

Raveneau was in the bomb shelter with Lindsley and the hatch was open. Daylight filtered in, as did voices, though Raveneau couldn't tell who they belonged to and as they moved the voices were gone.

Lindsley's flashlight beam slid across the wall on to the wooden seat near the generator. 'What's that for?'

'You sit on that seat and work those paddles with your legs. That draws fresh air in manually. It also recharges the battery.'

'What's that leaking next to it?'

'Battery acid.'

Lindsley moved his light off it and found the metal bathroom door. 'Where does that go?'

'It's a toilet. Didn't Professor Lash ever bring you down here?'

'No. We stayed in the house, though when it was warm he liked to sit in the garden. Did I tell you if he hadn't gotten sick we were going to collaborate on a book or that's what he wanted me to believe? We talked for a year about the first book. I did research for him. We actually talked about collaborating on more than one book.'

'He lied to you.'

'Oh, he did more than lie to me. He used me.'

'What was the collaborative book going to be about?'

'It doesn't matter. He was never really going to do it.'

'Would he have written one with Ann?'

'Ask him.'

'Did he ever talk about doing a book with her?'

'Not that I remember, but ask him and he'll say, "No–ooo." Does he say, "G–o–o–d to s–e–eeee you, In–spec–tor?" '

Raveneau flicked his flashlight abruptly and in time to catch Lindsley's grin and his abrupt shift away from it.

'I've seen enough, Inspector, and I appreciate you showing it to me. I hate to think that Ann might have been in here. That's a terrible thought. On Lash and me and the book thing, the last time I saw him was after the house had sold and he was just a few weeks from moving out. We talked on a Saturday morning and collaborating on books was still the plan. I waited to hear from him when he got settled in his apartment in the assisted living place, but he never called and he didn't return my calls. The caregiver, his doctor, his lawyer, no one would tell me where he was. They were sure the professor meant to call me before moving, they said, but with all the moving and the big change, he was overwhelmed.

'I waited. Finally, I found out where he was. Maybe he was freaked because he knew this bomb shelter would get found. Maybe it was the finality of it, that he would never live in a house again or ever have anything normal anymore. Or that the disease was going to kill him.'

'Did you know him as well as he says?'

'I don't know what he said.' Lindsley grasped a rung with his left hand. 'I'm going to climb up. Let's talk in the sunlight, but yeah there was a time when I thought we knew each other pretty well and were good friends. Now I don't believe any of that was ever true. He lied to me all along.'

'Have you visited him where he is now?'

'I have but probably won't ever again. When I first met him we would sit in his living room and drink whiskey and talk about American history. Now it's hard for him to talk and we don't have much to say to each other anymore. He's not going to write any more books and I finally figured out he used my ambition to string me along for years.'

'Did he pay you for the research?'

'He did do that.'

'Are you certain he never mentioned this shelter?'

Lindsley sighed heavily. 'Man, give it a rest. Whatever you think of me, just give it a rest. I was a grad student who realized he wasn't ever going to end up a professor but who might do OK writing books that popularized history if I could get some help getting my name out there. And we got along. It was great to be in his circle and we got as far as working out the chapters of the first book and the arc of it. But he was always going to write it himself. The way he told me the collaboration was off was by saying that in his condition he couldn't do it. Those weren't the exact words but it was that.'

'He's in a tough spot.'

'Oh, yeah, I know, it's very bad now, but back then he still had some hope. The book was going to be a follow-up on the one he did that included Ann's ideas. This was going to be a history of the Indian Wars through the eyes of five who were there and wrote about battles and decisions. Sounds dry but it wouldn't have been. He probably didn't want me to know where he was moving because he still thought he could write it.'

Lindsley's voice has risen as he talked and it echoed faintly in the shelter, and though Raveneau doubted la Rosa could make out the words, she had to be wondering.

'That's what happened,' Lindsley said, and then climbed the ladder.

'If you write the book now are you going to give Lash any credit?'

The vehemence of the answer surprised Raveneau. Lindsley's voice was very emotional and loud. 'I'm going to expose him. I'm going to show the world what a fucking fraud he is.'

When they got back into the sunlight Lindsley's gaze roamed from him to la Rosa.

'Do you know what I can't stand? Do you know what I can't handle? I can't stand that he might die first. I want him to stay alive and then

I'll come visit him and I'll read my book to him. I'm working on the book now. I'm writing it and he's just got to hold on. I want him paralysed, trapped, and me reading and the people taking care of him thinking he's loving it. Thanks for the tour, Inspector. I'm out of here. Good luck with everything.'

Raveneau watched his quick steps up the garden stairs and the way he broke to his left and went around the side of the house.

'See that?' Raveneau said to la Rosa. 'He does know his way around here. It wasn't all in the living room.' He considered that a moment and added, 'And he wants us to know that. He gave me a little more today. He gives me a little more each time. He gave me a reason why he might have been jealous of Ann and another motive for framing Lash.'

'What's he say about Lash?'

'That he hates him, and I'm starting to believe him.'

Seventeen

Sunday dawn Raveneau was on his redwood deck with coffee and a laptop open reading into Coryell's dissertation. Attis had quoted several times from page twenty-nine and he read that first.

'No society can move forward carrying unreconciled genocide. It leads inevitably to detachment and the inability of a society to envision its future.'

He skimmed forward looking for hard facts and stopped at the heading *'Trail of Tears'*, then read her distillation on the forced relocation of the Cherokee, Chickasaw, Choctaw, Muscogee, and Seminole tribes with the passage of the Indian Removal Act of 1830. The Choctaw were first to go. They were removed in 1831, Seminoles in 1832, the Muscogee or Creek in 1834, and the Chickasaw in 1837. A year later it was the Cherokees, the last of those called the 'civilized tribes'. That opened twenty-five million acres for settlement of what would become known as the Deep South.

Coryell focused on the Cherokees who came last. The Cherokee tribe resisted and were relocated to a concentration camp in Tennessee prior to a forced walk to the Oklahoma territory.

Four thousand died of disease, starvation, and cold along the way. He read those stats, laid the dissertation down, and went to get more coffee.

He read about the Navajo and Coryell's theory that it wasn't about numbers killed but the thing done to a people. The Navajo dead numbered two hundred on the eighteen-day march from Arizona to eastern New Mexico. That was very poor land, and they eventually returned home to the land between the four sacred mountains. That wasn't in here but Raveneau remembered reading about their return.

He looked up from the laptop as Celeste walked out. She leaned and kissed him and passed on by and walked down the wooden plank way leading toward the stairs, and halfway down she walked out across the flat roof to the parapet. Raveneau's apartment sat up on top of an industrial building in China Basin. The view from that parapet looked north-east across China Basin. She was standing out there with a coffee, and he walked over now and stood with her.

Three hours later he was sitting in the FBI San Francisco Field Office watching the video feed as Lisa Berge was interviewed. One male and one female agent, both similar in age to Lisa, shook her hand and thanked her for coming. Berge seemed flustered.

'I'll be honest,' she told them, 'I don't think much of any government organizations and didn't have any choice but to come here. SFPD is trying to intimidate me and I'm sure you're talking with them. I think this is one big set-up by people who don't really know what they're doing. So ask your questions and let's get this over with.'

Special Agent Alyssa Fry didn't challenge her on that and it looked like Fry was going to be the alpha here. She opened a notebook and tapped the table with a pen, though lightly, as if musing about something, or waiting for a signal from Berge. If so, she got it a few seconds later, though it didn't have anything to do with the answering machine.

'What if we got rid of all government agencies with policies? I had to leave my driver's license with your guard when I got here. He said it was policy. That's all the explanation he gave me. It's policy. What good do these policies that the rest of us are paying for achieve?'

'Lisa, will you allow that it's a complicated world and we're fighting a war on terror and need to protect our offices.'

'If you ask me, what you're trying to protect are your jobs and the right to retire when you're in your fifties. Then you have pensions at eighty or ninety percent and you go find some sweet new job to sugar coat it. The rest of us don't get that.'

'We make some sacrifices along the way and we put our lives at risk.'

'Then why aren't more of you killed?' Berge stared across the table then said, 'I didn't lie to Inspector Raveneau, but I didn't tell him the truth. I listened to the recording on the answering machine and took out the tape and flushed it down a toilet.'

'What was the message?'

'I couldn't make any sense of it. It was about something happening in San Francisco due to an expansion. It didn't make any sense.'

'Did you write anything down before you destroyed the tape?'

'No, the inspector already knew what was on it.'

'How many times did you listen to it?'

'Once.'

'Just once.'

'Yes.'

'And yet you're saying you didn't understand what was being said in the message?'

'Yes.'

'When you didn't understand what was said, did you consider replaying it?'

'No. I had heard enough.'

'What was the voice like?'

'It was a man with a deep voice.'

'How old would you say he was? Give me a range.'

Berge thought it over and then said, 'Thirty to forty.'

Raveneau, who was sitting next to Mark Coe, said, 'That's what I heard too, but it wasn't Brandon Lindsley. It might have been this Attis Martin. The quality wasn't good and some effort went into disguising the voice. Sounds to me like she's been coached to say she didn't understand what she heard.'

Raveneau abruptly stopped talking as Fry asked the next question.

'And you only listened to it once?'

Berge nodded.

Fry said, 'I need you to answer.'

'I was the only one.'

'You were in a hurry. The homicide inspectors were on their way and you needed to deal with it.'

'People make threats all the time. It doesn't mean anything is going to happen.'

'And it's not good for a property to get known as a place where someone the police arrested was living.'

'He wasn't living there. No one was living there. I don't think anyone ever used that apartment in the year they had it leased. We have inspections every six months and required cleaning. As far as we know, no one has ever stayed there.'

'Did you tell the homicide inspectors that?'

'I told them everything, but they're not very bright. Especially him.'

Coe chuckled.

'Did the client always pay on time?' Fry asked.

'Yes, and you have the records.'

'I have to say, Lisa, you have a lot to manage. My husband and I bought a duplex and we live in one of the units. The other is rented and just that one is a job. I can understand how you have to make some quick decisions. Is that what happened? You made a management decision?'

'I would call it that, but I can't tell if you're being sincere or patronizing me.'

'Tell us again what you remember about the recording, and this is important because you and Inspector Raveneau are the only people who have heard it.'

'I think I've already told you.'

'Would it make a difference if I said the FBI believes this threat is real?'

'What happens if I remember more?'

Coe chuckled again. He punched Raveneau on the shoulder.

'That would only help, Lisa,' Fry said, 'and there's no risk to you here. We appreciate you coming forward and coming in on a Sunday. The truth is we depend on people like you and always have.'

'He said if you borrow money you owe it and that if you kill people it's the same thing, you owe for it. And the last part, which I didn't really understand, the western expansion you were talking about. I didn't understand what he meant. My family has been here forever. We were pioneers and there are others like us, so I have no idea what he was talking about.'

'After Inspector Raveneau called you, what did you do?'

'I drove straight over there.'

Raveneau nodded. He believed that.

'Was that because you were worried?'

'Yes, I was worried, of course I was worried. I didn't really know what to expect. We had another situation once where the police didn't tell the truth about why they wanted to get in.'

'So you were thinking about that?'

'Yes.'

'Did you remove the tape as soon as you heard the recording?'

'Yes.'

'You said you flushed it down a toilet. Was it

in that unit?'

'Yes.'

'Did you touch the iPhone holder?'

'No, I didn't. I took a book but the inspector didn't ask about a book so I haven't said anything about it. I asked my lawyer and he said I was within my rights as long as the tenant was notified of eviction and the book was returned later.'

'Where is the book now?'

'It's in a bag in my car.' She added, 'In the trunk.'

'How much have you handled it?'

'Not very much. I opened it up and looked at it.'

'Why don't we go get the book together and then come back up?'

'Will I get my driver's license back when I go out?'

'I'll make sure you do.'

She was parked in a garage and it took twenty minutes before they were back. The book was in a plastic department store shopping bag and was moved into a clear plastic evidence bag and brought back up to the interview room. Raveneau and Coe read the title through the plastic: *'Retribution and Redemption: The Probable Use of Nuclear Weapons In the 21st Century.'*

'Has anyone other than you touched it?' Fry asked, and her voice was much quieter, almost soft as she studied the title and held it so the video feed would capture the cover.

'No.'

'Has it been in your trunk in this shopping bag

the whole time?'

'Yes.'

'Have you talked to anyone else about it?'

'No one.'

'Did you remove anything else from the apartment?'

'You already asked that.'

'I'm asking again.'

'I didn't take anything else.'

'Have you had any more contact from the renter?'

'No.'

Raveneau saw that Lisa Berge was completely unfazed by the book's title. All that mattered to her was her world. He turned to Coe. 'No one saw her coming. That book was meant to be found and that's the one pattern we're seeing. They want to engage. They must think we have it and it explains something about the meeting I had with Brandon Lindsley and the threesome at Grate's Place.'

'You're locked in on these guys without much to go on.'

'That's true, but they're the ones engaging us. It's too much to ignore.'

Neither said anything for a moment, and then Coe said, 'Ben, you know we're going to have to get involved now in a bigger way.'

'Well, let's talk it through after you've met with your ASAC. Call me and I won't be at Homicide. I've got to go see someone in Marin.'

Eighteen

Marion reached for her cane and rose slowly as the doorbell rang. Though she knew the homicide inspector meant well, she was burdened by this visit and it was difficult to smile as she opened the door.

'Come on into the kitchen, Inspector. I've made tea. I can make you coffee.'

'Marion, thank you, tea is fine but I don't need anything other than to talk with you. I need your help.' Raveneau brought out the photos before sitting. He asked, 'Have you ever heard the name Brandon Lindsley?'

'No.'

'He was a grad student at the same time as Ann, though he was younger. She may have mentioned his name at some point.'

'I don't recognize it.'

She watched her hand tremble as she lifted the saucer and teacup and brought it to him. What were these photos about? What mattered was confronting Albert Lash, and though she was angry that that wasn't what he was here about, she was also fearful. Some part of her inside felt as if it was dissolving.

'I'm going to show you six photos because he may have used a different name with you.'

He spread them out on her kitchen table, all of the faces younger men, and one she knew well. She touched it. 'He's a friend.'

'How long have you known him?'

'For years.'

'That's Brandon Lindsley, that's who I was asking about.'

'That's not the name I know him by. He's writing a book and he knew Ann and I've known him so long I didn't mention him when you asked last time about people who admired her.'

'What name does he use?'

'His name is Alan Siles. He lives in Mill Valley. Once a month we meet at a restaurant there or I cook here.'

She heard herself and it sounded as if she was defending Alan yet she also saw the truth the inspector was showing her. She saw in the inspector's face that Alan had deceived her, yet she'd had more fun with Alan than with any other person in the past few years. He seemed to care so genuinely about Ann and was so interested in her memories of Pine Ridge and relatives who were on the reservation. She had helped him with his book and she looked forward to their meetings and to their dinners at the restaurant. Alan was her friend, maybe her best friend. They emailed each other regularly. These truths flitted through her head in rapid succession and they fell away and she felt short of breath.

She stared at his photo. It was almost inconceivable that Alan wasn't who he said he was and she hadn't really even considered him when the inspector asked her before. She had so little respect for the police. This one who felt guilty was sincere but what chance was he going to have after all this time? They failed with Lash when they had their chance and she had dismissed the idea that Inspector Raveneau could ever be right and now she had to accept that she was wrong. I've failed Ann in every way, she thought.

'I'm coming home, Mom,' Ann had said.

'No, you're not; you're staying where you are. You have a sickness and cowardice about beating it. You need to find strength.'

'I'm coming home.'

'This is not your home anymore.'

She felt Raveneau's hand on her shoulder.

'Marion?'

She nodded. She looked out at him as though through a tunnel.

'I'm not saying there's anything wrong with him, but we're looking at him. Has he ever brought anyone with him?'

'He did once but only once and I don't know the name of that man.'

'I have another photo to show you, but it's on my phone.'

She watched him fumble with his phone. The police were stupid. They were stupid everywhere. It was Albert Lash who killed Ann and what they found in this bomb shelter was going to prove that. She had to remember that but felt so shocked right now.

'This is a friend of Brandon Lindsley. Do you recognize him?'

'No.'
'Are you sure?'
'Yes.'
'Then tell me what you can about Brandon. I'd like to know what he has said to you about Ann's murder. What does he think about all the mistakes the police made?'
She wasn't going to answer that. Did she need to? They had talked about everything and often about Professor Lash and she wasn't going to tell the inspector what they said about the San Francisco Police.
'We've talked about what you would expect.'
'Does he agree that Lash killed her?'
'It was always obvious he killed her.'
'Does he agree?'
'Yes.'
'Marion, stay with me. I'm not saying he doesn't or that he's wrong. But I know his name isn't Alan Siles and that he lied to you about that.'
'How do you know that?'
'He pays his taxes as Brandon Lindsley. He has a driver's license in that name and this afternoon we found where he moved here from. He grew up in a suburb outside of Chicago. We have other reasons for wanting to learn more about him and I'm asking for your help. Have you talked with him about the night Ann disappeared? Has he questioned you at all about that night?'
She nodded.
'Have you talked with him about it?'
'I have.'
'I have some ideas about that night I want to

run by you and this won't be easy to hear, but maybe these are some of the things you've talked about. Ann left the cottage and may have been walking to her car when she was abducted, or she may have been in the back garden still.'

'She went to Professor Lash's house and knocked on the door and he let her in.'

'How do you know that?'

'I told her she couldn't come home.'

'Did she say she would knock on his door?'

'No.'

'How do you know she did?'

'I know because I told her she couldn't come home.'

With that something broke loose inside her. She looked at him and then stared again at the photo of Alan. Was that really not his name? She told everything to Alan and now he wasn't who he said he was? She couldn't understand anyone doing that and it devastated her. She tried to answer now and couldn't and the inspector sat in silence and waited. When she spoke her voice broke and the words did not sound as if they came from her.

'Yes, she was coming home. I told her no but she said she was coming anyway. My sweet beautiful daughter was scared and wanted to come home and I said no. I thought it was all in her head, same as I told you last time. I wouldn't let her come home. I told her she had to stay to get stronger, to solve her problems not run from them and not let her imagination affect her so much. If she had come home in the earlier part of the night, she might never have gone back.

She would be alive right now.'

Her body was wracked with sobs as she bowed her head. It took her several minutes to stop, and she wiped her eyes and her face and it was the inspector who spoke.

'She must have loved you just as much to want to come home.'

'I blamed you for missing her call, but it was always me. I wouldn't let her come home. I'm so sorry for things I've said, for what I've done.'

She shook her head, wiped her cheeks and tried to breathe and then couldn't stop the tears. She couldn't control herself anymore. She tried for so long. She carried it for so long. She couldn't any longer.

Nineteen

As Raveneau drove through the toll plaza and back into San Francisco the Missouri sheriff called and pulled his thoughts from Marion Coryell's anguish.

'Sending out bone samples to you made its way into the local newspaper here. I'm getting some blowback. I don't know who leaked it. I never try to find out anymore, but safe to say some people don't like the idea we kept DNA samples and are now shipping them to San Francisco, of all the degenerate places in the world. So I need two questions answered. Did your crime lab get what we sent and how soon can we get them back? Well, three questions. The third is, when do you expect results?'

'I know the guy that runs the lab and he left me a message earlier that they arrived and he took samples. I'll ask him to ship the rest back to you tomorrow morning.'

'What about results?'

'I'm pushing and I can tell you they think the skeletal decay is similar between what we have and what you sent. Of the leads we've got, and we've got five or six, yours is most promising.'

'I feel like a contestant.'

'I'm with you and I hope you win. I'd like to get it answered, and if they are yours, how did they get from Cagdill to a bomb shelter in San Francisco?'

Some of the bounce was gone from her voice when she answered that saying, 'I've got a story I should have told you before now, but I was waiting to see if this panned out as anything first.'

Raveneau listened as he drove along the Marina Green. He turned into the lot looking for a place to park and with the warm weather not expecting to find one but got lucky.

'The caskets washed up on both sides of the highway and we put markers on them. I think I told you that. We couldn't drive to all of them. We had to walk through the river mud and we sure weren't going to be able to move them until a backhoe got the muck off the highway, but the hoes were all working on levee breaks. The river was still up and we had a basketful of other problems and taking care of the caskets didn't happen as fast as it should have. We taped off the area and blocked access and made sure they weren't going to get damaged, but let's face it, caskets sit six feet under in mud, so what the heck.

'Very early the next morning a scraper was due to clean the road, and Jacobs, the farmer I told you about who owns the fields alongside the highway, saw a light. Did I tell you all of this already?'

'You told me there was a farmer who saw someone but keep going.'

'He saw a light and went out to investigate and it didn't take him long to figure it was someone looking at the caskets. His guess was that it was somebody wondering if they had a relative washed up on the side of a road. He worked his way down to the edge of his property. It was a cold morning, it was early and the highway was muddied up, so old Jacobs was curious that anyone would be out there at that hour. He got close enough to figure it was a man but not close enough to give us a good description. He thought the vehicle was a either a Jeep Cherokee or something similar in shape. He didn't have his cellphone with him and had to go all the way back to his house before he could call us, and he did some chores on the way back, so by the time we got out there all we found were tire tracks and footprints. I have plaster casts of those.

'It's been a hard one to have unsolved. If it was grave robbing and this individual stole jewelry and watches and such, well, that would have been one thing. But stealing skulls made it very emotional for people. I've had a lot of pressure to get it solved and some crank calls because of it, not all of them friendly. It's why I put you on speakerphone the first time we talked.'

'I figured it was something like that.'

'I've been made a fool of once on this already. A handful of high school kids tricked me. One of them reported skulls out on a bluff overlooking the river and I raced out with my siren on. They took videos of me with their cellphones and posted them to Facebook, but not one would rat out who made the call to the Sheriff's Office. So when you called that went through my head before anything else.'

'But I told you who I was.'

'You also told me you were from California.'

Raveneau got out of the car still talking to her, easing back to just exactly where they were at number-wise with the samples sent and also asking how serious her concern about the blow-back was. He didn't want anything to derail these DNA tests.

He looked out on a dark blue bay and an orange-red light along the western horizon behind the Golden Gate Bridge as he talked with her. He gathered she was at home and that her house was small and up on a bluff over the Mississippi. She could see the river from her porch. She told him she had a ten-year-old daughter she was raising and said nothing about her ex-husband. He thought he heard the clink of ice in a glass just before he hung up with her.

Now he walked out the path to the anchorage of the Golden Gate Bridge. When his cellphone rang again it was Celeste.

'Hey, are you still coming here or should I bring some food from the bar and meet you up on your roof? How long until you're home?'

'An hour.'

'Where are you now?'

'Walking.'

'Thinking?'

'Quit thinking so much, it's a beautiful evening.'

'I'll see you soon.'

Twenty

When Raveneau had negotiated the lease for the one-bedroom rooftop apartment, the wood deck off the sliding door was much smaller and several of the redwood deck boards had rotted through. His landlord, a tough Vietnamese immigrant, shook off repairing the deck, but they kept the conversation going and over time Raveneau cut a deal with him. Now the deck was lined with potted citrus trees whose fragrance floated in through the open slider most nights. He often slept with the door and windows open. Up here, he didn't worry much about intruders.

Tonight in the warm still air he and Celeste sat

outside at the deck table eating crostini she'd brought from M33 along with salad and red wine. Raveneau rarely talked about an ongoing case, almost never when he was on-call, but cold cases were different and this one different again and when she prompted him he said, 'In our office for a long time there was a feeling that Albert Lash knew more and may have killed her. One of the two inspectors who caught the case was a good friend of mine – not so much anymore – but definitely then and for a long time. We joined the force together, came through the police academy in the same class and both of us wanted to make it to homicide someday. He got there first.'

'Who's that?'

'Hugh Neilley. Hugh worked the Coryell murder with another inspector now retired named Ray Alcott. I've combed through the murder files. They did their best, but it's all a big zero if you don't solve it, and Hugh left the Homicide Detail not long after the investigation files ended up in our cold case closet.'

Raveneau saw Celeste start to ask and answered it first. 'Hugh had a drinking problem and his marriage had ended so there was no one waiting for him to get home at night. No one will ever acknowledge this, but it got worked out so that the southern precinct made him an offer and Hugh promised to get his drinking under control. They took him in there so he didn't have to resign and he worked out a story he could live with. He's a lieutenant now at Southern, has been since January 2005.

'Her remains were found in 2003 but we didn't get DNA confirmation until early April, which is a fairly normal lag. It was a Marin case, and when the suspicion came that it might be her the investigation became joint, and once it was joint and we knew it was her we took over the investigation. We wanted it. We wanted to solve it.

'Now in all this Lash was very helpful and we did a kind of dance with him. He was working on a book where he needed police interviews and we wanted to know everything we could about him. Hugh spent time with him during the active investigation and I know he was up at Lash's house regularly even after he moved to Southern. Lash poured some expensive liquor and wine and had a cook and started a poker thing with some of the officers. The book was about San Francisco as seen through the eyes of the SFPD, so he was especially interested in the career officers who'd been around for awhile. Hugh fit.'

'What about you? Did you go there?'

'I did and Lash is a charming guy. He's generous. He's quick and fun and has a lot of stories of his own. It was easy to accept his invitations and drink his twenty-five-year-old single malts and his top-flight wines and tell ourselves we were getting closer to him to learn more about him.' Raveneau paused. 'If Hugh was sitting here and I said this, he'd punch me, but I'll tell you I think Lash got the better of him. He drew him in and compromised him with his generosity. Hugh would go there on a Saturday night when he was off shift and call me Sunday in a froggy hung-over voice to tell me something suspicious he'd learned about Lash the night before. He knew my interest in the case and that made him feel better, but it was all bullshit.'

Celeste studied him, her dark eyes filled with curiosity. 'I've never heard Hugh Neilley's name before.'

'We meet for a drink now and then, but he's got plenty of friends he's closer to. Hugh and I make a point of an occasional drink, but we don't have much to say to each other anymore.'

'I understand about the drinking but I thought once you made it on to the Homicide Detail you stayed there.'

'Yes and no, but there was also a rumor that someone well up in the brass saw him at Moose's deadass drunk and talking about a case to somebody he didn't know. There was that rumor and there were other rumors, and eventually it got to be too much.'

After a beat, Raveneau added, 'If he and Joan hadn't gotten divorced I think it would have been different. They were high school sweethearts and there's probably no one else for either one of them. I shouldn't say that but that's how it seems to me. Hugh took on a lot of debt in the divorce because he wanted to hang on to the house which had been his parents' house. His dad built it. He was a builder. That's how he got into this thing now where he's going to run a demolition company when he retires. He's got his nephew working as a foreman.'

'At Lash's old house?'

'Yeah.'

‘Seems a little weird.’
‘It’s something.’
Raveneau poured her more wine and picked up his glass. One good thing about working cold cases and no longer being in the on-call rotation was he could drink at night. He told Celeste more about the skulls stacked against the wall in the bomb shelter. None of it was secret anymore. The media had found a way in and the department elected to reveal the phone threat, calling it ‘as yet unsubstantiated, but being treated seriously’. Raveneau read that as don’t try to sue us later because we let know you ahead of time.
‘What do you think of this threat?’ she asked. ‘Isn’t there always somebody threatening something?’
‘Sure, and this may not be any different, but it ties to the bomb shelter. We’ve got some people we’re looking at, but I’ve also got a bad feeling about it. It’s a self-righteous threat, somebody who has assigned themselves the job of making us all pay for a wrong, in this case what we did to the Native American tribes. It connects with what Ann Coryell wrote about. I haven’t told you this, but I met Ann Coryell the night she disappeared. I was two streets over re-interviewing a witness in a murder case and when I left I saw three police cruisers out in front of Albert Lash’s house.’
‘Did you know it was his house?’
‘Yeah, he was a popular writer by then and always trying to get media attention. I’d seen his house on TV and if you’re a cop long enough you come to know who lives where. I stopped to

see what was going on and that led to walking through a eucalyptus grove just over a low stone wall and in the Presidio. I walked it with Ann Coryell. She had called 911 twice that week claiming to hear a woman in pain screaming. The responding officers got there fast the first time, but they were more skeptical after the second and third calls. When I was with her she was both distraught and embarrassed. I thought there was a pretty good chance she wouldn't call 911 if she heard the screaming again, but she might call me. So I gave her my cell number. She called me that night and I missed the call. I slept through it.'

'What did you do before you went to bed?'

'I made a sandwich, watched TV, and drank a couple glasses of red wine. If not for the wine I would have heard the phone vibrating.'

'You don't know that.'

'I would have heard it.'

'You can't do that, Ben.'

'I'm pretty sure, and the way it worked out I was the last known person to see her alive. Most of her remains were found thirteen months later up on the western slope of Mount Tam.'

'I've heard and it's still awful.'

It was, and now he lay awake near Celeste and the heart-calming warmth of her skin and soft breathing. At five o'clock he was out of bed making coffee and reading Ann Coryell again, a section titled, *'Suppression of the Ghost Dance and Wounded Knee.'*

Coryell's style in her earlier writings was to lay out the facts with few adjectives. Wounded

Knee Creek, Pine Ridge Indian Reservation, South Dakota, December 29, 1890, US Army Seventh Calvary intercepts five hundred Lakota Sioux under the leadership of Chief Bigfoot. Calvary officers later claim the soldiers fired in self defense but of the three hundred dead almost two hundred were women and children and cavalry dead and wounded are almost entirely victims of friendly fire. So again, Coryell style, no judgment and the facts speak for themselves.

Raveneau read until dawn and then showered, brewed fresh coffee and he and Celeste left together. He took an unexpected early morning call as he got in his car.

'Hugh, what's up?'

'I need a favor. My nephew got in a fight last night with two off-duty officers and broke the nose of one of them. He's in jail and telling me it wasn't his fault and that he was defending himself. One of the two he fought with has been called in before for unnecessary force, so maybe that's true, but I've got to stay clear of it. Can you go see him and find out what the fuck happened, and then tell me straight what you think? And tell me no right now if there's any conflict with your investigation.'

'I'll talk to him this morning.'

'Thank you, and I'm asking you because you know the whole story. You know what a struggle it's been with him. I've done all I can for my sister's kid and if he's not going to stand up, and if there's always an explanation and an excuse, if he's really no good, then family or no family I can't keep helping him.'

‘Two off-duty officers?’

‘That’s right, and Matt’s in jail expecting me, not you.’

‘OK, and so we’re clear, I know you called because you guessed I’d jump on it. I’m not jumping, but I’ll do it and not out of friendship. But you already know that too. I’m doing it because I’ve got questions about Matt. I’ll go see him and then you and I are going to meet.’

‘Not in the homicide office.’

‘We’ll meet somewhere else and it’ll be tonight.’

‘You don’t know any more than we did when we put that file in the cold case closet.’

‘I’m getting there, Hugh, and one way or another I’m going to figure out who knew about this bomb shelter and when.’

‘I know what you’re doing.’

‘And what’s that?’

‘You’re undermining the investigation Alcott and I did so you can feel better about how you let her down. But you’re not going to ever get away from that. That’ll always be on you. You don’t need to go see Matt. I’ll deal with it.’

‘I’ll go see him this morning.’

Hugh hung up without saying anything more.

Twenty-One

'Your uncle asked that I come see you.'

'Where is he?'

'He's at his desk. He's busy.'

'Why would he call you?'

'We're old friends and he knows I understand what a hard time he's had getting you to stay out of trouble.'

'You ought to hear what he says about you now.'

'Well, I can hear it from him. I don't need to hear it from you. What happened last night?'

Baylor shook his head. He smiled. 'Sorry, Inspector, but this just doesn't make any sense. My Uncle Hugh totally trash talks you.'

'We still go way back and not all of those times were good times so don't worry about it.'

Matt Baylor stared at the homicide inspector. Why did Hugh send this guy when he didn't even like him? What he needed was a lawyer who would sue the police department's ass. He touched the bruise on his left cheekbone where the cop arresting him clubbed him and didn't like the way Raveneau was staring at him. Truth was, he hated cops all the way down into his gut and that included two-faced Uncle Fucking Hugh, who was going to save him from a life of ruin and build a retirement fund for himself by sending him out to tear crap down and then bitch about it taking too long. Hugh, who never dealt with the Mexicans who all wanted to friggin' get paid the same day or had to drive crap to the resource center so some prissy-ass could check it in and make sure it all got recycled.

'So you're here to hear my side and then help me. Is that it?'

'I'm here to get your version. I don't care much about helping you or listening to attitude. Either tell me what you claim happened or don't. I'll give you another fifteen seconds to decide, but there's no pressure. I've got plenty to do today and I'm fine with walking out of here right now.'

'What are you going to do with it?'

'I'll see Hugh tonight and tell him what I heard. You probably know better than I do what he'll do with it. Doesn't he usually post a bond and hire a lawyer when you get arrested? When you got busted for selling dope, he paid for your lawyer, right, and you're working it off but you're resentful about that now. You weren't that way when you needed a lawyer, but that was then. So what do you want to do here?'

Baylor didn't say anything but he hoped Raveneau could read his look. He wanted Raveneau to know what he was capable of and let him think about that. But the fucker just looked at him and smiled like he was going to laugh.

'So what happened last night?'

'Forget about it.'

Raveneau reached for the door.

'I was at a bar and around midnight these two guys came in and started talking at this chick I'd been drinking with. They were drunk and when I went to use the bathroom one of them took my seat. He wouldn't get up when I came back. My drink was right there in front of the stool when I went to piss and he pushed it down the bar and Rachel was freaking a little. These guys were drunk.'

'Did you know Rachel before that night?'

'No, but we connected. She had already given me her phone number. It's in my cell and I can show you. She wouldn't have done that if it wasn't real.'

'Go on.'

'He wouldn't move and I kind of bumped him and when he went to push me I grabbed his arm and pulled him off the stool on to the floor. Then the other one jumped on me and I had to fight them both.'

'The other one says he identified himself as a police officer.'

'That's bullshit.'

'They're saying you kicked the head of the guy on the floor hard enough to knock out some teeth.'

'I don't know what happened, but they started it and the other one was swinging at me.' He turned his head so Raveneau could see the bruise. 'Look at this.'

'Then what?'

'The bartender goes for the phone and the one I'm fighting whips his badge out after he lands a few on me. Then other cops arrive and they baton the shit out of me before they put me in their car. I was sitting there having a good time with her before they walked in.'

'Did the one who took your bar stool identify himself as a police officer before you got into it with him?'

'I told you already, no, he didn't.'

'Is Rachel going to back you up on this?'

'She's probably totally freaked out.'

'What about the bartender? How much did he see?'

'I don't know.'

'A couple of witnesses told the officers who arrested you that you were wearing boots and kicked the one on the floor in the head as you held the other one off with a chair.'

'No way, and those guys started the whole thing. They're lying. Do you want to see the bruises on my back? I can barely stand up, dude.'

'If we call Rachel is she going to answer?'

'I don't know.'

'She's your best witness. Should we call her?'

'They took my phone when they booked me.'

'I can get your phone. Is it worth calling her? If she backs up your story that's going to help a lot, and it wants to happen before they figure out what to charge you with.'

'Sure, I'll call her.'

'I'll go get things started, and then you're going to have to OK releasing your phone to me.'

Baylor thought about that a moment before deciding it was his best chance. Rachel sure as fuck wasn't going to answer the phone. The cops busted her last month for prostitution, but if this bozo Raveneau thought she was legit that might help. He nodded at Raveneau. 'Whatever I've got to sign to give you access to my shit, that's cool.'

'All right, I'll be straight back.'

Twenty-Two

It took half an hour to get Baylor's phone released. Raveneau walked back with a guard but not before thumbing through the recent calls on the phone and scanning the stored photos. He stopped on three taken on Tuesday the day after the bomb shelter was found, and then went back one more day to Monday where it looked like Baylor took photos from inside the bomb shelter though none came out very well.

Raveneau returned to the day after photos. All three were taken from above looking down. In one was a silver necklace and locket, in the next an old hunting knife with an ornate handle and a cracked leather sheath alongside it. The third was a photo of two rings, one on its side, one standing; the one standing was a gold ring with carvings, the other silver with a turquoise stone. Each photo was taken with the ring or knife or necklace lying on what looked like a faded yellow white blouse. Around the edges of it was gray countertop and familiar.

When Raveneau handed it to him, Baylor took the phone without saying anything. He was shackled yet that didn't slow him down. He quickly found her number and Raveneau wrote the number down then put Baylor's phone on the table and called from his phone. In Baylor's phone directory her name was Rachel. No last name and as the phone was ringing he asked Baylor, 'Rachel what? What's her last name?'

Baylor hesitated.

He knows her last name and doesn't want to give it to me, Raveneau thought. He knows her name and she didn't give him her phone number when they were sitting at the bar. He already had it. 'Come on, you've got to remember her last name.'

Baylor waited him out. He knew her voicemail was coming. Her voicemail said, 'This is Rachel. Leave me a message.'

Raveneau left one. In it he identified himself as a San Francisco homicide inspector and gave his cell number. Baylor didn't like that much. Passive hostility radiated off him.

'Is she going to call me back?'

'I don't know. She was crying and in total shock.'

'What about the bartender?'

'He was a jerk. I think he knew the cops.'

'I'll wait for Rachel to call me and I'll let your uncle know you've got a witness and maybe he'll give her a call too.' Raveneau stared, sizing him up again, now asking, 'Is that OK with you?'

'Sure. Whatever.'
'Anything else you want me to tell him?'
'Ask him to get me out of here.'
'Hasn't he always had your back?'
'You really don't know, dude. It's not like he tells you, if he tells you anything. I've done a lot of squirrelly shit for him too.'
'Like what?'
'Forget it.'
'OK, then let's talk about something else before I leave. The first time I climbed down into the bomb shelter I could read your boot prints pretty easily. Remember, you had a guy with a hose wetting down the demo dust. You tracked mud into the bomb shelter. We questioned the crew and we're confident no one else went down there, only you, and you didn't work too hard at erasing your tracks, so I'm guessing you didn't care that I knew you went through the belongings on the blankets. But now I want to know where the things are that you took and I want them back. Did you sell them or do you still have them?'
'I didn't take anything.'
'Yeah, you did.'
'Why doesn't anyone believe me?'
'There are photos in your phone and I just looked at them. Did you post these photos to Craigslist? Will I find them there?' Raveneau waited for him to answer though he didn't expect him to yet. He gave him another long beat and then said, 'If I get those things back then that'll be it. I'll let it go, and if not, you've got a new problem.'

'It's not legal for you to go through my photos like that. You fucking tricked me.'
'Do you still have everything you took?'
After a silence, Baylor said, 'The knife sold.'
'To somebody you know?'
'No, some dude.'
'Could you find him again?'
He shook his head.
'What about the other things?'
'I've got them.'
'Where?'
'At Hugh's place. I'm staying there until I get another apartment. I had a screwed-up roommate who was playing music all night and I was out the door to work early every morning. I wasn't getting any sleep.'
'Where are they at your uncle's?'
'Hidden.'
'Hidden where? The kitchen countertop is in the photos. Should I tell Hugh they're either at his house or in your truck? Where are the keys to your truck? I'm sure he'll look in both places and you don't want him breaking a window to get in. Actually, you know what; it'll be easier if I just get the truck impounded. I'll do that.'
Raveneau got ready to leave again. He needed to get a guard to return the phone to storage, but knew same as ten minutes ago he wouldn't get as far as the door before Baylor said something. That was about Hugh. Baylor needed Hugh to get him a lawyer and help him navigate his way out of this bar fight.
'I don't want him to know,' Baylor said. 'I'll get them back to you as soon as I get out. I'll

meet you and give them to you.'

'You're out tomorrow if not today and I want them as soon as you're out. What about Rachel? What do you want to do with her? What's the message I give to Hugh?'

'Just say I have a witness. I'll give the lawyer her name and number.'

'Is she going to back you up?'

'She saw what happened.'

'I got that. But is she going to back you up? I'm going to put my cell number in your phone.' Raveneau did that and kept talking. 'I'm taking you at your word, Matt. Now you've got my number and you can call me as soon as you're out.'

'I don't know why I took them, anyway.'

'Sure you do, but I want them no later than tomorrow. We'll go from there.'

As he left the jail, Raveneau figured he had a pretty good chance of getting them back and he was glad it was the knife that had sold. The knife he could live without. But the other things, they might matter, and truth was there was no crime scene when Baylor took them. Baylor could erase the photos in his phone, change his story, and stonewall him. But chances were he wouldn't.

Twenty-Three

Hugh was at a North Beach bar he liked. It was also a bar that would comp a police officer a drink or two and Hugh was gregarious and full of stories once he got going, and Raveneau didn't doubt there were times Hugh didn't see a bar bill. He was several drinks in when Raveneau caught up to him and chatting with the bartender. Hugh didn't turn until Raveneau settled into the seat next to him. Raveneau read that as anger. The bartender took it as a cue to move on, and without any hello or preamble Hugh started in on his nephew.

'I'm just about at the end with him. He had some really bad years after my sister and Danny were killed and that was understandable. He fell in with the wrong people. He wasted a lot of chances, and he's about burned up his last with me. What did you think of what he told you about this bar fight?'

'I think the off-duty cops had been drinking before they got there and they elbowed their way in on the woman Matt was hitting on or already knew. Have you heard the name Rachel before? He says he met her last night and they hit it off and she gave him her phone number. I got his phone released and called her. I left her a message and he knows her, but he's not talking much about her. If she backs him up the whole thing might go away.'

Hugh considered that a few moments. He took a quick swallow and said, 'He must know her because no woman is going to sit down at a bar and give her phone number to a guy with a tattoo of a skeleton running up his neck without knowing something about him first. I'm hearing that the one who went to the floor, DeAngelou, has got more than a few teeth loose. He's got a broken jaw, and I've got a worthless nephew that I'm glad my sister isn't here to see. I'm going to have to get him a lawyer and get him out. I'll do that again because I need him working. I'll get him back to work and I'll find his replacement and he and his lawyer can deal with whatever comes out of last night.'

'He won't see charges. The officer who is already carrying the excessive force investigation is going to want to make it go away. That's DeAngelou. He'll decide it's not worth it. And his jaw is cracked, it's not wired shut. He'll be OK, and they were drunk. That's what the bartender told me.'

'How did you find out all this so fast?' Hugh turned, looking at him from the corner of his eye. 'Or rather why are you taking so much interest?'

'You asked me to.'

'Right, and I hung up on you this morning, too. I apologize for that. I'm not doing so well. I'm way too hair trigger and jumpy. This demolition business isn't adding up the way it needs to, and

Matt and I are going to part ways and he's still going to be into me for eighteen grand. That's a lot for me.'

Hugh took another good swallow.

'He was my sister's only kid, and she was my only sibling. I've got nothing left for family when I show him the door. I really saw the demolition business as the way to bring him around. I'm not saying he would need to spend the next ten years tearing things down and breathing God knows what, but I saw it as a way to get into construction. He could get some education, learn to read plans, and take it from there. Housing will come back eventually. It always does. But he just doesn't want to do real work. Worse than that, he looks around and thinks everyone else has got an easy ride. He doesn't think you or I do anything except talk all day. He doesn't respect people and I can't change that.'

Hugh didn't let up. He didn't want a conversation. He wanted to kill the night by talking it away and keep from answering any questions.

'You and I are counting on a pension system where they are still pretending they're going to make eight percent a year on the invested money and they're making half that at best. We're screwed. It's all going to blow up, and having this demolition business seemed like my best shot, but it's not working. Nothing is working for me.'

Hugh swallowed the last of his drink and wagged the glass so the old bartender could see.

'Now Matt's in jail and we've got jobs we'll

get fired from within a week unless they're manned. If we get fired, those contractors will never use me again. My other choice is to use the line of credit on my house and post bail for him.' He turned and looked at Raveneau. 'I already have a line of credit on the house and they're warning me they may call in the loan.'

Raveneau ordered a glass of red wine. Hugh's bourbon and ice got replaced, and as the red wine arrived Hugh looked at it and shook his head.

'Look at you, the wine sipper. Who would have guessed you'd turn into that?'

'Not you.'

'That's sure as fuck true.'

'But you don't have to worry about what I drink. You've got a lot on your mind already without worrying about what I drink or have for breakfast. You've got other problems with me.'

'That's what it's starting to seem like. You don't have much of an investigation so you're trying to create one out of thin air. What's next? Are you going to tell me that Alcott and I should have known about the bomb shelter and what was in it?'

'No, but I don't want to wrestle you for information. We've got a new situation, but I don't feel like you want the Coryell case to be open and active again.'

'Of course I want to see it solved. I just don't want to get hit when we're not there to defend ourselves. You know, this nephew of mine, this son of my sister's, might have been better off if he'd been in the car with his mom and dad.

That's a hard thing to say, but that's about where I'm at now. He's probably going to prison for a year.'

'He's not going anywhere, and we've talked about him enough today.'

'If he goes to prison even a year, he'll get shaped by the environment. He doesn't have enough of the right kind of will. He talks like he's tough but he's a pliable little shit and susceptible to all the wrong people. He'll come out with a shaved head and a swastika tattooed on his cock.'

Hugh continued on as Raveneau got impatient. He was tired of it. He laid money on the bar and signaled the bartender. 'Let's talk outside,' he said. 'We're not getting anywhere in here.'

Outside, Hugh said, 'I'm going to say one last thing about my nephew before we get to Coryell. About a year and a half ago, Matt beat a homeless man he claimed was stealing from his truck, but that's not what a witness saw. It got pleaded down to nothing and he did community service to try to erase the rest. He kicked the man unconscious and stamped on his hands until he broke every finger. I talked to a guy who didn't want to get involved but who saw the whole thing. He said Matt went berserk on the guy. So it's not that surprising to hear he got into it with two off-duty cops. That's going to figure into whatever decision gets made and I hope you're right about DeAngelou wanting to make it go away.'

'Are you through talking about him?'

'I'm done. You don't give a shit anyway.' He pointed. 'There's a place up the street here. We can talk in there, but what do you want from me tonight?'

'The names of who else was at Lash's parties and not just cops.'

'I may not remember any names. I can tell you who on the force was there and you can talk to them. Who do you remember, Ben? You were there.'

'I was there twice: once when it was just Lash and me, and once when there were two other police officers.'

'Well, talk to them, talk to Lash. He's the guy who should know who was there, but what difference does it make? How does this all connect?'

'I don't know that it does.'

'He had students in and out of there all the time. I just don't remember their names.'

'What if I showed you a photo?'

'Have you got it with you?'

'In my car.'

'Well, get it and I'll meet you inside.'

Raveneau retrieved the photo and as he came back in he saw why Hugh liked the bar. It was long and dark and of a different generation. They ordered drinks and found a corner.

'I saw Lash a few days ago,' Raveneau said. 'I think he wants to answer some things before he goes.'

'Lash will never confess to anything.'

'You know him much better than I do, but I get the feeling he wants to talk. There's no avoiding some of what we found in there.'

'Sure there is. He can die tomorrow and then

what are you going to do? Where's the photo?'

'I've got it.' Raveneau touched his coat pocket. 'It's right here. Lash kept diaries. Those are at his sister's. She's not cooperating with us, but she may with the FBI. They're working with us now and if they label this a terrorist plot they can pretty well get whatever they want of Lash's from the sister. I think that'll happen too.'

'And why is it you're telling me all this?'

'Because I need your help.'

'What is it you think you'll find in Lash's diaries?'

'I don't know yet, but there were other grad students in and out of Lash's house. It wasn't just Coryell.'

'There were plenty of them. I just don't have any names for you. I didn't become friends with any grad students. But they were there.'

'The photo I'm going to show is of one of them.'

'All right, and are you going to tell me now that Alcott and I should have been looking at him and we missed him like we missed the bomb shelter?'

'All I know is he's contacted me and gone out of his way to do it.'

'There was one kid who was background in those poker games Lash set up. I got the feeling he was working on something with Lash or learning from him. He talked about writing books himself, but he and I didn't connect.' Hugh pulled what looked like a prescription bottle from his pocket, opened it, and took out two pills. 'Acid reflux. Let's see the photo, and does this person in it remember me?'

'He does.'

'Are you looking at him or is he helping you with Lash?'

'I don't know yet what he's doing.'

'But you want me to look at his photo.'

'He ties to Lash. He may also tie to this threat you're hearing about.'

'Lash dropped me from the regulars list and cancelled the poker game as soon as his book got good reviews and was selling. I never had any close relationship with him and he sure beat us. All that time he sat there knowing about the bomb shelter and that bloody cot you found. He really did beat us and then made money writing about the department. Now he'll give us the finger as he goes out the back door. He's going to get away with whatever he did. You ought to give up on this one, Ben. This is one that not even you are going to bring home. You've felt guilty all these years, but let it go. He beat us but we're going to outlive him, so we'll get the last laugh.'

Raveneau didn't say anything to that. He pulled the photo, laid it on the bar, and Hugh picked it up.

'Brandon Lindsley wasn't around when she disappeared. He had an alibi. We checked.'

'He's not in either murder file.'

'Not everything makes it in. You're not in there either, but when I told you Alcott wanted to question you I wasn't kidding.' He laid the photo down. 'How did you find him?'

'He found me.'

'Lindsley approached you after the bomb shelter was found?'

'Yes, he found me up on Mount Tam not far from where her remains were found.'

'Then maybe you've got something there, and I wish I could help you, but I don't really know anything about him. We ruled him out early.' He paused. 'Maybe we shouldn't have.'

Twenty-Four

Raveneau brewed coffee, soft-boiled an egg, toasted two pieces of bread very dark, and then ate in the darkness out along the parapet. He poured a second cup of coffee and watched the dawn before heading into the office. On the drive in he took a call from the contractor, Ferranti, and forty minutes later Ferranti was in his car. They drove down to the Starbucks in the Letterman Center near Lucasfilm in the Presidio and carried coffees back and stood outside Raveneau's car in the morning sunlight.

'I like Lieutenant Neilley. It's his nephew I don't connect with. He's OK when he's working but I try to deal only with Neilley. The first two jobs they did for us were fine. They weren't great but they got it done. This has been completely different and what I heard yesterday is bad news. One of his laborers talked to one of mine and said not all of the dump loads are going to the Resource Center.'

'What's that mean?'

'That not everything hauled away from the job is going where it's supposed to. It says they're having money problems and don't want to pay what it costs.'

'So where is it going?'

'That's why I wanted to meet. We're required to show how the debris coming off the construction is diverted. It's in my contract, so it's also in Neilley's. It's about less going into landfill. This laborer says some of the loads got dumped down off Skyline Road, but Hugh has been giving me all his tags so somebody is lying.'

'What do you mean this laborer says? How would he know if he's working for you, not Hugh?'

'He says one of Baylor's laborers got an extra hundred bucks cash to help and the next morning Baylor fired him – told him he wasn't needed anymore. So that guy told one of his friends to tell my laborer.'

'Sounds like you'd better talk to the laborer who talked to your laborer.'

'I did. That's why I'm telling you.'

Raveneau thought over that as he drove to the Hall. He would have told la Rosa about it, but a call came from the manager of the assisted living facility where Lash was and the manager sounded shaken. She worked to keep her voice calm.

'Albert Lash is in the hospital with symptoms of radiation poisoning. A doctor just called. She wanted to know if Albert had been any place where he was getting radiation therapy. They're sure it's radiation but of course we don't do any radiation treatment here and he hasn't gone anywhere in a month. When someone needs an X-ray or treatment requiring radiation we schedule a visit. Albert hasn't had anything like that ever. That's why I'm calling you.'

'Maybe they're making a mistake.'

'The doctor sounded sure and I'm calling you because he had a visitor a couple of days ago.'

'Did the visitor sign in?'

'He signed in and we have videotape. It's not very good but there's eight seconds or so when he's in the elevator and then just outside it. Some of our residents wander at night and can forget which floor is theirs, so we always watch the elevators. Albert got sick and we thought it was a virus that's been going around.'

'Why don't you give me the phone number of the doctor you talked with this morning?'

Raveneau phoned the doctor as he started driving but cut that call off before it rang as another call came in, this one from Brandon Lindsley.

'What's up, Brandon?'

'Some not so cool police action today.'

'What happened?'

'My apartment manager got in my face. Usually the only thing that gets him going is spilled laundry soap. He said a homicide inspector has been asking questions about me. What am I supposed to do with that?'

'I've been making a lot of calls. You know how it is when someone suddenly appears on the side of a mountain and then feeds you a story.

I'm just doing what you expect me to, at least for now. But I definitely want to know who you are, Brandon, and all about your friends.'

'You already know who I am and what I'm about. I'm writing the book I told you about.'

'Why don't we take it to another level, Brandon?'

'I'm ready for that.'

'That's going to mean the conversation is a little more challenging.'

'I hear you and I am your guy, but I've got to ask a favor before we go any farther. I need you to call the geek who manages this apartment complex and tell him you were just fishing and that you have an unsolved case I'm trying to help you with. He needs to hear something. Maybe you want to tell him you're looking at me as a possible suspect. If you do that, let me know so I can get a lawyer.'

'I'll call him. I think he left me a message yesterday anyway. Now let me ask you something – why did you move to California?'

'That's the best question you've asked. So you are digging. I do a lot of research myself. I know that sense of discovery when you hit on something. Who are you talking to in Chicago?'

'People who worked the case.'

'Thanks for the vote of confidence. I made a big mistake with you.'

Raveneau talked on another few sentences before realizing Lindsley was gone. He started to call him back and stopped, decided to wait. He called the hospital and left a message for the doctor treating Lash. She returned his call a half hour later and sounded perplexed.

'Untreated it may have killed him and could still. In his condition it's going to be hard. He ingested a liquid with radioactive material in it. That's not like eating an apple.'

'Can he see visitors?'

'He wouldn't even know who you were, but I'll try to keep him from dying, Inspector.'

Twenty minutes later he was at the assisted living facility crossing the foyer where a handful of residents were sitting watching a TV, or maybe not. It was hard to tell where their focus was. He watched the elevator videotape a half dozen times with the manager and agreed with her – the man was aware of the cameras and dressed to hide his identity, baggy long sleeved shirt, billed cap, head down until he left. When he stepped outside another video camera caught him by surprise, or seemed to until he took his dark glasses off and looked directly at the camera.

'Do you recognize him?'

'His friends call him John the Baptist. I don't know what his true name is. He's delivering a message of sorts and I'm not sure what to do with it yet.'

'Arrest him!'

'We'll start looking for him and we will arrest him when we find him. I'll be in touch. Thanks for making a copy of the tape.'

Twenty-Five

The next morning they got a positive DNA hit on two of the skulls. Raveneau called the Missouri sheriff and once again he got the feeling that it all made sense to her, and would in Cagdill, that a California whacko pilfering caskets stole the skulls. It was a believable ending to the town's ordeal. As he got off the phone with her, he sat with la Rosa.

'Radiation poisoning,' la Rosa said slowly, as if pondering a chess move.

'Everything in his room was tested last night and they got a strong Geiger reading off a liquid prescription he takes for a stomach problem. The routine is to give him two tablespoons every night before bed, so the working theory is the visitor switched bottles. The visitor is the one Attis Martin called John the Baptist.'

'Can we just call him John Doe?'

'Sure. The videotape will need to be cleaned up and enhanced. Coe is on his way here and we'll give them the tape, but you should watch it first. Coe will make us a digital copy no later than tomorrow and now that radiation is in the mix the FBI is assigning another dozen agents to it. They're stepping in on that part and the meeting today is about how we're going to work together.'

'There's a first time for everything.'

'They'll try to identify John in the photo but when you see the video you'll see he's not worried about being identified. That should worry us. I'm sure he was at Grate's so that when the time came I could ID him.'

When Coe arrived they sat in the homicide detail kitchen where two tables pushed together and covered with a striped tablecloth provided enough room to spread everything out. Coe was bright and quick, and regardless of what he felt about local law enforcement he was always deferential. He and Raveneau had worked well together on a case last year that went to the wire and still woke Raveneau at night.

The FBI and SFPD budgets were far apart and this was never more apparent than meeting here in the kitchen with other homicide inspectors coming and going, putting sandwiches in the refrigerator or getting milk for their coffee.

Coe held a white coffee mug in his right hand as he wrote notes with his left. His image conjured something out of the past for Raveneau, an archeologist in desert shade at the end of a long day, an early-twentieth-century cartographer before the advent of radar, Coe in a white shirt with the sleeves neatly folded back almost to his elbows, his gun tucked in at the small of his back, suit coat draped over the adjacent chair, ramrod straight, and like himself slowly getting locked into a former era.

'What have you learned about Attis Martin and Ike Latkos?' Raveneau asked.

'We got a strange call about her.'

'What kind of call?'

'A back-off call, meaning she may have helped an agency somewhere along the line, and with her talents it must have been cyber help. I don't think the agency was the CIA and I'm sure I'll be hearing more soon and I didn't tell you two any of this. We're not having much luck yet with Attis Martin, but I'll get you a list today of what we've come up with. It's understood you're pursuing the murder investigation, but we need some ground rules on the rest of this.'

'Everyone at the table at Grate's Place is inside our investigation,' Raveneau said, and they hashed out all of it now. Fed and SFPD surveillance would coordinate on tracking Lindsley's movements, but Raveneau would do the talking with him. The FBI would handle the Lash radiation poisoning and find where the radioactive isotopes came from.

Coe leaned forward. 'Albert Lash contacted us in 2005 about a man named John Algiers. Here's a photo.' He turned it so they both could see it and tapped it. 'That's him. He attended one of Lash's book tour events and later contacted Lash through his website. Lash notified us and kept up communication with him for over a year and a half. They had an ongoing conversation about mass killings and how they happened. He was very interested in talking about genocide and Lash's theory, or what you say was actually Coryell's theory. He kept up a correspondence with Lash from various places in the world and bounced his ideas for mass extermination off of

Professor Lash, including dispersal methods for radiological weapons, though the highly radioactive material he was writing about he was unlikely ever to acquire.

'Algiers wrote to him in spurts, sometimes three and four times a day for two weeks and then nothing for a month. His understanding of physics was well beyond what Lash knew so we brought in a physicist to help us understand the letters, same with biochemistry. At some point he got frustrated with Lash and in his final communications denounced him as an intellectual fraud and his books as those of a print whore. We have a profile, we've made guesses, and I can copy you that. Lash's publisher still maintains the website. There was a communication that very likely was from him about a year ago. It was an aggressively personal threat to Lash.'

'All right, so he's a possible too.'

'I don't know what he is, but you need to know about him. From word usage and references we put his age at late forties and we believe he has worked or is working as a scientist and is wealthy.'

'That can't be a long list.'

'It's not and we have a good idea who he might be and I don't think he's in any way a fit here, but he connects to Lash.'

They moved on to Lash's sister and the documents stored at her condominium.

'We're not having much luck getting to those diaries,' Raveneau said. 'She might respond to the FBI better than she does us, but I doubt it. She's protecting her brother and believes we abused him last time. It's going to take a better warrant than we can write from our end, but you've got the terror angle. Maybe the FBI can wrap terror around his diaries.'

'You have such an inspiring way of putting that, Ben.'

'Thank you.'

'How seriously is the Bureau taking this particular mass killing threat?'

'You were right last year, so my ASAC is sitting quiet. Otherwise, we'd need a lot more to go on than we have now, and frankly, there's skepticism about the capability of the gentlemen you met. But the new cure-all prescription they wrote for Professor Lash does give them some street cred. Bottom line is temporarily there are more agents but we'll need some results very soon.'

'Where are you at on Lash's hot drink?'

'We're working through a list of possible sources and doing that with more than just our field office.'

'Berge?'

'We agree with you that the Delaware company making the rent payments is a shell. A Bank of America account was opened over a year ago in the company name and one deposit was made with enough money to cover the lease for a year. It was all done by mail. There's no video, no record, but we're still digging. I don't think we're going to get anything more from the property manager. What's her name again?'

'Lisa Berge.'

'That's right. I don't think she's got anymore

to tell us, and that's about it. Thanks for the coffee, you two. Let's talk later this afternoon. Don't take any free drinks from strangers.'

Twenty-Six

'Hey, it's me, Missouri, and if you've talked to your medical examiner you already know what I'm going to tell you.'

'I haven't, so tell me,' Raveneau said.

'Four more of the skulls match. You may get me re-elected county sheriff.'

She laughed and her laugh made him smile, but what he heard in her voice was relief and he felt the same. Now at least a piece of the puzzle was figured out.

'But that's not the only reason I'm calling. I've got a new witness, a young woman who has come forward with a story about how she and her boyfriend were there and saw the skulls taken.'

'Why did she wait so long?'

'Afraid of what her mother might do and I don't blame her. I grew up with her mother. She was out there with her boyfriend. He was about to deploy to Afghanistan.'

'Is that where he is now?'

'He is but I know how to get a hold of him and she's here and still worried about how others will react, so I've made a deal with her. We keep her identity secret. Are you OK with that?'

'I'm fine with it.'

'I've got her statement and I'll send it to you as soon as we get off the phone, but let me read you her description in case there's something to talk about. Oh, and I guess it takes you to get the skulls released to us. They said you have to sign off on it.'

'I'll do it today.'

'Perfect. OK, so here are her words. Ready?'

'Go ahead.'

'I snuck out of the house to meet my boyfriend. He couldn't take his car because his dad would have heard it. We rode bikes out to the river road. There was a moon so it was OK and when we got closer there was mud on the road so we left the bikes in trees and walked. Just in time too because there were headlights coming and we hid as a car passed us. Jody says it was a Subaru.'

Different than the farmer, Jacobs, Raveneau thought, but the shape at that distance was similar in some ways.

'He parked and wasn't super close to us, but he was pretty close and we could see him put on a light on his head like those things people wear when they go down in the caves. He took this backpack with him, you know, wearing it. He's tallish and not real big, sort of thin. We couldn't see his face and he walked this really still way that creeped me out. He was like a zombie. That's what I remember most and how weird it was with the light on his head when he bent over a casket. We could hear when he opened them and it was freaky. Jody wanted to go stop him, but I didn't let him do it.

'We knew he was putting something in his backpack but we didn't know what it was until later when we heard the news and I'm really sorry I didn't come tell you sooner. He made like three trips to his car and on the last time he put the backpack inside and drove away. It wasn't like he was in any real hurry or afraid of getting caught. He was fussing around in the back of the car like he had groceries or something he didn't want to spill over when he drove away. He cleaned off his shoes and was careful to get everything the way he wanted it before he left. Then he just drove away slowly.'

'Three trips,' Raveneau said. 'Jacobs' account is at four thirty in the morning. Can you try to pin the time down with her a little more? And what about a partial license plate?'

'They couldn't see well enough.'

'Could she tell if they were out of state or were they Missouri plates?'

'She says no.'

'Let's try to get in touch with the boyfriend. If he knows it was a Subaru, maybe he registered something about the plates.'

Raveneau was standing by the fax machine when la Rosa came in. As they talked, the fax machine began to clack. Raveneau picked up the statement from the teenage witness and handed that to her, and the next fax had a list of the skulls now identified. One of the names on the list all but jumped off the page, yet he still had to read it two or three times before handing the list to la Rosa. 'Check out the names.'

La Rosa read and then read aloud, 'Attis Martin. This is a break.'

'It is except there are no secrets here. They'll know in Missouri if they don't already know who has been identified and that's going to find its way into a TV report or some media. Our guy here, Attis version two, is going to find out.' Raveneau had another thought. 'We'll have to release something here about identifying the skulls and that should shutdown the serial killer talk.'

'Does this interrupt their plot, if there really is one?'

'Who knows.'

La Rosa shook her head like she was trying to get rid of something and then pushed her hair back. 'This is all just too weird.'

It was but they were starting to figure out what to do with it. Raveneau let Coe know four more skulls were identified and that they had a Missouri connection. At his desk he looked over the list of names again. Then he got a text from Brandon Lindsley. Lindsley wrote: *'New information.'*

Raveneau texted back and told la Rosa, 'I'm going to meet him at his apartment this afternoon.'

'He's texting you an hour after we learn one of the skulls belonged to an Attis Martin. This is going to sound crazy, but do you think there's any chance he knows we just got this fax?'

'No.'

'The timing spooks me. That cot in the bomb

shelter was used how many times?'

'There are four blood types.'

That report was on Raveneau's desk this morning. A positive, A negative, O positive, which was the same type as Coryell but probably too old, and the last was AB negative, which was still among the common eight types but more rare. Coryell was O positive but not only was the DNA match negative but the working theory was the blood that drenched the cot mattress did so over a span of more or less twenty years, though that was rough science, an estimation and the best they could do.

Raveneau hoped they were going to learn a lot more from the cot. But they could say now that whoever placed the skulls and cellphone did so years after anyone bled on the mattress, and Raveneau gravitated to the probable, that the mattress and skulls were not necessarily connected; same location but different events.

La Rosa was still on Lindsley's timing. 'Within minutes of this fax, he's texting you.'

'I've been texting with him all day and yesterday, too. He's starting to worry.'

'If he's worrying he knows more than he's told us.'

'Oh, he does, and that's the dance we're doing. I'm trying to bring him over. That's what he and I are going to talk about this afternoon.'

'I'm coming with you.'

'On this one I've got to go alone. I've got to be one on one with him. I get the feeling the clock is running down on whatever Attis has planned and we've got to get Lindsley to come across.'

Twenty-Seven

Lindsley lived in the upper unit of a two-story apartment building on Miller Avenue in Mill Valley. The building was one of those you might notice driving by but were unlikely to remember. It sat back from the street with parking in front and around to one side. It was shingled with white trim and a green asphalt roof that had faded. There were stairs but no elevator and Lindsley was on the second floor in a two-bedroom that faced the street and the commercial enterprises lining it. If he wanted to get a coffee to-go, walk to the dentist, or get his nails done, he was all set.

He was ready when Raveneau called and said, 'I'm here,' and then knocked on his door a few minutes later. A friend of Lindsley's who was visiting was a little less ready. She acted shocked and angry and Raveneau heard her say so as she dressed in Lindsley's bedroom with the door partially closed. Lindsley grinned through her stream of invective and looked happy. He wove anxiety into his text messages, but Raveneau didn't read it on his face right now.

Lindsley wore jeans, sandals, and a long-sleeved, green T-shirt with a black and gold dragon emblazoned on the back. His friend opened the bedroom door a moment later, let it slam against the wall, and left the front door wide open as she walked out. She offered one last loud word. 'Asshole,' echoed in the corridor.

'That's my new neighbor,' Lindsley said. 'I didn't tell her you were coming over.'

'I got that.'

'Let me shut the door.' He did and when he turned it was as if Raveneau was talking to another person. Lindsley's face changed. 'I want to make a deal,' he said. 'I've learned some things from Attis the police need to know about.'

'Start with where he is.'

'I don't know. Everything is prepaid cell-phones now and the conversations are short.' Lindsley crossed the room, slid a phone off a bookcase shelf and tossed it on his couch. 'He gave me that. He said every-thing is on the go path and we've started the countdown.'

'Is he launching a space shuttle?'

'I'm not messing with you, that's exactly what he said and I know from other conversations everything is timed around when Ann Coryell disappeared. We're almost there. It's just a few days from now. All I can do is try to help you find him. Take that phone if you want or I'll keep it and call him when you tell me to. Tell me what to do. I'm not asking for anything other than to be protected.'

'Protected from what?'

'From going down with them when they get arrested for whatever insane thing they have planned.' Lindsley tapped his chest then crouch-ed on the edge of his couch. 'My ambition is to write popular history books just like Lash only better. I know these guys from an online chat room and I've seen them socially a bit over the last I don't know how many years, but they've got their own deal going. I'm not part of whatever they're planning. Whatever it is they're pretty sure it's going to work.'

'How do you know that?'

'From listening to Attis, from the attitude, you need to find them. Watching me isn't going to do it. Look at this over here from the window.' He waited for Raveneau to walk over. 'See that white van up the street? You have to stand where I am to see it. Is that SFPD or is that someone else? I don't think SFPD would be staking me out over a cold case.'

He turned and stared and didn't look like any history PhD candidate Raveneau had ever met. Lindsley's face was surprising, something raw about it when he got animated, none of the nervous agility of his friend, Attis Martin. And when sitting quiet Lindsley's face had a blunt solid look to it like stone, his eyes faraway, returning nothing.

'I don't want to make you angry,' Lindsley said, 'and Attis is no genius, but he's bright and he's smarter than you.'

'Great.'

'I'm just telling you, and Ike has probably already hacked her way into whatever he needs. They're not afraid of you. About a year ago they were analyzing police surveillance techniques supposedly that was just out of curiosity, but it was about this. They give me little bites always sort of testing me to see where I'm at. They've thought ahead. They've planned.'

'For what?'

'I don't really know. I just know I don't want to be part of it or them.'

'Well, I'm all ears, and by the way that van isn't ours. It probably belongs to the florist it's parked out in front of.'

'Their van has their name on it.' He turned from the window. 'You're underestimating them and it's a mistake.'

'I'm still waiting to hear what they're going to do.'

'They're planning to try to kill people.'

'How do you know that?'

Lindsley shook his head. He didn't want to go there. He wanted to allude to but not reveal what he knew and Raveneau wasn't going any farther that way.

'Until you come across, we're nowhere,' Raveneau said. 'Do you have knowledge that they placed the iPhone and the skulls in the bomb shelter and that the phone threat came from them? It's that simple, Brandon. You've got to give us something and we'll want it on tape and then we'll start working with you. We won't make any promises until we know everything, but if you show good faith we will too.'

'Attis asked me once years ago if I knew about a fallout shelter. Somehow he knew about it. When I introduced him to Professor Lash it seemed like they already knew each other, so maybe he and Lash had contact I never knew about.'

‘When did you introduce them?’

‘It’s going to make me a liar.’

‘Think of it as a spiritual cleansing and crossing to the police boundary.’

‘I introduced them a long time ago at a party at Lash’s house in 2002 when Ann was still alive.’

‘Was she at the party?’

‘I don’t remember.’

‘OK, a decade ago in 2002 and Ann was still alive. When was this party?’

‘On Memorial Day.’

Raveneau felt a rush of excitement and hid it. It just might be and it would give them an opening and he knew what was coming next, but he asked the question anyway. ‘Was Attis a student?’

‘Yes.’

‘OK, so what’s his real name?’ When Lindsley hesitated, Raveneau said, ‘We know it’s not Attis Martin.’

‘Alan Siles.’

Raveneau nodded, showed nothing. Alan Siles, the name Lindsley used with Marion Coryell, and for a moment he wondered if Marion had called Lindsley and confronted him. But he didn’t think so. She was humiliated to the point of shame for having been taken in and tricked by Lindsley. She was very proud and he doubted she would carry that humiliation any farther. It would soon turn to hate.

Lindsley cleared his throat. ‘We weren’t friends. I didn’t hang with him and I didn’t know what he wanted with Lash other than to meet him. He didn’t tell me anything.’

'Did he know Ann?'

'Yes.'

'Are you certain of that?'

'Yes, and what's funny about this keeps going through my head is that Albert knows all of this. He could tell you.'

'He doesn't know about the plot. Was Siles enrolled at Cal?'

Lindsley nodded. 'He was a visiting student from McGill. He had some project he was working on and was at Cal for that. I don't know if he stayed or went back or what, but Albert would probably remember. He has a very good memory for students.'

'Canada, McGill University.'

'Yeah, where Leonard Cohen went.'

'I need you to flesh this out. Did he get to know Lash, was he at the house often after you introduced them, and where else did you have contact with him?' Raveneau sat and wrote notes. At some point he'd have to take Lindsley back to the homicide office, but not yet. Lindsley didn't want to leave here and he wanted him to keep talking.

'I don't know how close he and Albert got. Close, I think, and he was around and he didn't really talk to me much. Most of my contact with Alan in the last five years has been online.' Lindsley paused. He glanced over at Raveneau and then stared at the big window facing the street as if inwardly debating. 'You're right, Alan knows about the bomb shelter and he's been in there. He talks to me like I showed it to him, but that's his way of trying to keep me in line. Do you know what I mean? It's like a threat where I'm supposed to hear that he doesn't really care what happens to him and he wants me to know that he can take me with him just by saying whatever he wants to the police. Albert must have showed it to him or maybe they went down into it together.

'After Lash sold the house and the house was in escrow, Alan knew who had bought it. He knew it was a Chicago couple. He knew they had hired an architect and planned an extensive remodel that was going to need all the approvals that would drag out the process for a couple of years. He knew there'd be a big gap between when they moved out and the start of construction. He said that to me once and it was obvious that mattered to him and I was supposed to ask why. But I didn't.'

'When was that?'

'I don't even remember. We were getting coffee somewhere in San Francisco.'

'You need to remember where.'

'I'll try. Alan was very into her. I know he went into the guest cottage after Lash moved out and no one was living there.'

'He broke in?'

'No, there was a key hidden near the guest house. I knew where it was and I told him one time years before but after she was dead. I guess he remembered and no one collected the key when Lash moved out. You don't get how into her Alan is. He wanted to get into the cottage so he could meditate in the space where she lived. He was trying to contact her by going to where he said her energy was strongest. He would come up through the trees from the Presidio or that's what he told me.' Lindsley exhaled hard. 'I do not want to go down with these guys. They're going to say I was part of everything but that's bullshit.'

'Were you there when the skulls were brought in?'

'No, but they showed me later.'

'OK, stop there, so when you and I were in the shelter that wasn't your first time there. You've been in there with Alan Siles and you saw the skulls?'

'Yes, and that was the only time. They said they were from a graveyard.'

'Did you think about contacting us?'

'I had a really bad experience with the police when I was sixteen. You are the first cop I've had any contact with since and I wish I hadn't done that. In my life, police have been nothing but bad news and stupid and lazy.'

'Well, as you said, we're not that bright.'

'Don't underestimate him. With you, I followed you. I made a guess when you didn't go back toward San Francisco and you got on the Fairfax–Bolinas Road. I knew if I was right you'd be parked at the trailhead and you were. The rest was easy.' Lindsley turned from the window. 'Alan expected to be questioned before now. He's not sure why he hasn't been and no one has figured out where he's living, so now he's starting to get a little nervous. You need to make him think you know where he is. I could tell him something. Tell me what to say and I can call him. I can make him believe me. But I don't know where he lives or where John or Ike live. I'm sure the ID she gave you is bogus.'

'It is.'

'Every six months she has a new name, and John has never said ten words to me. I used to think he was totally drugged up and taking a bucket of antidepressants every day. John might be his true first name and I think he sleeps in his car somewhere because that's what Alan told him to do, make himself invisible. If Alan told him to lay down at his feet, curl up and go to sleep, John would do it. He does whatever Alan tells him.'

'Does he work?'

'Yeah, that's the strange part. I think John does work somewhere part-time. I don't know where or what. Ike had a sex change in Mexico so her past is as a male.'

'You've told us that and let's hold right here because what needs to happen now is you ride back to San Francisco with me and we do this more slowly in an interview room with my partner. I'll call and tell her we're coming and we'll go through it all slowly. We'll get some food if it runs long or we'll go to dinner later. There are agents at the FBI who will want to talk to you also. You've done the right thing, Brandon.'

'I can't go with you. I can't go to a police station. I wouldn't be able to talk there and I'd be afraid of one of them seeing me leave here with you.'

'He's not watching you.'

'I'm not going to a police station.'

'The Homicide Detail is an officer on the fifth floor. It's not like a police station. It won't feel like that.'

'I've been in an interview room. I was questioned for forty-eight hours. I'm not going with you unless you arrest me.'

Raveneau backed off a little and as they talked more he asked Lindsley, 'Are you willing to wear a wire?'

'No, Ike has equipment to detect that kind of thing. She brags about it.' Lindsley blew air out and shook his head. 'We're talking about someone who can get into your cellphone and turn on the microphone.' He pointed at Raveneau. 'That could be your phone. I'll do whatever, but she scares me.'

'Same as Alan scares you.'

'All right, I'm afraid of everybody, but I'll tell you what, I'm most afraid of law enforcement ineptitude. I don't want to get framed in the big hurrah when Alan and the freaks go down. Then I'll be in court shackled and listening to some serious-faced law enforcement dupe tell the jury I colluded. I can't defend myself from that. It'll be like standing on train tracks facing down an oncoming train. Juries are stupid and the media feeds the public the same way people throw seeds to pigeons in a park. Everyone is going to assume I'm part of whatever plot they have going.'

'You can keep that from happening by helping us stop them.'

'I need something formal. I need something in writing and I need a lawyer.'

'We can work with you through your lawyer, but you'll still have to give us everything you know and we'll need you to keep talking with Alan Siles.'

'They want to kill a lot of people. That's all I really know about the plot. They think that's the cleansing she wrote about. They don't really understand her.'

'How are they going to do that?'

'I have no clue.'

'Have dirty bombs been discussed?'

'Yes, somehow they have access to medical waste and they are really into wind direction. Having the wind blowing the right way is something they talk about. They've let me hear that or Alan wants me to hear it.'

'Do you think that's what it is, a dirty bomb?'

'Could be. They've talked dirty bombs and the last time was a couple of months ago over beer and pizza. But they weren't specific, it's all hypothetical, as if they are just discussing an idea. John sits silent and Ike and Alan talk and Alan tries to draw me in. I can tell you where and I remember the coffee place now, but I only want to be interviewed by you, no one else, not your partner, not anyone.'

'There need to be other witnesses. At least one should be my partner.'

'Then she's going to have to come here.'

'All right, I'll call her and I'm going to do that outside and then I'll come back up. You OK with that? You'll wait here?'

'I'll be here.'

'I'll be about fifteen and then I'll be back.'

'I'll be here.'

'You're doing the right thing.'

Raveneau walked down the stairs and called la Rosa from the asphalt lot.

'He's talking. You need to get here.'

Twenty-Eight

As they waited for la Rosa, Lindsley started to hyperventilate. Raveneau was unsure if that was real anxiety or an act, but suggested they take a walk, and once outside in the sunlight Lindsley proposed getting a coffee. But that was the last thing he needed and Raveneau eased him off that and they kept walking. They were a block and a half away from Lindsley's apartment building when la Rosa drove past. Raveneau watched her turn into the apartment lot and then called her.

'He wants to take a drive.'

And that's what they did. Raveneau drove through the many curves of the mountain, Lindsley in the backseat, la Rosa talking with him all the way up and about everything, the clear blue day, the beautiful if unusually hot start to the fall, the blood that seeped through the cot mattress and the obvious purpose of the restraints that held down whoever was on the cot.

'When you were in the bomb shelter you must have seen it?'

'We were in there with flashlights and candles.

They invited me and I was only there once. I don't like caves. I don't like being underground, and I think Alan sees himself as a messianic figure and is a little bit insane.'

'Did you have a flashlight?'

'I did.'

'You must have looked around.'

'Sure, I shined the light around but it was hard to look away from the skulls. Alan said one of them was Ann's.'

'Did he show you which one?'

'No.'

'Did you count them?'

'Count the skulls? No, I didn't count them.'

'You must have seen the cot.'

'They took me there to make me part of what they were doing. That's what it was about, OK? Alan was either bringing me on board or testing and taunting me. He knew I wouldn't go to the police.'

'How could he know that?'

Raveneau heard the quieter softer turn in la Rosa's voice and he was right there with her. How could Alan Siles know, or why was he unafraid of Lindsley tipping the police anonymously? Lindsley needed a good explanation for that.

'He told me construction was going to start and the bomb shelter would get found and then we could all watch Lash squirm. That was one thing we shared, for sure. I don't know what Lash did to make Alan hate him. I've never asked, but I've understood. I felt the same way and I was thinking about Ann and it seemed like the cleanest way for the police to come to it would be if it got discovered by the builder. I agreed with Alan. It was going to get found and the police would go straight to Lash, and I guess I also didn't want to have anything to do with the police, like I was saying earlier.'

'Did you find the stacked skulls disturbing?'

She was asking, *didn't you find the skulls and the chance Ann Coryell's skull was here and the bloodstained cot too disturbing to ignore?*

'It was terrible. It was very bad but he said construction was starting within a month and it did. If it hadn't I would have called you. I would have done it.'

'Of course, and you're telling us you knew about the skulls in the bomb shelter about five weeks ago, but you don't know how many were in there.'

'We stayed about ten minutes. It was night and we went back out through the Presidio. We walked through the trees down to the road and then to the car.' Lindsley said the next thing to Raveneau. 'That's the same car you saw outside Grate's Place.'

'The Chevy Malibu,' Raveneau said. 'OK, got it.'

La Rosa asked, 'What were the candles for?'

'They were probably for me and for nothing. They brought those candles in that night and I doubt any of them have been back. I'm sure they haven't. The skulls were meant to get found and they were.'

'Give us a date.'

'OK, I've got to pull out my phone and look at the calendar. It's bizarre I can't just rattle off the date.'

He fumbled with his phone and maybe with his story as Raveneau piloted them out the ridge road, the ocean below and off to their left, the grass on the mountain's flanks dry, golden, and brittle after months without rain. The road undulated and he took it slowly and he kept quiet, listening as la Rosa worked her way forward and back with Lindsley. They followed the ridge out and were close now to where he and Lindsley stood and talked near the Pantoll Trail. Raveneau eased off to the right side of the road as they reached the junction. He and la Rosa lowered their windows and there was just enough of a breeze and it was cooler with the redwoods. He left the car running.

'I have a question,' Raveneau said.

'You won't like the answer.'

'Do you want to hear the question first?'

'You want to know how I knew where her remains were and I could tell you I was up here like some other people who were just curious about the police activity after a body was found. I was up here, but that's not how I knew about the body. I didn't know it was her, but I knew there were remains of a woman up on the mountain and he told me where.'

'Who told you?'

'A guy named Bob Taney I buy dope from. I smoke. He deals with a guy who grows really good stuff and he told me some teenagers he knows and sells to were looking for a place to party and they walked down the slope and found the remains. They went back there several times and didn't tell anybody and it was Taney who tipped the police when one of the guys told him. That was three months after they first found her, or something close to that. If you check you'll find the first call was an anonymous tip from an unknown male who never came forward.'

Raveneau already knew that was true. 'Can you get Taney to talk to me?'

'I can try.'

'We're not interested in the dope dealing. If I can I'd like to get to the kids who first found her.'

'He's not going to want to give you their names.'

'Probably not, but I'd like to talk to him today if I can. Are you willing to call him?'

'Right now?'

'No, go on, so far Taney has told you about a woman's remains up on the mountain. But it's a big mountain.'

'The kids gave him pretty good directions and he gave them to me. Ever since she disappeared anytime I read about an unknown woman's body getting found I wondered if it was Ann. This was in my backyard so when Taney called the police he let me know and I went up there that day and there was just a park ranger walking around. The next day there were dogs. That's when they found her.'

'You saw it.'

'I did.' Neither Raveneau nor la Rosa said anything and Lindsley spoke again, saying, 'You ask for dates a lot, Inspector Raveneau. You should write today's date down. This is the day I told you Attis Martin's real name is Alan Siles and it's the same day I told you he's gone. All three of them are gone.'

'What do you mean they are gone?' Raveneau asked.

'Emails, cellphones, all the connections, chat room aliases, all those have gone dead. Whatever computers they were using before they're not using now and I've heard Ike talk. They won't touch a single electronic anything that they've used before. They've switched completely to the throwaway cellphones and I'll bet they never use one more than once. It's happening.'

'What is?' la Rosa asked.

'The day Alan talked about. It's about disruption, confusion, fear, and death on a scale big enough to provoke change. I'll give you an example and when you catch Alan Siles he can give you the year and the date. He knows all the names of the US officers in charge.

'This happened in the Powder River Basin. Federal troops rode into a Sioux village of two hundred teepees and slaughtered everyone they could catch and burned the village. Not necessarily an unusual event, just what they did that week. It was ahead of winter but not by much and they destroyed the pemmican and any other stored food they could find. That way anyone they missed, the winter might get. Alan researched plenty of those sorts of events. He was very interested in how the tribes responded to what they were largely powerless to stop.

'In this case it was the Sioux tribe and the

soldiers were there because the Sioux had stolen horses and ponies and killed settlers squatting on their land. This was before the treaties got modified again and the land that was Sioux land got even smaller. The Sioux knew as the soldiers entered the village that it wouldn't stop. Alan wants people here to feel that powerlessness. You heard him, Inspector Raveneau. You heard what he reads into Coryell's writing. He's righteous. That's what you're up against, a righteous man, and it's about making people see themselves and the past differently. People think because it happened so long ago that's it's gone. He's going to show them it's not gone, it's not forgotten.'

Raveneau drove slowly down the narrow Fairfax-Bolinas Road toward Lake Alpine and then to Fairfax, and la Rosa picked up the questioning again.

'Brandon, help me out here,' she said. 'What can three people do to kill a large number of people? Are we talking about multiple dirty bombs? We've got a wind that's supposed to come up hard; is that the weather change he's looking for, for the spread clouds from dirty bombs?'

Lindsley ignored her and said to Raveneau, 'I almost talked to you the night we met at Grate's Place. I actually followed you when we left there. When I went around the corner I ran to my car and then raced back and found you. I tried to follow you home but I lost you or maybe you noticed me. Is that what happened?'

Lindsley glanced in the rear view mirror and

caught his grin.

'Why San Francisco?' la Rosa asked, and this time Lindsley answered her.

'Symbolic edge of America's western expansion and the Gold Rush growth of San Francisco symbolic of the greed and plundering that characterized the age. We wrote the history but the truth remains.'

'You're quoting Coryell with that last line,' Raveneau said.

'Right on, Inspector, you're the man, and that's why Alan wants you on the big stage with him. Don't forget he told you that you're the witness. You're the one who will later explain it all.'

'And where are you?'

'They've left me behind. I had my chance and I didn't take it. Now I'm betraying them and I'm with you. I'm one hundred percent with you but I've got to convince you and that's not going to be easy. Where are we going next?'

'To the FBI office in San Francisco.'

'Really?'

'Got to.'

'I thought we weren't going to do that.'

'We'll be there with you.'

'That disappoints me.'

That's where Lindsley went quiet. That's where things turned. Later, Raveneau would think a lot about that.

Twenty-Nine

Coe asked Lindsley if he was willing to take a polygraph, what the Feds now called a PDD or psychological detection of deception test, and Lindsley buried a smirk and said, 'Why not?' So now early in the interview they were eliciting control questions from him to use in the test.

Raveneau doubted anyone in the room really believed in a PDD other than as a tool for interrogation, yet he watched Lindsley closely as they put the cuff on and the questions started. Raveneau had his own theory that he didn't share with Coe until they were outside and looking for someplace cool to sit and have a sandwich.

'We need shade,' Coe said.

Raveneau ordered an albacore sandwich that smelled old after he peeled the wrapping back. He was only good for a couple of bites before abandoning it for an iced coffee. They talked for a while about the opinion of a psychologist who had watched the interview. Coe ate slowly, his forehead damp with sweat and something clearly on his mind.

'At least we know who we are looking for now,' Coe said, meaning that it was confirmed that Attis Martin's true name was Alan Siles.

'We're going out to the public today. Someone knows where Siles and the other two are. We'll get a lot of calls. What's your read on Brandon Lindsley?'

'Scared but still trying to control the situation.'

'The psychologist thinks we're dealing with a psychopath. He beat the PDD test.'

'That doesn't surprise me.'

Raveneau took another drink of the iced coffee. He needed more ice. He leaned back in the shade knowing that Coe wanted a better summation of what Raveneau and la Rosa had learned from Lindsley today.

'Does Lindsley really believe a plot is under way?' Coe asked.

'If he didn't I don't think he'd be talking to us. He gave us a lot today.'

'Such as?'

'You've already heard them all, but I'll tick them off again. That all emails and phones are dead and they're gone from the Coryell chat room they've haunted. That he knew about the remains of a woman on Mount Tam before the police. That he was in the bomb shelter with Alan Siles and the other two a month before construction started and that Siles suggested Coryell's skull was there.'

'But it's not.'

'It wasn't among them. Lindsley is worried that Alan Siles has enough to tie him to the plot so that if they go, he goes down.'

'He's right to be worried.'

'I also get the feeling he doesn't think Siles will come in alive.'

'Is something going to happen today, tomorrow, is it under way?'

'Siles told him it's go-time and left him with the throwaway phone he showed you.'

'What do you believe?'

'That Lindsley doesn't trust Siles. In some ways he's afraid of him and he doesn't like us, but he felt he had to come forward today. He believes we won't be able to stop what Siles has planned.'

'Great.'

'I believe they're planning to act.'

'So do I.'

Coe took a last bite of his sandwich and laid the rest down in the cardboard box and chewed slowly his last bite before saying, 'We're going out with UNSUB warrants on all three. We might get a little blowback later if Lindsley has set us up, but I'm not worried about that. When we ask for help from the public we'll have to explain in more detail what we're after and what we're concerned about. We'll have to say we have no proof but a reason to believe the plotters may attempt to detonate dirty bombs. That's going to generate a media hurricane and that brings me back to how credible Lindsley is.'

'He lied before. He may be lying now. He beat your PDD and yet he's not the problem. This Siles has communicated he's going to act and we don't know where he is.'

'So what if we take the position we're not certain, but there's enough evidence to be concerned? We'll cite the phone threat, run their photos, and ask the public for help locating these three individuals. We'll ask anyone who has ever seen them to call us and we'll go out with your cell number since you brought him to our doorstep.' Coe smiled at the idea of giving out Raveneau's cell number. 'And where are the ageing homicide ace and his cool as ice partner going to be as I start answering questions about radiological weapons and an ex-UC history professor who swallowed isotopes? Are you going to be there?'

'I'll be there.'

'Do you want to be the one to tell them they might get dirty-bombed because of the Indian Wars of the nineteenth century?'

'I wouldn't want to steal your thunder.'

'Then maybe you can explain the western expansion.'

'Don't worry about any of that. The TV networks will come up with experts within half an hour,' Raveneau said.

'And what if this is some big hoax?'

'Then they'll never forget you.'

'That's what I'm thinking,' Coe replied. 'We have agents at food processing plants and at businesses where they deal with medical radiological devices and we've narrowed it to a list of twenty-five in California, but I get the feeling we're not going to get anything from that list. We put out these warrants and do the press conference and then they come out of hiding and get in front of the cameras and explain that they never were going to hurt anybody and it's all about focusing attention on the plight of the Native American and a broken reservation system that stripped the tribes of their dignity and purpose.'

'She hit right at a truth,' Raveneau said.

'Who?'

'Coryell.'

'You're funny about her. Are you going to go to the boundary place? I bet if you go there you get out of this heat and wind.'

'Some stuff doesn't stay buried. You said "true believer" earlier talking about me. I think that's what we've got in Alan Siles. He's a true believer and he took the name of a dead man.'

'That's just identity theft, and I don't trust much about this Lindsley. I see an act. Nothing about him is fixed. He's completely liquid. We caught a serial killer in Iowa that we chased for seven years. He was working three jobs, one as bartender, completely garrulous, easy-going, one as a building manager, monosyllabic, hostile, vindictive, and a third as a volunteer school crossing guard. Not quite volunteer. He got a little stipend and kids and the parents loved him. Gentle, watchful, you know, keep an eye on the kids while the parent ran an errand. Same guy. Lindsley reminds me of him.'

Coe shook his head and stood. 'You ready to go?' he asked.

'Not yet. What about Ike Latkos and the other federal agency?'

'She did work for a US agency and the operation was successful, but it was awhile ago and they're not with him – her now – anymore. Not an issue.'

Raveneau took another drink of iced coffee and then slid the cup into the trash. Coe expected him to go back up to the Field Office with him but Raveneau shook his head.

'I need to go see an old friend who may be able to help with all this. I'll call you later.'

Thirty

Hugh Neilley lived across the street from John McLaren Park in the two-story, three-bedroom house his parents left him. Several of his neighbors had known Hugh most of his life. Raveneau's guess was they saw Hugh as an outgoing man, generous with his time and protective of the neighborhood. Once a week he took an elderly neighbor to buy groceries, as he had for more than a decade.

But in many ways he was a complicated and private man. When his marriage ended, Donna, his ex, told Raveneau she didn't know if it was the drinking, the sarcasm, or both, but she was done. She quit on a cold December night when Hugh's brother officers gave him yet another ride home after a night out and Hugh hadn't spoken a word to her since.

Hugh believed it a mark of masculinity that he could turn his back on anyone who crossed him or he fell out with, even Donna. Some went from being the best people in the world to being the worst and as Raveneau knocked on Hugh's door he knew he and Hugh were on that path.

'I'm not even going to ask why you're here, but come on upstairs.' When they got upstairs Raveneau followed him into the kitchen. 'What's on the great homicide inspector's mind tonight?'

'Ferranti told me you bought the job. He had some other things to say that I want to ask you about as well, but that's not why I'm here. I think you know why I'm here.'

'Make yourself at home.'

Raveneau pulled out a bar stool at the island and sat as Hugh stood across from him, palms pressed down on the tiled surface, face reddening as he launched into Ferranti.

'Fuck him and his three hundred dollar jeans and Hollywood haircut. He's all over me now that Matt's not there. He beat me down on price, whined, wheedled, and whittled me down until he got what he wanted. You can bet he's charging the owner twice as much. That's how guys like him operate.'

'He told me a laborer claims two loads of debris you were hauling away got dumped off a slope on Skyline Boulevard.'

'Yeah, yeah, yeah, this laborer knows how we operate or was it the guy Matt had to fire that came up with the story later? Ferranti is also telling me my hauling tags are fraudulent and some other bullshit that's going to let him keep my money when we're finished. Can you imagine me doing that?'

'You don't drive the truck.'

'I don't want to talk about this.'

'Did Matt dump loads off the side of a road?'

'If he did, I'm ruined.'
'Is Ferranti lying about the dump tags being forged?'
'I've got to ask, are you a homicide inspector or a building inspector? Which is it? It's not clear to me.'
'I've got someone who says he was in the bomb shelter a month before the start of construction, and that this UNSUB the FBI is looking for, Alan Siles, expected the skulls to get found as the construction work started. So I'm more interested than ever in how everything went down, what Matt took from there, the delay calling us, illegal dumping, everything. Where are the things Matt took out of the fallout shelter that were going to make their way back to me and haven't?'
'They're here and you'll leave with them.' Raveneau saw questioning and uncertainty enter Hugh's eyes. 'I planned to bring them to you tomorrow. They're not coming from Matt because I asked him to leave them behind when he moved out of here. As soon as he got out on bail I let him know he didn't live here anymore and he was through working for me.'
'Stop right there, how long have you known he took these things from the bomb shelter? Did you lie to me before?'
'No, I didn't lie. I didn't find out until after you confronted him. He confessed to me as part of a bullshit apology. I don't want to talk about him anymore and you'll leave with the things he took.'
Hugh turned around and opened the cabinet.

He pushed several things aside, bottles and cans clinking and then turned around with a container and without a word slid it across to Raveneau. The label read *'Blue Diamond Almonds*' and below that the word *'Bold'* and, underneath that, *'Blazin' Buffalo Wing.*'

'Open it up,' Hugh said.

'Hand me a bowl.'

Raveneau emptied the contents into a bowl and two gold rings, both with jewels on them, slid in among the almonds. So did a necklace with an onyx-eyed silver eagle.

'This is not what he said would be here. He told me one ring was gold with carvings on it and one was silver with a turquoise stone, and there should be a locket.'

'He lied to you to fuck with you. That's him. That's my nephew. There was a knife but he sold it.'

Raveneau stared at the jewelry but didn't touch any of it yet as he debated his options. He didn't have many.

'There you go, Ben, now you've got what you need to solve the case. Take them to Coryell's mother and maybe she'll recognize them. Good luck with it and I'm sorry Matt took them, but that's the last apology I'll make for him. So don't look for anymore. If he dumped loads I'll pay my fines.' He tapped his chest with a fore-finger. 'I've made a lot of mistakes, an awful lot of mistakes, but I really don't need you reminding me. Anything else before you leave?'

'I want to keep talking.'

'You want to keep prodding and probing, so

I'm going to keep drinking. Do you want one?'

'No.'

'I don't have any wine anyway.' Hugh pushed a glass up against the refrigerator ice maker, his back to Raveneau as ice clacked into the glass. He poured from a bourbon bottle and Raveneau listened to liquor flow over the ice and Hugh say, 'Ben. Ben. You may be sorry where all this goes.'

'Where what goes?'

'You're putting pressure on me. I needed you to help me keep Matt out there. I needed you to help me get him out of jail and keep him working. I needed you to tell the contractor you've known me forever and I'm a straight shooter, not to cozy up to him so he'd open up that tiny little suspicious mind of his and share his dark theories with you. I needed you to just sit tight on the things Matt stole until I had the situation in hand. Now you're going to ring them into evidence and the smirking bastard there who checks them in is going to have a new story to tell. The only thing you've really done to help me is to tell me straight up to step away from my nephew and let him stand on his feet as a man. I listened to you on that.'

He took a long drink as he turned around then put the glass down on the island. 'I followed your advice on a lot of things over the years and you used to never give it until I asked for it. I always admired that. Mattie's the last of my family and that's it. He'll break from me now and maybe he'll straighten out and marry someone who helps keep him in the right direction and the family will rebuild through their children. But I won't be part of it. He and I have parted and that's the end of something very important to me. No more family.

'Now Ferranti, Ferranti is going to sue me for fraud. He's hired a fucking lawyer and filed a complaint with the city and police department. Matt dumped two loads. I didn't know that before. I know it now and I don't know how I'll pay for the clean-up or the fines or keep my license and the business going. My last ten years have been one downward spiral. I'm inside ninety days to retirement and I'm not going to have the money to pay my bills and keep going. I'm trapped. I have nowhere to go.' He drained the rest of the glass, turned and refilled it, then opened a drawer Raveneau knew held a pistol.

'Shut the drawer.'

'Just hang on here a minute; nothing is going to happen to you, old buddy.'

Hugh pulled his hand back but left the drawer open and took a long swallow. When Raveneau started to move around the island, Hugh wagged a finger and said, 'No. Stay there and listen to me. Matt is my nephew. He's got my sister's blood, but it's my honor he's taking down too. There's not going to be anything left for me when this is over. San Francisco will file a criminal complaint over the forged dump tags and I got a call an hour ago from a *Chronicle* reporter. That newspaper is so thin you can't see it when you turn it sideways, but this guy writes for the online version and he wants a scoop. He wants a quote from the career police officer before he's charged with dumping construction debris in the sacred watershed and trying to cover it up.'

He rattled the ice in the glass as he swirled the bourbon.

'I'm in a bad hole. I've fallen. The pedophile bastard of a priest where I go to church loves to say we're all fallen. He'll be delighted to hear this story. It'll make his fucking day. But I have fallen and there is no way to get back from here.'

He reached quickly, pulled the gun, brought it to his right temple, held it a moment and then lowered it, though not all the way and the barrel wasn't quite resting on the tile. The nose was up just slightly and turned a little more Raveneau's direction. Raveneau looked at it but didn't move yet.

'That's what I should do. That's probably what I will do, but I'm going to let it all play out first. I'm in a very bad space where anything could happen, anything at all, Ben. I think you should avoid me because I feel like you've betrayed me. You're circling me. You're asking questions that suggest you think I was a drunk and a fool and Lash used me or worse I helped him. I honestly don't know what I'm capable of right now. Why don't you take the jewelry and leave? You're making progress. Take the jewelry to that bitter old woman and let her rub her hard fingers over the silver and tell you how the drunk homicide inspector failed her daughter.

'But hurry, because right behind that one is a new cold case, perhaps one that has sat fifty years. But a rag in someone's attic with DNA on it might let you solve it. You'll get another one before you're done. Get out of my house because you've got what you came for and this is not a good place for you to be. I hope this jewelry helps you and too bad you can't solve them all before they nail the coffin shut on your career. Too bad about that, Ben. Too bad you're running out of time and cases. Too bad you missed that phone call from Coryell. You might have saved her life and you wouldn't have to do all this.'

'Let me have the gun.'

It was another twenty minutes before he did, and Raveneau called Hugh's doctor and his ex-wife. Donna got there first and led Hugh into the front room. He heard them talking and at one point Hugh sobbed. When the doctor arrived Raveneau let him in and as the doctor went up the stairs Raveneau left. He took the rings and the necklace with him after sliding them into an evidence bag. He didn't know how close Hugh came to pulling the trigger. He wasn't sure yet what had really happened, but he was sure that if he stayed he'd be asking Hugh questions and there would be a better time later. This was by no means over.

Thirty-One

Raveneau headed to Toasts, or rather M33, to meet Celeste. Wind or not, the warm weather brought people out tonight. Margaritas were selling. So were rum drinks, and there were people at all six sidewalk tables despite gusts that lifted litter from the gutter and sent it spiraling overhead. He watched a young woman's hair wrapped around her head by the wind.

'I'll be awhile,' Celeste said. 'At least half an hour, maybe an hour. It's been crazy since around five o'clock.' She plated a salad and wiped away a drip along the edge of the plate.

Raveneau saw a table clearing outside. He pointed. 'I'll be out there.'

He took a glass of wine out with him. He sat with his back to the wind, and if the wind were cold it wouldn't even be worth the try. But warm fall wind was a Bay Area phenomena – the heated valley air from the dry north kept the cooler moist marine air offshore. He rode out the gusts as others gave up and went inside. He had the wine and a chance to think and then a text from Brandon Lindsley: *'Paranoid. Meet you later?'*

'You home or in the city?' Raveneau replied.

'City. Under surveillance and freaking.'

'What did you expect?'

Raveneau took another swallow and a waitress came out and put a small pizza down in front of him, explaining Celeste sent it. She asked if he wanted another glass of wine and he shook his head. He typed, *'Why r u paranoid?'* When there was no answer he laid the phone on the table. As soon as he did, it lit up.

'The wind. Want to meet?'

'Maybe.'

Raveneau rested his phone on the table ticking through once more what they knew. They knew the caskets weren't uncovered by the Mississippi floods until last spring, 2011. The skulls came from those caskets and were moved across the country and into the bomb shelter after the Mississippi flooding, and they knew the house was unoccupied from the time Lash moved out. Escrow closed before the flooding. The new owners' house plans ground slowly through the approval process. Which left a window of time and it probably happened as Lindsley described, though who knows what his real role was.

Lash wasn't there for any of that. Once again, the good professor was exonerated though somehow Lindsley was the link. It was also possible the compulsive Lash wrote something in the mythical diary. They needed those diaries, if they existed. He picked up his phone, looked at the texts from Lindsley as another came in: *'This is the wind.'*

'OK. What do we do?'

'where r u?' Lindsley replied.

'Is it tonight?'

'don't know.'

'think u do,' Raveneau sent. He waited and when there was no response laid his phone down on the table again and picked up the wine. He ate a bite of pizza and his phone buzzed.

'meet me now?'

Raveneau followed his gut. He didn't respond. Not long after he got a call from Coe.

'We've been texting,' Raveneau said. 'He wants me to come get him and go drinking. I could do that. Are you on him?'

'We're all over him and we're reading your messages. He's back in his apartment with the lights off, but he's at the window every few minutes. I guess he doesn't know about our thermal gadgetry.'

'I don't either, and what don't you wiretap?'

'Good question. I think we've got it all covered now.'

'He's talking wind and radiation and wind dispersal but I'm starting to think he doesn't know what's going to happen, just that it is. He's guessing. Not too many years ago he was a grad student in history and now he might be wrapped up in something that could put him behind bars for the rest of his life and he is scared.

'So maybe an FBI team ought to grill him tonight rather than me drink with him. Go upstairs, knock hard on his door and make it feel like it's now or never for him. He warned about wind. The wind has arrived and that's enough reason to question him. I'll meet you there.'

'I'll call you back.'

Raveneau ate the pizza and when Celeste came out they moved inside and took a table in the corner. The crowd thinned. They talked and ate and then Coe called. They were already on the way to the San Francisco Field Office with Lindsley in the back seat, one FBI vehicle in front, one behind.

'It probably felt like a rendition to him,' Coe said. 'He jumped about five feet when we came in. We took him out like a suspect.'

'What did he say?'

'The first thing he did was ask, "What's happened?"'

The interrogation went on for four hours and it wasn't harsh but it was frank. Outside the gusts in the hills now topped forty and Mt. Tamalpais and Mt. Diablo were recording wind speeds in excess of sixty miles an hour over their summits. In the city the gusts rattled the light poles and shook the electric lines of the street cars.

Lindsley, he was a bright guy, and they showed him cases where informants cooperated and helped prevent something from happening, and how much better it went for them later. Leave it to the Feds; they even had a graph that showed how much better you did if you cooperated. He was asked what will Alan Siles say about you? Will he say you tried to manipulate us at the point you got scared? How will you answer that? Will all three of them swear you were part of the plot?

As each half hour passed, an FBI interrogator noted it and said, 'Nothing has happened yet. You can still do this.'

But Lindsley didn't give up anything. He stayed right where he was in the text messages to

Raveneau and pitched the same message he had before, that he came forward because he was worried. When Raveneau got home it was after midnight and the wind rattled metal awnings out over the street. The gusts shook the sliding glass door on to the deck and blew over one of the potted lemons. He slept three or four hours and thought it was sirens that woke him or his phone, but it was neither. It was the wind. He walked out on to the wooden walkway and crossed the smooth roofing to the parapet, his heart loud in his chest as he smelled smoke, and not the smoke of a building burning but dry grass and oak.

Of course there had been warnings for weeks of fire danger, as there always were this time of year, especially as the anniversary of the Oakland Hills fire of 1991 grew closer. He scanned the hills across the bay. He didn't see any fires. Yet the smell was strong and the wind came from the north-east and Raveneau didn't have a good view in that direction. He checked the time. 04:10. He tried the Internet then TV and radio and called the Southern Precinct. The first squib showed online at just about the same time the Southern Precinct called back.

'Inspector?'

'I'm here.'

'We have a report of a fire on Mount Tamalpais. Check that, we have a report that Mount Tamalpais is on fire on both the west and east sides. That's all we know right now.'

'The whole mountain?'

'Yes, sir, that's what it says.'

Thirty-Two

Raveneau once sat in on an interview of an arsonist arrested after setting fire to five dilapidated houses in San Francisco over a period of three months. In one a homeless man squatting on the third floor died. The arsonist, a thirty-eight-year-old assistant manager at a tech facility named Steve Lahore, apologized for the death. He was aware from news reports that a man died in the second fire he lit. But that didn't stop him from setting more. All that stopped him was getting caught.

When confronted with possible murder charges, he was more interested in talking about how he planned the burns so that even a three-minute-response fire department wouldn't get there in time. He was proud of his work and forthcoming with details but what Raveneau remembered most vividly was how he rhapsodized about the 1929 fire on Mt. Tamalpais and how wooded and thick with underbrush the mountain was now. He fidgeted in his seat as he described the fuel load, the underbrush and trees that had thickened in the eighty years since that burn.

The right conditions brought out the arson bugs. They got them anxious and excited when the wind rose in the dry part of the year. Raveneau couldn't help but think about Lahore as he heard the Tam fire was spreading very rapidly and already arced over the whole mountain. He hurried back in, showered, and dressed.

A half hour later the burn smell was stronger. He scrolled his cell and found the phone number of a Petaluma fire captain, reasoning that he wasn't waking anybody up. They would call everyone in. He punched in the number but didn't hit Call yet, held his finger there for a moment before pressing the phone to his ear. First thing he heard was a big engine working hard.

'Steve, it's Ben Raveneau.'

'Ben, hi, you're calling about the fire?'

'Yeah, what's going on?'

'There's a fire line that reaches from Highway One all the way up over the mountain and down to Lake Alpine, and we're rolling there. That's about all I know other than it started an hour and fifteen minutes ago and all at once.'

'I'm heading your way.'

'No, you're not, you'd be out of your mind to, and why would you? Winds are gusting to sixty at the summit. They're thirty-five miles an hour down at the base. This fire is exploding. The whole mountain is going. There's evacuation under way in Mill Valley and you wouldn't even be able to get here, and why would you want to?'

'We're working on something that might tie to this.'

'What are you talking about?'

'There's a possible tie and the timing coincides with a threat made. Look, I'm heading your direction, but I'll stay out of the way.'

Raveneau crossed the Golden Gate after picking up la Rosa. They had Coe on speaker-phone as they looked at the orange halo over the mountain and tendrils of fire curling and rising fifty, a hundred feet into the air and twisting and leaping in the roaring wind. It was like a scene out of a volcano erupting or a nightmare of the end of the world. He had never seen anything like it and the idea of firefighters battling seemed absurd. Even in the pre-dawn darkness you could tell how fast it was moving, funneling up through steep ravines and dry oak and pine. On the open flanks a line of orange flame danced across the long slopes of dry grass and brush.

A fine white ash fell on the windshield and the air filled with sirens as they exited and made their way toward Mill Valley. Across the road a long line of headlights came toward them and Coe reported that the highway patrol was getting ready to close 101 due to ash and smoke. Coe was off the freeway now trying to work his way around that, having left his house in Novato ten minutes ago.

'There's a police roadblock ahead,' la Rosa said quietly and Raveneau nodded and continued to talk with Coe.

'You know what their orders are,' la Rosa said. 'This is a full-on evacuation.'

It was, and Raveneau kept Coe on the phone in case they needed his help. The police line was at Redwood High School and a uniform officer held a hand up for them to stop and then waved them forward signaling for them to turn into the high school. La Rosa lowered her window but it was clear the officer did not want to talk.

'The surveillance team is still on location,' Coe said, 'but they can't vouch for where Lindsley is. He could be in his apartment still. The police are using loudspeakers to tell people to leave immediately and the smoke is thickening and they're not certain he's still there.'

'We'll go up to the apartment.'

'They say embers are falling and at least one small fire started on a roof not far from where our team is. At some point we'll have to pull them.'

'Give us ten minutes. We're close but we've got to talk our way in now.'

'I didn't say they've lost him. They think he's in his apartment still and they'll send an agent up to his apartment if they need to. You don't need to go there.'

'He'll be gone. It's his excuse to move.'

'Then that's another reason you and Elizabeth can turn around.'

'This is them. This fits. This was what the wind talk was about and it may have been why Lindsley wanted to drive up the mountain before we brought him in. They were never going to get enough radioactive material. This is what they had planned all along. We need to find Lindsley right now.'

Raveneau looked over at la Rosa showing her homicide star and talking to a pair of California Highway Patrol officers. He heard their questions and could tell they were about to be waved through, but still said to Coe, 'Get two agents to go up now and knock on his door. They can knock on every door on the apartment floor and be concerned citizens. Lindsley won't know. Let's find out now if he's still there.'

'We'll do that if we need to. I'm going to let the surveillance team make that call.'

After Coe hung up, Raveneau said, 'They don't know where he is. It's like a refugee camp out here. It's chaos.'

They were waved through now and Raveneau drove slowly past the police units and the high school and through the first stoplight where the wind gusted so hard the stoplight swayed back and forth. Smoke was like a thin fog in their headlights. It wasn't too thick yet, but was enough to make la Rosa cough.

'We'll be a long time getting out of here,' she said. 'We may want to do what Coe suggested.'

'We're almost there.'

'And what if he's not there?'

'Then it's a manhunt in an evacuation.'

They got closer and then went past and Raveneau couldn't tell if Lindslcy's car was there. It had to be. A bullhorn on a police car slowly passed them and made clear the evacuation was mandatory, cutting in front of them, blocking their way, telling them to turn around. And that was fine because they were past the apartment now. They made the U-turn the officers wanted, nosing their way into the stream of traffic and a hundred yards later making a right into the apartment lot.

But before they left the car and went up to check, Coe called back.

'There are new fires, fourteen of them, and one that's now burning on Mount Diablo with multiple simultaneous ignitions similar to this Tam fire. I'm being told that seven of the new fires are in the East Bay Hills and they're spreading very quickly.'

'We're headed into the apartment building. I'll call you,' Raveneau said and broke the connection. He turned to la Rosa. 'There are fourteen new fires and they're going to overwhelm the fire departments. If this wind keeps up, a lot of houses will burn. People will die. Let's go see if he's there.'

Thirty-Three

A flustered and frightened apartment manager came straight at them. He shook his head and said everyone was out and he was leaving soon. He wore a fluorescent orange coat that came down to his thighs and carried a sixteen-inch flashlight. Raveneau slowed him down and got him to go upstairs with them. After they got no response knocking on Lindsley's door, the manager unlocked it. He called, 'Mr Lindsley, Mr Lindsley.'

'Could be hurt,' Raveneau said, and moved inside with la Rosa. He called Coe when he was sure Lindsley was gone, and then told the manager, 'We're going to be a minute or two. We're

OK. We'll pull the door shut when we go.'

With the smoke, sirens, confusion and an evacuation under way it was believable Lindsley had slipped away. Raveneau stared at the line of cars and the fog-like smoke that colored the early sun a brown-gold as Coe continued to insist that Lindsley was probably still there in the building. Coe had the surveillance team on another line and they were sure he hadn't left.

Two agents on the FBI surveillance team came upstairs a few minutes later. The apartment manager was still there and Raveneau described the young woman with Lindsley on his last visit here. The manager recognized the description and led Raveneau down the corridor and then knocked on her door. When there was no answer he unlocked it, but it was empty as well.

'He walked away,' Raveneau said, and texted Lindsley. He sent a second text, this one to Alan Siles: *'Let's talk.'*

Raveneau got back on the phone with Coe after the FBI agents went downstairs with the apartment manager. 'We're not going to find him,' Raveneau told Coe. 'Are we covered if your agents search his apartment with our help?'

'They need to be in the apartment.'

Raveneau could hear the agents coming back up. He looked out the street window as Coe gave him a fire update and saw that the cars parked on the street and in the lot below were beginning to get a coat of white ash.

'There are fatalities,' Coe said. 'An elderly couple trapped in their house in the Oakland Hills. That fire has already burned twenty-two homes. Between them they'll burn hundreds of homes.'

The white ash probably meant they were in the path of the fire and Raveneau didn't need any convincing. If the winds didn't let up, it would burn its way down the mountain and could easily get here. With the strong winds, tanker planes might not even be able to fly. Later today the fire could reach Mill Valley. He got off the phone and as the two FBI agents returned he and la Rosa and the agents searched Lindsley's apartment, knowing as they did that by tomorrow the apartment building might be gone.

Soon after they started they learned that two major fire lines up on the mountain had merged and that all of the homes and along the ridge and the Mountain Home Inn were gone. Winds were still gusting to sixty over the summit. On some roads the smoke was too thick to drive through and new fires were starting well ahead of the main fire line as glowing embers were carried and scattered by the wind. The Tam fire took its first victims while they were still in the apartment. Nine died in five cars that were trapped on a narrow street trying to get out when an ember generated fire grew rapidly and swept down the slope above where the cars were blocked by a fallen oak that had toppled in high winds. The fire burned nearly horizontal with flames reaching one hundred fifty feet as it came over the crest and started down on this side.

A firefighter came upstairs. 'OK, folks, time to go.'

'We'll be down in a few minutes.'

'My orders are to get you out now.'
'The man who lives here may know how these fires started. You need to give us a few minutes more, and I never told you what I just said.'
'Five minutes. I'll wait here with you.'

Thirty-Four

Raveneau found the book he was looking for hidden behind others in a wood bookcase left of windows facing the street. It was slim with an orange cover and was one of two hundred printed after Ann Coryell's death. In the circles Lindsley traveled it was hallowed. Compiled inside were unedited original essays, a series of blogs, and excerpts of the fabled thesis of Ann Coryell. It was put out by a small press that appeared, published it, and vanished again all in 2004, the year her body was identified. Raveneau learned of it then but didn't try hard enough at the time to get a copy.
One theory was that Lash financed it and someone else put it together, but Lash denied it and Raveneau believed him, especially after he plagiarized her for one of his books. The true publisher was still a mystery. There was no title on the book, no name of author on the spine or cover. This copy was thin and faded. Raveneau opened to the cover page and read, *'The Writings and Teachings of Ann Coryell, De Haro Press,'*

and then closed it and hurried through the rest of the search.

He stayed with the bookcase and both agents undid the bedroom, emptying a closet, stripping blankets and sheets, then lifted away the mattress. They walked a desktop computer and a laptop down to their vehicle.

The firefighter said, 'Time's up.'

Raveneau turned to the couch and pulled off beige cloth-covered cushions and found only loose change, a handful of quarters and dimes, a paper clip and cap for a pen tucked back in the cracks along with plenty of dirt.

The firefighter's voice got deeper and louder. He rapped his knuckles hard on the door frame. 'Let's go!'

Raveneau stalled and did one last check as la Rosa moved out into the corridor. He checked the small kitchen. When he turned the firefighter was right there, yellow coat and helmet, and Raveneau nodded. He followed him. He checked his phone, read the text messages. Mt. Diablo fire out of control. More dead in the Oakland Hills. New fire in San Bruno. It wasn't even eleven o'clock, less than eight hours since the Tam fire started and the governor was declaring a state of emergency and the smoke was so thick that commercial air traffic was being re-routed.

'Did you find what you were looking for?' the firefighter asked, though he didn't turn around to do it.

His boots clumped on the stairs, and Raveneau said 'no'.

As they crossed the Golden Gate, Coe called.

'I understand you found the book you've talked about. Can you bring it here on your way in?'

'I can but I'd rather not stop.'

'We'd like to get it from you now.'

Coe's message was the fires were terrorist acts until they knew otherwise.

'We'll bring it to you.'

Outside the FBI Field Office, Raveneau double-parked. La Rosa stayed with the car and Raveneau rode the elevator up. The Feds wouldn't have found the book and they wouldn't do any more than thumb through it now, so it was a complete waste of time delivering it but he didn't begrudge the Bureau anything.

They did all the heavy lifting on terrorism investigations after 9/11. Other agencies provided information. Other agencies watched. Raveneau forgave the Feds their regulation haircuts and tight smiles and pronounced stares as if their seriousness made them better investigators. He forgave the task force meetings with folded chairs and power point talks that droned on, and forgave the chain emails, the eternal 'Reply to All' that beat the life out of a day.

He knew a police captain who kept bees and viewed the FBI culture as analogous to a beehive. The bees were the agents who went out every day, but were never allowed to make decisions on their own. They flew home to the hive every night and reported to the drones who were called SACs and ASACS. The Director was the queen.

'Letting you help search the apartment was like asking a shoplifter to help stock a store,'

Coe said, meaning it to be a joke though it fell flat this morning.

Raveneau flipped through the remaining pages of the book and found a few had handwritten notes in the margins before he handed it to Coe. He asked, 'Can you copy and scan these for me this morning?'

'Is that Lindsley's handwriting?'

'I don't think so. I'm not good at comparing handwriting but his isn't even close. If you read these notes, they're sharp critiques. They're dismissive and disdainful. Maybe it's Albert Lash's and Lindsley on one of his visits to Lash's house decided to take the book. I'll call Lash's sister today. With the fires I may be able to change her mind.'

'If she does we'll send a couple of agents with you.'

'You've got your hands full this morning. Make those copies for me. I'll talk to you later.'

Thirty-Five

The SFPD website went down first. Raveneau figured that would worry some fraction of the public and make an equal group happy. But not long after that they lost the ability to access any police databases on their computers. When that happened Raveneau and la Rosa left the office and rode up to the top floor and then climbed the stairs to the roof.

They weren't alone. Others had made their way up and there was a post-earthquake feel as strong gusts swept the roof. The burn smell was sharp and pungent and across the bay the fires looked, if anything, stronger and larger, dark smoke billowing then flattening, tongues of flame visible as a house caught or a stand of trees. Overhead the sun was a bloodshot eye.

By early afternoon more was understood about the incendiary devices. The first remnants were recovered from the Tam fire not far from the junction of the Fairfax-Bolinas Road and Highway 1. Raveneau leaned on another old friend, Bill Staten, an arson investigator who had left SFPD four or five years ago and now consulted for insurance companies.

Staten picked up in the first ring. 'Knew I'd hear from you.'

'What are these devices?'

'Think of high quality accelerant in a plastic drinking bottle like you might carry on your bike, if you ever exercised which you probably still don't.'

'I walk.'

'Extending out of it is a high quality underwater fuse. Taped to the bottle is a cheap electronic timer and a reliable igniter to light the fuse. With this wind and the dry conditions that's enough, because when the accelerant ignites it'll give you six to eight feet in height and four in width. Not for long, but it'll burn very hot, real hot, and I was surprised they found anything worthwhile. I think what probably happened was the wind was so strong that it moved the fireball with it right away. Dry as things are right now, eight to ten seconds is enough to start tinder burning. Five minutes in the brush well-started, but the real engine is the wind. Whoever started these was thinking wind and counting on what we usually get in the fall. They just happened to catch a very strong cycle.'

'What have you seen?'

'I saw the remains of one the incendiary devices this morning and the thinking is they're all the same at all of these fires. They're cheap and easy to make. They're portable. It could be one person but with this many locations distributing them works better with a pair, one getting out of the car and one driving. They probably scouted locations and were ready when the time came. One guy gets out with the device and goes up the slope. Five minutes later he's back in the car, or maybe he uses his cellphone and another driver picks him up.'

'You're assuming it's the threesome we're looking for?'

'Me? No, not me, I'm not making any assumptions. This accelerant evaporates very easily and at low temp so you don't distribute these until you're ready, and in this case that seems to be as they knew the wind was rising. You go out with a map and make the rounds as the wind is coming up. They've got preset timers. That's why Mount Tamalpais went up all at once and maybe they've done their homework. Could be they know what departments will respond and where and the timing with the next ignitions was built around that. You know they're not even trying to fight the Diablo fire right now other than to keep it out of the populated areas. It's burning its way up the mountain. There are no crews available to stop it.'

'What's the size of one of these incendiary devices?'

'Roughly the size of a football, and they had them ready.' Staten paused. He cleared his throat before continuing. 'We get these winds every year in the spring and fall. In the spring nothing will burn, but it's all different by now, huh. Where are you? You're in the news. You've been right in the middle of all of this. What can you tell me?'

'Not much. We're talking with someone who is affiliated with the three you're seeing on TV and there's every reason to think those are the perpetrators. I'm up on the roof of the Hall of

Justice looking across the bay at fires in Oakland and the Berkeley Hills. I can see smoke to the south down the peninsula and Marin is dark with smoke. I can see Diablo burning. It looks like a volcano from here. And there's something burning farther back in the East Bay, and also farther. They've slowed the inbound/outbound at SFO and in Oakland.'

'There are fires all the way down to where I am. Three new ones in the last hour.'

Raveneau couldn't remember where Staten had moved to when his hourly billing rate crossed over three hundred dollars an hour, but it was somewhere south and near the coast.

'Ben, you can't talk to me?'

'Not yet, not really, other than it's almost certainly the three the fugitive warrants went out on.'

'Well, that was pretty obvious already.'

Staten was disappointed and Raveneau remembered how moody he could be. Good chance he only picked up the phone because he thought he was going to get something in return that he could pass on to his clients. Raveneau asked Staten now what he was working on.

'A fire with three fatalities, all of them kids. Their mother was badly burned. The fire started at five this morning when they were asleep and they got trapped in a canyon. The insurer I'm working for excludes terrorism coverage, so they're hoping that's what it is. Call me when you can talk.'

Late in the afternoon Raveneau rode with Coe who was driving and not saying an awful lot about where they were going yet, except that they were headed to Mt. Tam. The SFPD website was still down, the victim of a denial of service attack it was supposed to be invulnerable to, but the department computers were working. Someone got a hold of a local legend, a guy named Tim Chee. Chee got the SFPD system up and going again. At the mayor's office there were problems with the landline phones and there were other quirky failures in the city computer systems.

They crossed the Golden Gate with Coe talking about another person of interest, a medical technologies engineer let go four months ago for failing to properly track a waste disposal though his guess was that was negligence and not nefarious. Two agents interviewed the man and he was still unemployed and very regretful.

Coe took a call and Raveneau heard enough to not need an explanation. Lindsley had turned up. He was in a Marin high school gym designated as an evacuation center, arrived there fifteen minutes ago and said the FBI needed to be notified.

'He's only ten minutes from where we are right now,' Raveneau said. 'Let's go there.'

'We're picking him up and bringing him in and you and I are going somewhere else. We're going to see a body.'

'Whose?'

'We're hoping you can help with the ID.'

'What's the matter with the rest of you?'

'It's a male and his face isn't what it used to be. We're hoping that seeing the rest of him you'll have an easier time IDing him.'

'You're telling me you know already who it is?'

'We think we do, but I want you to take a look.'

A four-wheel-drive fire vehicle escorted them through the worst smoke as they wound their way along the coast, and they reached Stinson Beach and continued on down past the lagoon. Off to his right and looking up Raveneau saw much of this face of the mountain had burned off. In the ravines he saw stands of charred trees and white ashes. They crossed through another roadblock just past the end of the lagoon and another as they turned up the mountain. Raveneau saw only one fire crew on watch for any restarts. The fire was over here. There were pockets of green, and in the winter there would be mudslides because there wasn't anything left to hold the soil. But above Mt. Tam columns of black-gray smoke still boiled up.

'It's burning down the other side,' Coe said. 'It may reach the town.'

The road up was narrow and windy and the pale gold rye grass and the trees still green underscored just how much was chance. On their right, everything was burned. As they neared the top of the winding two-mile road he saw the redwoods along the spine were fine and for some reason that made him feel better.

He turned. 'How do you know it wasn't a homeless person living in the watershed who got caught by the fire?'

'I don't want to say too much yet, but you'll

see why. I'd rather you look at him first but I can tell you he appears to have been on a mountain bike on a single track trail. They found him as they followed the line of where the fire started. Not much question about what he was doing. Wind is supposed to die tonight or at least let up.'

Raveneau nodded. Everyone he had talked to today gave him a weather report. Winds were expected to abate, but the heat would continue. There wouldn't be any marine air, just less wind.

'Dogs scented to the incendiary materials found eight locations and we've gathered what was left. On the ocean side they had the paved road. They may have used a car to carry the incendiary bombs. On the other side they were all near a single-track mountain biking trail – and not much of a trail. The park people tell us it was an illegal track mountain bikers scratched together. The victim we're going to see was on a bike and wearing a backpack. He's on the watershed side up above the lake. We're not far away now. You know your way around here anyway, don't you?'

'I do.'

They started down the road to the reservoir, drove eight or nine steep falling turns and pulled over where another vehicle was partially blocking the road, then climbed the embankment into the trees with a firefighter who led them in, talking as he did.

'We climb up and across, and then we'll pick up a trail.'

As they got closer they saw lights and heard

voices, and as the track looped and headed toward the lights Raveneau tried to picture it. What he saw was the rider getting out of another vehicle after spreading five of these incendiary devices off the right side of the Bolinas-Fairfax Road as it climbed up the ocean side, maybe placing these devices at dusk when it wasn't too dark to drive without lights. Or maybe the mountain biker placed them all. If so, he went up the steep road in a howling wind and then down the single track on the other side. That or he was dropped at the ridge and the vehicle turned around and went back down the way it came up. The vehicle would be something ordinary, a Toyota pickup, something that blended in, maybe salt-worn from the ocean and with a rack.

Up on the ridge the rider starts down, starts placing the devices. Behind him the timers are ticking and maybe he spends a little too long trying to make certain he's got them placed correctly so they'll ignite what's around them. Maybe he falls a little behind and lets the bike roll a little faster, but it's also darker on this side and he hits a root or a rock. He goes down.

He asked the firefighter now. 'What happened to him?'

'He went over the bars and landed badly. We're guessing he was unconscious when the fire started.'

'You're thinking he rode this trail in the dark with a light?'

'Yes.'

'Why would he do that? Why wouldn't he place these in daylight?'

Raveneau didn't get an answer that satisfied him. It only told him they were guessing, but he didn't ask any more questions either because as they came around the turn there was the FBI Evidence Recovery Team, a couple of park rangers, more firefighters, and the body.

Thirty-Six

The mountain bike was a Specialized, carbon fiber, and expensive. The front wheel was twisted, the tire flat and half stripped, seat torn and turned sideways. From blood on a rock and a gash the bike's gear ring left in a scorched bay tree they determined where he was ejected. He struck the rock hard bursting off the incendiary devices in the backpack. The backpack was pulled tight, the waist band cinched. One shoulder strap tore loose on impact but thc backpack stayed on as he tried to drag himself.

The head of the FBI Evidence Recovery Team turned to Raveneau. 'He broke his right arm and collarbone when he hit the bay tree and it looks like he had trouble with his legs after he hit the rock. Gritty guy though, look how he dragged himself trying to get back to the trail. He thought he would get back on his bike.'

'How do you know he rode down here at night versus earlier in the day?'

'His helmet had three lights screwed on to the

front of it. That's the only part that didn't melt.'

Raveneau studied the scuff marks and gouges in the dirt and came up with a different idea. 'I think he was just trying to get the backpack off. He wasn't trying to go anywhere. How many of those devices were in it?'

'Two, and one ruptured when he hit the rock.' The head of the ERT, Cabrera, stared at Raveneau.'You just got here, but you've got it all figured out? Do you want to hear our version or do you just want to look at him?'

'No offense.'

'No problem. I deal every day with people who've been doing the same thing for so long they think they're experts.'

'Show me what you see.'

'Then let's start a little higher up.' Raveneau followed him up the narrow bike trail and after they hiked around the first turn Raveneau saw the long run down the rider had before he hit the next turn. He came into that turn with a lot of speed but made it through.

'He was flying,' Cabrera said. 'Why do you think that was?'

'The incendiary devices were timed to go off at the same time and he was running late.'

'Exactly, and he was probably a good rider but it was night and this is an illegal single-track trail and poorly marked. He made it through the turn down there before losing control. He couldn't see his bike after he crashed and was trying to get back to it. He only had two more of the devices to drop and the bike was his way out of here. He needed to get back on it and he must have thought he had enough time. Otherwise, he would have shed the backpack.'

'Unless he couldn't get it off.'

'Come on, one strap was already gone, and it's a backpack, they're made to come on and off easily.'

They walked back down and Raveneau saw the shoe still clipped on to the bike pedal. He looked at the marks in the dirt again and the blanket over the body.

'The shoulder strap broke and one of the incendiary devices burst when he hit the tree. It was the right shoulder strap, same as his broken arm. He flew backwards through the air and struck in the mid lumbar and with the backpack turned he didn't have any cushion.'

Raveneau wasn't seeing it quite the same way and normally an autopsy would largely resolve it, but that might not be the case here due to the severity of his burns. There was something that didn't quite mesh in the way they were putting it together. He walked up to the tree, looked at the gash, the grease stain, and the tire mark, and saw where the ground was gouged. He agreed the bike struck the tree and the rider shattered his arm and was ejected and had the bad luck to hit the rock. Maybe he was unconscious after that. When he came to what would he do?

He would be disoriented and in pain and probably the thing that made him ride too fast would come back to him. He might go for his bike like Cabrera claimed or he was too badly hurt for that and there wasn't enough time. Raveneau stood at the rock where the blood was and looked up the steep slope at the bay tree and the bike down below it. The bike had a light and he walked up and looked at it, felt for the switch. It was on and the plastic lens glass was broken but the pieces were all still there, so the light might still be on as the bike came to rest.

If so, he saw it, and let's say he felt his injuries and checked the time and smelled the leaked accelerant. That would have scared him, that and the time going by.

Raveneau turned back to Cabrera. 'I think he was trying to do both things, trying to get rid of the pack and get to the trail to walk or ride out. He may have knocked himself out when he hit the rock.'

'You ready to take a look?'

Cabrera pulled the blanket off. When the incendiary devices in the backpack ignited the rider was near a dry pine tree. The pine probably turned into a fireball. The backpack and helmet melted but for the front section that was intact because his head shielded it from the incendiary's intense heat. The backpack became white ash. His shirt burned away and the skin cooked. Vertebrae in his upper spine and a blackened section of skull were visible.

Raveneau stepped back. He asked, 'Did a branch of the tree fall on him?'

'Yes. We moved it off.'

It was grisly, and where his head was turned the right side of his face was still covered. Raveneau wasn't in any hurry to see that. They were letting him talk and come to it his way, but were already past that themselves and only being patient with him.

'OK, show me his face.'

Cabrera pulled the rest of the blanket and two of the ERT rolled the body. Half of the face was gone. Raveneau got closer. He used one of their flashlights to look at the other nostril. It was still intact and that made sense to him since Staten had said these type of incendiary devices generated a fireball that lit the surrounding tinder but also burned itself out quickly. He reached and moved the head just a little and saw he'd breathed smoke and soot, his nostril dark. He must have hid his face as they went off and when the pain became too intense his head twisted toward the fire.

The dead man's mouth was locked open, a rock between his back left molars, and he had shattered his teeth biting down on the rock. It was as Coe predicted and Raveneau studied what remained of his face and then looked at his hands. He pulled the cycling glove on the man's left hand and turned his wrist and saw the scar he wondered about at Grate's Place.

'Looks like he tried to cut his wrists,' Coe said. 'Is that what you were looking for?'

'It is. This is the one they called John the Baptist.'

'Are you certain?'

Raveneau stared at what was left of his face. The helmet plastic dripped and ran down where his right ear had been. The face was badly disfigured but the body shape was right. So was this wrist scar and the remains of the thin beard under his chin. Only a little remained on the one side.

'It's him.'

More video got shot and another round of photos and they worked him into a body bag. They were yet to zip it shut when he and Coe started back to the car. As they did, Coe questioned him again. 'Are you absolutely certain?'

'I can't be that, but it's him.'

'He suffered.'

'He really did.'

'If this is who you say it is then we're past debating who set these fires and we'll look for more help from headquarters.'

'The debate is over.'

The manhunt that already included every law enforcement agency in the Bay Area would reach out across the country now. With the fires in Colorado in June and the other wildfires in the west and LA with its Santa Ana winds, the hunt would get attention. Alan Siles and Ike Latkos would get apprehended and quite possibly killed during the arrest. That wouldn't surprise Raveneau at all.

'What is this really about?' Coe asked. 'I can't get my head around why they are doing this. I don't think anyone in our office understands it.'

'Do they understand fanatic, zealot, and ideologue? Siles says he believes in a place called the Boundary. Siles isn't the first to incorporate paranormal into his reality. We're dealing with a true believer.'

'Not with Lindsley.'

'No, not with Lindsley, but maybe as Siles says, Ann Coryell wasn't really murdered. She was freed.'

'He said that to you.'

'Pretty close to that, and he knew her.'

'Do you know what Lindsley was accused of when he was sixteen?'

'I do and he gave me a chance to talk about it with him but I haven't yet. I've been waiting on a call from a retired Chicago assistant prosecutor, but there's no time for that anymore. We need to push Lindsley harder. He knows more than he's told us. It's time to rock his boat.'

Thirty-Seven

De Haro Press was the name of the publisher who brought out the book on Coryell's writings and then vanished. Raveneau was still trying to figure out who was behind that book, though now he believed he'd found the source of the publisher's name. If he was right the name tied to the nineteenth century and so maybe tied to Lash, Lindsley, or Siles.

By June of 1846 tensions between ambitious American settlers and the Mexican rulers of the province of California led to minor skirmishes between irregular Mexican forces and those called 'bear flaggers' for their newly adopted flag that carried a bear, a star, and the words 'California Republic.' When two Americans were killed and their mutilated bodies left near what is now the town of Healdsburg in northern California, a retaliatory band of one hundred and thirty men, many of them bear flaggers, searched for their killers.

Taking charge of these men was John Charles Fremont, an ambitious man dubbed 'The Pathfinder' for his surveying expeditions as a lieutenant in the Corps of Topographical Engineers. With him was the famed Indian scout, Kit Carson, and perhaps Fremont believed the time had come for greater boldness.

In prior months while camped at Sutter Buttes he'd been content with a campaign of terror directed at local Indians he suspected of plotting against settlers. But now he took charge of the 'California Battalion.' Under his lead the battalion spiked Mexican cannons in San Francisco and prepared for a war of independence. They were camped on the Marin shoreline on the morning of June twenty-eighth when Fremont made a decision that ten years later may have cost him the US Presidency when he ran as the first candidate of the newly formed Republican Party.

That morning two nineteen-year-old-twins, Francisco and Ramon, rowed a boat from Point Molate on the eastern shoreline in what is now Contra Costa County north toward Marin. With them was an older man, Jose Berryessa. Why they crossed the bay that morning is unclear. Possibly they were bringing messages intended to help Berryessa's imprisoned son. Whatever their motives, they were intercepted by Fremont's band of bear flaggers in Richardson Bay, and reading now, Raveneau saw where Ann Coryell's beliefs connected to the story.

After the three men were captured, Kit Carson informed Fremont and asked what he should do with the prisoners, and Fremont perhaps empowered by the hubris of the moment responded that he had no room for prisoners. Carson returned to the bear flaggers waiting on the beach with the prisoners. He relayed Fremont's message and helped shoot Jose de Los Reyes Berryessa and the two brothers.

If Fremont had been a less ambitious man the summary executions might have been forgotten, but ten years later on September 27, 1856, the *Los Angeles Star* ran a story that left readers wondering if a possible Presidential candidate had ordered three men murdered. With that story the *LA Star* planted the seed of doubt, and James Buchanan, a Democrat, won the election.

Fremont never escaped the stain. He was unable to discount the testimony of numerous witnesses. What he thought might have been forgotten in the birth of the great state of California wasn't forgotten. As a consequence, Fremont's stature diminished and four years later, ahead of the onslaught of the American Civil War, another man, an Illinois lawyer, Abraham Lincoln, became the first Republican President, and Fremont's political career ebbed.

Raveneau clicked out of the de Haro articles and returned to making phone calls, working his way down a list of those who called in to say they had information about Alan Siles, Ike Latkos, or the third man the public knew only by his first name, John. Finding out who the now dead John actually was had become critical. He was the best lead to the others and it was possible that lead was in the twenty-two pages of names and numbers that was Raveneau's share of tip calls to make. When Coe dropped him they left it that they would talk tomorrow, and he stayed in the homicide office now making calls until eleven that night.

Much later, he fell asleep on the couch at home and awoke to a late night call from Coe.

'We've got a new problem, a health problem. Three of the Evidence Recovery Team who handled the body, the bike, and backpack, as well as two at the lab, are sick.'

'What are their symptoms?'

'Nausea, diarrhea, fever, and other symptoms consistent with radiation poisoning. That's now confirmed and why I'm calling you. The victim's body is hot. He ingested radioactive material and enough to kill him. The guess is he was in bad shape when he went down on that bike. It's probably why he went down. They're saying he must have dragged himself with pure adrenalin. You need to get checked immediately, Ben. This stuff accumulates in the thyroid. Bring the clothes you wore last night with you, but put them in a bag in your trunk.'

'Great.'

'Your place is going to need to be swept too. Did you shower?'

'Yes.'

'Good.'

Raveneau brought the clothes and they were

scanned and he was fine and about the clothes he was told, 'Leave them here and go shopping. The reading isn't serious but you don't want to wear these anymore and you don't need any X-rays for awhile.'

'How many have I had?'

'About a dozen.'

'How long was the dead man exposed?'

'Probably less than an hour and closer to half an hour, but that's just a guess. The sport drinking bottles in the backpack are hot. If radioactive particles are small enough they can be suspended in a fluid and easier still if the fluid had other particulate in it. He drank it and he carried it and probably spilled some, and those bottles melted and the fluid evaporated so that spread the radioactive material.'

A subcontractor working for the Feds followed Raveneau home and swept his apartment with a Geiger counter and also Visa, the cat, who lived on the rooftop and had been in and out. Visa was clean but the apartment read higher than background radiation and Raveneau ended up making calls from home as he waited for a team that specialized in this kind of cleaning.

That ate a lot of the morning. By mid afternoon a number of the smaller fires were either out or under control, though that wasn't the case with four majors, the Mt. Tamalpais, the Mt. Diablo, what was being called the Castro Valley blaze, and a fourth in the Oakland Hills. The Tam fire did reach Mill Valley and burned commercial buildings along the north-western edge of the town. And there were new fires, but fire crews believed most were caused by the fire jumping or by embers carried and the wind continued to lessen. So there was hope of more containment by midnight. Eleven deaths were now attributed to the fires. Three hundred fifty-three homes had burned and thirty-six other structures.

That afternoon the FBI called a press conference and briefed the media on the mountain biker suspect found dead in the Lake Alpine watershed. They said though it was not yet confirmed they believed the as yet unidentified dead man had placed the incendiary devices on the eastern watershed slope carrying them in a backpack. They believed it possible he had an accomplice, as other incendiary devices were placed on the western slope, and asked anyone who had seen a vehicle in the vicinity on either the day of the Tam fire or the day prior to please call or email.

As the press conference turned to questions from reporters it got a little heated with the Feds, and it was no longer just Coe. Coe was in the background as a spokesman defended the Bureau's inability to find Siles or Latkos. Another reporter jumped in with questions about Brandon Lindsley. They were all over Lindsley's past now and Coe took the mike and made it clear Lindsley was cooperating with both the San Francisco Police and the FBI.

Coe looked to the back of the room where Raveneau stood near a door. This was the plan. This was the signal they wanted to send Alan Siles. But as Coe delivered this he was challenged on it. A reporter said he'd been told yesterday by someone who should know that Lindsley was a suspect and Coe caught Raveneau's eye in the back of the room and reaffirmed, 'Mr Lindsley's working with us and with the San Francisco Police. He has provided valuable information that we are acting on right now. We expect his help to lead to the capture of the other two very soon.'

'Shouldn't have said that last,' la Rosa whispered, but it was already done.

Thirty-Eight

Rhe next morning the retired Chicago assistant district attorney, Stan Pierce, called Raveneau and began to talk as if they were old friends. Pierce referred to his website as he talked and Raveneau brought it up on his computer monitor.

'Bottom line, Inspector, is Lindsley murdered his parents when he was sixteen and got away with it. His best friend helped him and they stuck with each other. The detectives thought they'd get the friend to talk, but he never did. They tried everything and neither talked. Lindsley inherited three and a half million dollars from his parents. He probably paid his friend, Jules, later, though I don't yet have proof of that.'

'What do you mean, you don't yet?'

'I haven't quit. He killed them for their money

and to get them out of his life. There was nothing impulsive about it. He planned it carefully. He didn't feel any remorse, any guilt. He put on a show of looking sad and crying and when he finished doing that he turned it off like a light switch. He didn't feel anything for them. You've probably seen my website.'

'I'm looking at it.'

'Kids killing their parents is comparatively rare and usually there's some reason, rage or a feeling of being trapped, something. Lindsley insisted he loved and got along with his parents. But he didn't. We had plenty of witnesses willing to testify, but we also had a district attorney who needed everything perfect or he wouldn't touch a case. Brandon killed them for their money but there's an irony to that. He was a young man very upset with the state of the world and thought of his parents as part of the problem.

'His father was an executive for a chemical company and his mother a tax lawyer for the well-to-do. After they were murdered he was asked what his mother did for a living. He said she helped people cheat on their taxes. I know that because it was me he said it to. He was sociable, got good grades, and his teachers liked him. If you've met him, you know he likes to talk. He's studious and deceptive. Underneath there's a monster looking out at you.'

'You're talking but you're not really giving me anything. Tell me what makes you certain he killed them.'

Raveneau wasn't sure Pierce heard him, continuing as if Raveneau hadn't said a word.

'We were just short of having enough evidence for a slam dunk and that's the only way Harris would go forward.'

'Who's Harris?'

'Albert Harris was the District Attorney. If you're on my website, you'll see his name. You're on the website now, aren't you? Harris was born in the wrong country. He should have been a prosecutor for Stalin. That way he would have won every case he tried and not ever needed to run for re-election. Lindsley got this best friend of his, Jules Owens, to lie for him. His parents were due to leave early in the morning on a four-day vacation and Lindsley was to stay at the Owens' house while his parents traveled. That's an arrangement they had used with previous vacations.

'His parents planned to drive to the airport very early in the morning so they dropped Lindsley at the Owens the night before. They went out to dinner after they dropped him off and were murdered that night. What happened was Brandon rode his bike back home at two in the morning, killed them, then rode back to the Owens' house, a distance of two point three miles. The bodies weren't discovered for another four days. He used a bike path and an old farm road. He was on a residential street for less than half a mile. It's all on the website.'

'Tell me what you know that isn't on the website.'

'There was just enough moonlight. He let himself in, took his father's pistol from the back of a drawer in the study downstairs and crept upstairs.'

Raveneau listened to Pierce's voice, wavering, but certain in his conviction.

'It's a big house I'm talking about. The master bedroom is on one end and the only thing that went wrong was his father heard footsteps and woke up. Probably that's because they were going to get up early to make a flight. Bill Lindsley's body was in the hallway. His mother was reaching for the phone when he shot her through the head. Three bullets in each, and he stepped in his father's blood as he left the bedroom and tracked that downstairs. He wore gloves for the shooting and showered before he left the house, taking his clothes with him.

'We never found those but I'm going back next spring. I have some idea of where to look for them. He and Jules Owens claimed they played video games all night and never left the house. Then there was the complication that the bodies laid there for days before they were discovered by him. Lindsley purposefully contaminated the scene when he went home for some clean clothes and allegedly found them. That was a day before they were due to return. He wanted to make certain he'd be the one to find them. He called the police.

'Now, Inspector, there are roughly fifteen thousand homicides a year in the United States. Maybe seventy-five of those are children killing their parents. I've studied this and some are for the reasons I mentioned earlier and some of these kids can't say later why they did it. Most of the younger ones don't know why. Some of it is impulse. I've become an expert in this and I'm willing to help you, but I think it's best if you read everything on my website first.'

Raveneau skimmed pages on the website as Pierce kept on.

'He cried. He feigned grief, but I'm certain he didn't feel anything. He thought of a way to get free of them and get the money. The money was the motive. He wanted to recreate his life. As soon as that inheritance was his he left the Chicago area. He moved out west with the rest of the kooks and I don't mean that as an insult.'

'Did he move straight here?'

'What?'

'Did he move from Chicago to here or did he move somewhere else first?'

'He left the country for awhile. By then he was eighteen. He had freedom and money and could go anywhere he wanted.'

'Where did he go?'

'To the French Riviera. He stayed there for six months. The hotel he stayed in is on my website as well as how much he paid.'

'How do I get to the case records?'

'What's been released is there. You'll see a tab that says case files.'

Raveneau clicked on that and was surprised Pierce had access to an unsolved case and had put up anything in the files, but as he scanned down he saw it was next to nothing. As Pierce continued to talk, Raveneau clicked through the other web pages. On each in the upper right corner was a headshot of Pierce, neatly cut white hair, glasses, blue suit coat, white shirt, red tie.

He looked like the Fourth of July. But annoying as he was to talk to, Raveneau could hear how the case changed his life.

Then abruptly Pierce shifted away from Lindsley. 'What are the conditions?'

'Where?'

'Where you are? What's the situation with the fires and apprehending the individuals?'

It took awhile to get Pierce back to Lindsley. But like a train, once he was back on the tracks he set off again.

'Lindsley is bright but not brilliant. He thinks he's brilliant but the only thing he's brilliant at is disguising who he is. He is imaginative and I don't know how he did it, but he got himself into college. He did well on the SAT and his score is there on my website. You'll need to click on his bio tab. He's manipulative. He won't try to sell you everything at once. He's smart that way. He'll sell you a little and then take a little back and then give you a little more. He's doing that now with you. I'm getting that from the news reports, though here at the lake I can't get anything live. But still, I recognize what he's doing.

'I don't really believe in the theories of multiple personality but the boy that I interviewed sometimes seemed inhabited by a different person. It was as if when I left the room for a few minutes ... Let's say I was interviewing him and needed to go to the rest room or get a glass of water or the Mountain Dew he liked to drink. He loved Mountain Dew. Sometimes I'd be back in less than five minutes, but the person I had been talking to was gone. A completely different person was sitting there now, but subtle, not night and day at all. Scary and exciting, I've never been around anything like it before or since. He's probably even better at it now. Let me put it this way, it doesn't surprise me a homicide inspector is calling me about him. I can get you copies of the case files, but you didn't get them from me. You may want to try the department first. I'll give you a name.'

Raveneau wrote down a name and phone number.

'I'm going to summarize our conversation on my website, Inspector.'

'Don't do that. Keep this one between you and me.'

'I'll leave your name out if you want.'

'Don't put anything up yet. You'll compromise us.'

'All right, I'll wait until you give me the go.'

'That might be a while.'

A very long while Raveneau thought and Pierce said, 'That's OK, I'll wait, and I'm going to warn you again, he's capable of anything. You haven't come out and said it, but you're telling me he might be involved in another killing, aren't you?'

'We don't know what's what yet.'

'Give me your email and I'll send you some things I haven't posted to the site yet.'

Raveneau gave him an email and half an hour later Pierce called to asked if he'd read the documents yet.

He hadn't. He scanned them now and saw they were Pierce's analysis of Lindsley's personality.

He thanked Pierce again, said he would read them as he could.

Half an hour later Pierce called back. 'Have you read what I sent?'

'Not yet.'

'I'll wait for your call.'

'If you don't reach me, leave me a message and I'll get back to you when I can.'

Raveneau broke the connection, laid the phone down, and stared at a photo of Lindsley that Pierce had just sent him. He was young in the photo and with his parents. He looked like he was about ten years old and it took Raveneau a little while to figure out that the hotels behind them were French. Then he put it together that this was somewhere on the French Riviera and they made a family trip there and Lindsley returned after his parents were dead and he had left Chicago. In this photo he looked very happy and leaned against his mother. What did it mean that he returned and stayed six months after they were gone?

Thirty-Nine

Raveneau put a call in to the Missouri sheriff. She was a little bit of relief in all this and when she picked up the phone it was good to hear her voice.

'Is this the same mountain where your victim's body was found?'

'It is and that area burned early. The fires were set along two roads – one that comes up from the coast road, the highway, on up to the ridge of the mountain, and down the other side. Her body was on the ocean side of the ridge. Listen, Jennie, you're going to get a call from a Mark Coe at the FBI. He may send you a photo of the man who died while setting the incendiary devices.'

'This is the fire bomber we've all been hearing about?'

'It is, and he's a John Doe but so badly burned I don't know if a photo will do it. We've also got testimony that Alan Siles has knowledge about how the skulls made their way into the bomb shelter.'

At noon Raveneau drove out to talk with the contractor Ferranti. He parked and stood looking at the smoke out over the bay. It was whiter and that was a good sign. The garden shed slab was gone, the bomb shelter pumped full of a sand slurry. A backhoe operator dug away the earth to a depth of roughly six feet around the access tube and the operator was using the hoe to bang into the access tube until the rebar was exposed. Raveneau watched him cut through the exposed steel with a blow torch and then knock the tube down. He cut the last rebar, hooked a chain around the tube and lifted it away. Raveneau felt a pang of worry that he missed something that he could now never get, but he also felt an almost superstitious sense that they were entombing a place of evil.

He climbed the stone steps back up to the house. New windows and doors were getting installed and he watched three guys lift in a big window and then found Ferranti. They sat down at a plywood table in what had been Lash's study and was for the moment a construction office. Ferranti looked happy to finally get the bomb shelter out of his way. He smiled but acted nervous and Raveneau guessed he wanted something. He was going to ask for something and didn't seem comfortable about it.

'Should I pull my complaint against Hugh Neilley?'

'I can't give you advice on that.'

'I'd like some anyway because what he did was dishonest and I'm not sure what to do.'

'You'll have to make that decision on your own.'

'He forged those dump tags and the question is do you want me to bury it because he's a cop and your friend? I mean, you have helped me here.

Do I owe you?'

'You have to do what you think is right.'

'He's your friend.'

Raveneau reached over and touched Ferranti's abdomen. 'You're the guy wearing the wire, so that means you can listen to this conversation over and over again. I just gave you my best advice. Replay when you have time and let your lawyer listen too. See what he thinks. As for me, I think you're as fucked up as Hugh. See you later.'

He called la Rosa as he left Ferranti and she knew this tone of voice in Raveneau. He was driving. She could hear the car engine, the wind blowing through the window. She thought Raveneau was of another time, maybe a better one, but one that had almost gone by. She realized in that instant she was never really going to know him. The difference was generational and she felt an acute sadness well up as he talked.

'I just left the contractor, Ferranti. He was wearing a wire and wanted to draw mc into saying he should back off Hugh. There's something there that we need to learn about.'

'How do you know he was wearing a wire?'

'I saw it when he moved and reached over and touched it. I'm wondering what he's heard about Hugh. I hate to say, we've got to know.'

'Where are you now?'

'On the Golden Gate on my way to Marion Coryell's.'

'Does she know you're coming?'

'She does, and an old friend of hers will be

there also.'

'What is it, an intervention?'

'She's got something she wants to tell me. Her friend is helping her find the words.'

'I'm surprised she's even in her house with the fires. Is it something she should have told us a long time ago?'

'I really don't know, and on getting back into the house, she told me they were allowed to go back in last night. I'll call you when I leave Marion's house.'

'OK.'

Except it wasn't OK, because now what he said nagged at her. Raveneau wouldn't have called unless he was seeing something. She continued working for another hour then scratched around on her desk until she found the number Raveneau got from pot-bellied Hugh Neilley, Southern Precinct lieutenant turned crooked demolition contractor. She swore as she dialed the number, but then quietly asked for a Lieutenant Sanger.

'This is Sanger.'

'It's Liz. I want to talk to you about Hugh Neilley, but let's do it away from the Hall.'

'I've always got time for you.'

She knew that but would just have to deal with him today. If there was anything, Sanger would probably know.

'How about in an hour?' she asked. 'I'll meet you outside.'

'An hour from now is tough, but for you I'll do it. I thought you'd never ask.'

So did I, she thought. 'Good. See you then.'

Forty

When Raveneau sat down in the kitchen with Marion Coryell and her friend, sunlight was bright on both of their faces. It also revealed age, weathered lines at the mouth and the eyes, a slight yellowing of her friend's eyes, and all the worry and sadness Marion had carried and now wore. But her voice was firm. What she had to say was not what Raveneau anticipated.

'Alan, I mean Brandon, brought me flowers and a copy of the book. That's when I first met him. He said he had a number of copies and was going to givc it away so she wasn't forgotten. He wanted a photo of Ann and I gave him one. I could have told you this last time we talked, but I didn't know you had questions about the book.'

'Did he say anything about who published it?'

'Not that I remember, but I think it says so on the book. I had the impression it was a friend of his.'

'That friend might have been Professor Lash.'

'Please don't say something like that.'

'They were good friends, Marion.'

'No, they weren't. They couldn't have been.'

'Why not? He lied about his name and about his relationship with Lash. Do you think that's where the lies stopped?'

'I may be wrong again but you have to understand how often we talked about Professor Lash. Brandon and I agreed about Professor Lash. We both hate him. Excuse me a minute, I'm going to get something to show you.'

She got up and left and Raveneau looked to her friend but got nothing there. Then Marion was back and carrying a photo album that in her arms looked heavy, though she had no difficulty setting it on to the table. She turned to her friend. 'You'll remember this.'

She showed Raveneau a photo of Ann as a graduate student standing on upper Bancroft with the campus behind her.

'I had two of the same and I gave him one.'

'Gave Brandon Lindsley one?'

'Yes.'

'Did he say why he wanted it?'

'He admired Ann.'

Raveneau studied the photo and asked, 'Can I take this and get a copy made?'

'I don't want to lose it.'

'I'll get it back to you.' Raveneau turned to the friend. 'Are you married?'

She smiled at that and said, 'George and I have been married forty-six years.'

'Do you and George keep secrets from each other?'

'Never.'

'Then you need to walk outside while Marion and I talk.'

She walked out and Raveneau told Marion that they had recovered a partially burned photo from the bomb shelter and that the photo used in the book might also be the same as the burned one. He tapped the photo in her album. 'I want to compare it with the burned fragment we have.'

She nodded then said, 'If you're going to tell me he doesn't believe in the things Ann wrote, then I don't know anything at all about anything.'

'He may well believe in the things she wrote. I'm talking about something different. I'm talking about a fragment of a burned photo we found in the bomb shelter. I want to compare it to the photo in this book.'

'Why was it burned?'

'There were candles in the shelter and it may have been accidental that it was burned. Why it was there I don't know yet, though we are getting closer.' He saw her reaction and added, 'Marion, I'm not saying Brandon Lindsley was her killer and her killer befriended you. I'm not saying that at all and I may be completely wrong about this photo.'

'You must have one of the books. I can't lose this picture of Ann.'

'We do have a book but the photo there is cropped. It doesn't show as much as this one. I'll make sure it stays with me.'

She gave him the photo after finding an envelope to put it in. Now she sat straight-backed in her chair, her face ashen as if the conversation had exhausted her. Raveneau left soon after.

When he walked out the sky was bluer and yet the smell of burn was still very strong. He called la Rosa, left a message on her cell, and then crossed back to San Francisco to a copy shop where he knew he could get a jpeg emailed to him before he left the store. Upstairs at his desk in the homicide office he opened the image and then sized it to match the photo found in the bomb shelter. When he did that he saw a match, but it would take someone better than him looking at it. He left another message for la Rosa. This time she called back and said, 'I'm on my way back to the office. I'll see you in a few minutes.'

When she walked in he held the photo from the bomb shelter up against the image on his monitor.

'Mom's photo?'

'Yes. An old friend of hers got her to open up a little more. The publisher of the orange book of her writings was given a copy of this photo and most likely they got it from Brandon when he was impersonating Alan Siles. Marion loaned him the photo to make copies about six months after Ann's remains were identified. He made one or more copies.'

Raveneau read her quizzical look and answered it as best he could.

'I don't know if it matters at all, but I think Lindsley gave a copy of the photo to whoever published the orange book. This is the photo that's at the back of that book, and the charred photo that came out of the bomb shelter may be the same.'

'OK, but why are we chasing it?'

'I don't think Lash was the publisher, and if it was Alan Siles then that deepens the connection with him and Lindsley. Why was it left in the bomb shelter? Was it discarded because it was burned or was that intentional? If it connects Lindsley to Siles at a point when Lindsley swears he only knew Siles in passing, that's information that might help us later. I just don't know how yet.' He paused. 'But there's something there and we need to know it. I'm sure of that.'

Forty-One

Raveneau picked up Jennie Crawford, the Missouri sheriff, after she landed at SFO. That was her idea, though it was the FBI who paid for her to fly out. She said it was the first time she had ever flown business class and that she hadn't been apart from her daughter a single night in three years. Not only that, she was uncomfortable leaving her daughter with her mom.

'What's the matter with your mom?'

'She's always got a cigarette.'

'What about your ex? Where is he?'

'JB works for a company that supplies goods to the military. If he was here, Julie could stay with him, but he's not and he never is. He's probably wherever the next war is being planned, figuring out how much his company can charge the Army for water. Let's not talk about him. What's that thing over there that looks like a chopped-off tea cup?'

'Candlestick Park. It's a sports stadium.'

'They should think about knocking it down.'

'They are.'

'Is the traffic always like this?'

'This isn't bad at all.'

'I wouldn't have asked you to pick me up if I knew the traffic would be like this. I'm sorry.'

'Don't be and I'm glad to meet you.'

'Likewise, though I really don't know why I'm here. I still don't understand why I couldn't get the FBI's questions answered with a fax and a phone. Where do they get the money for all this anyway?'

'You know the answer to the second question. Did you bring those files with you?'

'I did and they're yours first, but we should go over them together. I want to check into the hotel and shower. Any chance you want to meet at the restaurant your girlfriend has?'

'It's more like a bar.'

'That sounds even better. If she owns a good bar I'd marry her if I were you. Have you ever been married?'

'I was for a while.'

'Kids?'

'A son.'

Raveneau waited for the next question. He didn't want to answer it or change the mood in the car, and of all things this was still the hardest for him. For some reason his head always went to the lines of a poem. He braced, and it came as human and naturally as breathing.

'Where is he?'

'He died in Fallujah, Iraq.'

She nodded. She didn't say anything for seconds and he saw in her profile the grit that made her sheriff.

'I have a cousin who died there. I was older and I babysat him a lot and saw him grow up. He was on his way to becoming a really good man. In those long wars so many things happen. A lot is just luck, I think.' She was quiet then in a softer voice said, 'Fallujah was special. It's one we'll remember. I miss my cousin and I'm sorry I made you talk about your son.'

That was a bond for Raveneau. He was quiet for a mile and then picked up the conversation again, lightened things up and gave her a thumbnail city-tour on the way to the Sheraton, and then told her he'd come get her in a couple of hours and take her to meet Celeste and get a drink. He dropped her off and picked her up two hours later. One drink in she opened the file she brought. In it were photos of every casket that got pilfered. The caskets looked like shipwrecks in the river mud.

'Sometimes a burial site turns up on a farm or an old cemetery outside of where a town used to be, and it's been so long their people are gone. There's no one left to care. But that wasn't the case here. We knew the river was rising but we hoped the levee would hold. It didn't.' She paused a moment. 'Maybe I said this to you before. I've had it in mind that the thief of these skulls was looking for an opportunity like this.'

'That fits.'

'Some of them got cleaned.'

'That's right. Several got cleaned.'

'People at home are very offended by that. They want to see whoever did this go to prison and they want to understand why it happened. Whoever stole them took a pretty good risk of getting caught. That's always puzzled me. A deputy could easily have driven up that road just to make sure it was all still secure.'

Raveneau had no explanation for the man's lack of fear of being caught, other than the invulnerability delusion can create.

They ate sardines, cleaned, salted, and roasted. They ate a plate of crostini with quail eggs and prosciutto that Celeste brought over. She sat with them, drank a half glass of wine, winked at Raveneau, and left as Sheriff Crawford drank cold white wine and talked about her life and job and living on a bluff over the Mississippi. She was locked in a tight race running for re-election.

'The election is less than a month away and the fellow I'm running against has made catching who did this his main issue. He claims I haven't put enough work into it. Think there's any chance this will get solved before then?'

Raveneau did, and he briefed her on where things were at. They talked more and then as he drove her back to the Sheraton there was a report of yet another new fire. They listened to that report and as she got out of the car she leaned back in.

'They didn't fly me out here just to ID a body. They know something else.'

'That's what I figure too.'

'But they haven't said that to you?'

'No.'

'At home I know an FBI agent who refers to the police in Missouri as the locals, even St Louis metro. They're all tribes to him in a foreign country he's been stationed in, and he was born in Missouri. I'd show you how he walks and looks at us, but I've had too much wine.'

'Get some sleep.'

'You're a good man, Benjamin Raveneau. I'll call you when they get through with me tomorrow.'

It would turn out she was right. The FBI did know something and had for at least twenty-four hours. Raveneau didn't like that and liked it even less when he found out what it was.

Forty-Two

When Jennifer Crawford looked at the melted right side of the dead man's face, the stump of ear coated in melted plastic from a helmet, they said, and then the other side, she asked, 'How did Inspector Raveneau identify him?'

'You tell us.'

'I tell you? What's that mean?'

'What do you see?'

'I see myself throwing up in a toilet in about twenty seconds.'

'Have you ever seen him before?'

'Maybe, just maybe, and what is it you're going to tell me about that?'
'Let's do this first, Sheriff.'
'Am I getting radiation right now?'
'No, and a lot of it was on his body and clothes. He was washed.'
'This is cleaned up?'
She didn't listen to what either behind her said next and studied the face more closely. She recognized him and was trying to put a place to it. One of the agents was Newton, the Missouri FBI agent she was telling Raveneau about last night. That said to her she should know this man and she knew now she hadn't ever spoken with him, never cited him or pulled him over, or questioned him. But there was something in her memory in the background. A car accident? No. Something else and maybe it was the elderly man locked outside his house and lying dead in the cold morning. Was he the one who called it in that the detective later questioned? Thought on that a moment and turned.
'I think he was interviewed after a neighbor got locked out of his house and froze to death. He called it in and later our detective went back and interviewed him as a possible suspect.'
Newton tried to get the elderly victim's name from her and the name of the detective, Abe Burtle, now retired. She didn't give either. She said, 'Good to see you, Todd.'
'Yeah, I thought we'd catch up over dinner last night but I couldn't find you. I left two messages for you.'
'I got both. I was out with one of the locals.'

'Raveneau?'

She nodded and then followed Special-Agent Coe to his office. She liked Coe. She saw a little dance of light in his eyes. He needed a few meals and some sleep, but he wasn't a suit with a gun. Now they sat a table in a much nicer room than anything in the squat, square, poorly air conditioned brick building she worked from. She took in a flat screen TV and then as abruptly as if switching off a light switch she quit being a tourist. 'What do you need from me, Agent Coe?'

'All the help you can give us. We think there's a house in your county where he was living and that house may have radioactive materials stored in it.'

'Do you have a name?'

'John Royer.'

They watched her for a reaction and Jennifer thought Royer was right. That might be it.

'They tell me you may have recognized him. How would you go about finding out where he lived and who he associated with?'

'Get him out on Facebook. Run an article and put a photo front of the weekly. It won't take long.'

'At this point we'd like to avoid going public with this. That's part of why we flew you out. We wanted to talk with you face-to-face.'

'Why isn't Inspector Raveneau here?'

'We're devoting significant Bureau resources to a potentially catastrophic terrorist plot. That's what this is about. The fires may just be one aspect of what's coming. Inspector Raveneau and I work well together and certainly we'll bring him up to speed on this, but at this point we need to move as quietly as possible. You recognize our victim as John Royer and we're prepared to act on that today as you remember more about this elderly man locked out of his house. We need to find that house today if it can be done. For the next few days we'd like to do that by alerting as few people as possible.'

She turned to Agent Newton and visualized Newton's car driving fast as hell down a county road. Everywhere he went, everything he did was important, even now in his mid fifties. She took in the other agent again, young, trying to mind his manners and sit at the grown-ups' table.

'To do this right, I need to go home now.'

'We'll get you there. We'll fly you.'

'Are you really that worried?'

Coe leaned back. He folded his arms and then unfolded them and she figured he was going to lie to her, but then changed his mind.

'Jennie, the dead man you looked at was placing incendiary devices that created the biggest fire ever on that mountain. It burned houses. It killed people. It could have killed many more. It was a ruthless act and we have very good reason to believe he planned it in association with the pair we're still trying to apprehend. He may have committed suicide drinking a radioactive agent or they may have killed him. We don't know which yet but it's the second instance of radioactive ingestion and more evidence that they have access to radioactive isotopes. We know that they've talked about producing dirty bombs. We know they were waiting for a cyclical weather event and now we know why, but my point is if there's more to come there's a good chance it's coming soon. We feel we're racing the clock. They probably feel the same. They know the manhunt under way is going to get results eventually. One is dead. Two are at large. We don't have any choice but to take a radioactive threat seriously.'

'I'm just trying to get my head around it. Inspector Raveneau called me. That's where this started for me. He read about our caskets washing up and the skulls and the bones taken. Didn't he lead you to these men and identify the same body I looked at?'

'We still want to keep this within the Bureau for a few days.'

'It was several days. Now it's a few?'

Coe showed a much different stare. He set his mouth then consciously relaxed it. Terrorists were here to stay and radiation was a big deal and scary, but she had seen and heard enough now to be skeptical of those holding the levers. The 9/11 Commission made recommendations everyone agreed with and no one implemented. So she figured you've got to take everything with a grain of salt. They talk one way, but always do something else.

She did think the FBI had done well thwarting several attempts. She admired them for that and Raveneau was right, they're all we have. But a kid with a melted face and part of his skull looking like a burnt cracker with radioactive material intended for terror in San Francisco stored in a house in her county, really? And the one who picked up on it first and seemed to be figuring it out kept in the dark now, that didn't work for her. That felt like something she was familiar with and she didn't like it that Newton was here to help bring her along. He ought to be home looking for the house.

'I do recognize him and I might be able to get on the phone and come up with a name right here, right now. But I'll need some space. I need to explain things in a way people can hear them. You might not want to listen in. And then there's Raveneau.' She pushed her hair back. She stared back at Coe. 'You've got issues with him that are more important than finding these people.'

'I resent that.'

'Of course you do. That's why I said it.' She paused before adding, 'He's not ever going to do things your way. That's not him and you know that. If it ain't broke, don't fix it.'

'How did he compromise you so fast?'

'It's called respect, not compromise. I know the difference.'

'OK, Jennie, you win. We'll bring him to Missouri.'

'That's the right thing to do.'

They thought she was full of shit. But Jennie didn't care. 'I need a place where I can get on a phone and talk,' she said. She stood.

'No, you stay here,' Coe said. 'This is your room.' He pointed. 'That's your phone. Come on, everybody, out of the room, give her some space.'

Forty-Three

Raveneau missed a call from Sheriff Crawford as he walked into a South San Francisco bar that Hugh Neilley was a part owner of. Hugh owned six percent and that turned out to be enough for him to consider it his space and probably was why he chose here to meet. The bar was Irish-pub themed and you could tell because two walls were painted green and a leprechaun leered above the dingy corridor leading to the rest rooms. He didn't see Hugh and walked back and used a urinal that held a crumpled cigarette package, chewed gum, and half a dozen cigarette butts.

Then he went back out and looked over Hugh's investment as he waited. His take was that Hugh was lucky he didn't own more. The air smelled of rancid fryer oil, stale beer, and the dirty water used to mop the floor. And somewhere in here and not all that long ago was somebody's vomit. It was humid and the ventilation system was people coming in and out of the front door and right now no one was.

He checked his phone, saw Jennie Crawford had called and tried her back, but didn't reach her. He left a message and started getting agitated waiting here to have some heart to heart with

Hugh that felt contrived. It was a bad day for a four o'clock beer.

When Hugh walked in he waved at Raveneau but headed to the bar and clapped the backs of two daylight drinkers. The afternoon was hot and the fires dominated the flat screen TV over the bar. Hugh wore a black short-sleeved shirt and what got marketed to the middle class as designer jeans. Raveneau couldn't help but wonder as Hugh walked over if pulling the gun out of the kitchen drawer was staged.

'I'll get us two beers. How about Trumer? You like Trumer and we've got it on tap.'

'Trumer is fine.'

Raveneau pulled his phone as Hugh returned to the bar. He read a text from Sheriff Crawford: *'Call me as you can.'*

He texted her back: *'Call you in forty minutes.'*

'I'll be in the air.'

He called her as Hugh was paying and starting back with two pint glasses, one in each hand, and the one in his left dripping foam that ran down the glass and through his fingers. He looked at Hugh but listened to her.

'I helped them put a name on the body this afternoon,' she said.

'What is it?'

'John Royer. He lives in my county.'

'Spell it.'

She did. Raveneau wrote it down. 'How do you know him?'

'I didn't say I know him. I know of him. We had an incident he was questioned about. The FBI is planning to search his house tomorrow.

Do you want to be there?'

'Yes.'

'I thought so. Agent Coe will call you. We had an old man die of exposure when he got locked out of his house late at night during a storm. He was close to ninety, frail and getting a little confused, so everyone thought he'd wandered out and the door closed behind him. His tracks in the snow went out his driveway, then returned and circled around to the back of the house. We thought at first he went out the driveway to go get a neighbor to help and got confused because of driving snow and came back and looked for another unlocked door. The man who found the body was his neighbor across the street, John Royer. That's how it looked at first and then our detective started to look a little closer and there were some things that didn't add up.'

'Like what?'

'Like the old fella never locked his doors. The neighbors who had known him for forty years said everyone knew that. And Royer's answers were inconsistent and the detective found him odd.'

'So did I.'

She chuckled at that. 'The Feds are flying me back now.'

'I'll call Coe. I'll be there tomorrow.'

As Raveneau put his phone away, Hugh asked, 'New girlfriend?'

'No, the Missouri sheriff we returned the skulls to. The Feds flew her out and she's leaving now.'

'What's that about?'

‘It’s about the dead man up on Mount Tam. He may be from her county.’

‘Too bad he didn’t die sooner.’

Hugh took a drink of beer and wiped foam off his upper lip with the back of his hand and as they left the sheriff a tension settled over the table. Raveneau asked how the bar business here was going.

‘Not well,’ Hugh said. ‘It’s another business deal I shouldn’t have gotten into. Did you tell that prick of a contractor that I have issues?’

‘I didn’t tell him much of anything.’ Raveneau took a sip of beer. He thanked Hugh for the beer and then asked, ‘Do you have issues? Should I have told him that?’

‘Fuck you, Ben.’

‘Yeah, fuck me.’

‘The bomb shelter is filled in. It’ll have a garden over it and flowers. That’ll be the end of it, huh, no one else going down there ever. That’ll also be the end of your investigation and getting yourself puffed up about solving what the fuck-up detectives before you couldn’t. I know you haven’t found anything new because Ray Alcott and I didn’t find it and we were a lot closer to it when things happened and probably better than the pair of you.’

‘Is this the heart to heart you wanted to have? You’re going to tell me how fucking good you were?’

Hugh leaned forward on the table and it rocked a little as his big frame weighted it. More beer spilled and his breath crossed the table. ‘I’m seeing a doctor and he says stress may have triggered the gun thing. Money worries have had me upside down. He wants me to cut stress and that means eliminating what I can and one of those is what happened to Ann Coryell. I've told you everything I know. I can't help you any more on that one.'

'You haven't helped me, so keep on keeping on.'

'Are you going to be a jackass this afternoon? Why say something like that? Is my life one big joke to you?'

'No.'

'Then why is it every time I turn around you are asking questions about me or undercutting me? Ferranti said he asked you about fake haul tags and you wouldn't vouch for me.'

'He told me about the tags and after he did that I wanted to know how he came up with proof that you hired someone to make you some fraudulent tags. He says he's going to show me.'

'None of that is any of your business. I'll deal with him and you keep your nose out of my business.'

'OK, well, Ferranti says he's going to show me proof. When he does, what do you want me to do with it? Tear it up, give it to you, threaten Ferranti, what works best?'

'You're making a big mistake here with me. You really are. I'm trying to talk to you.'

'Go ahead and talk.'

Instead he started into a laborious retelling of his need to make the demolition business work coupled with the old saw of his certainty the police pension was going down. He was probably right about that, but others had issued the same warning for years, and it was a little like listening to a Wall Street banker on a Sunday talk show predicting where the economy was going. You knew as a TV viewer that the banker didn't have a clue. Everyone watching knew and it was like that with Hugh now, except that Hugh had some other goal that required grinding him down first.

'I want you to call Ferranti and say you talked to me and tags were nothing I did and that I fired my nephew.'

'You want me to make that call?'

'I'm asking you as a friend to talk to him. Tell him I'm rebuilding my company without Matt and I apologize for anything Matt did. You, because he knows you know me well and you have no interest in construction.'

'You're on your own.'

'You won't do that?'

'No.'

'I need someone at my back as I get around this problem. I'm not asking you to lie. Matt was my problem.'

'Your nephew dumped trash off the side of a road, and if he forged tags, deal with that. Ferranti, I gave him the OK to fill the bomb shelter and he's filled it in and the rest is yours. Go sit down with him.'

'He fired me. He says he'll see me in court. He's not paying what he owes and I need someone to vouch for me. You're saying you won't do that?'

'Vouching for you won't change anything. Sit

down with him and talk it out.'

'You're a cold fuck, you know that?'

'But if you did hire someone to make you fraudulent tags, then I think you should announce your retirement tomorrow.'

'Get out of my bar, Raveneau. We're done.'

'No, we're not done yet.' Raveneau picked his phone up off the table. 'Thanks for the beer. I'll be in touch.'

Forty-Four

Raveneau changed planes at three thirty in the morning and landed in St Louis at dawn. He picked up the rental and drove for an hour and a half before he called Sheriff Crawford. 'I'm close.'

'You need to hurry. We're out at the house and all that's keeping the FBI from going in is some equipment. They're waiting for lead-lined suits and a robot that lives in St Louis.'

'Is Coe there?'

'He sure is. He's standing with a group of agents out on the street. I'm looking at him. We had breakfast together in Cagdill. He ate pork sausage made here and eggs from a farm down the road.'

Raveneau pushed his speed a little as he got off the phone with her, but there probably wasn't any need. With the possibility of radiation risk the FBI would move cautiously and he wasn't that far away. He checked the GPS again and drove low hills and treed country and then open flat farm land, river bluffs as he got closer. Then he was just minutes from Royer's house.

The house had a decorative red-brick skirt and a front face modeled on George Washington's estate at Mount Vernon except much smaller and without any estate to back it up. A detached garage sat off to the left side. Both house and garage were clad with gray-painted wood siding that badly needed repainting. It needed other work as well but its Mount Vernon face said everything was still possible in America.

He parked down the street and talked with Coe and neighbors, several of whom had plenty of opinion about Royer especially now that he was dead. In plain speak he moved here because his wife's people were from here and he changed considerably after she died of cervical cancer. The cancer was discovered after she and John failed at getting her pregnant. She was twenty-six when she died. He was a young engineer working for a medical technology firm that required him to commute regularly to Chicago. Living here was a concession to his wife and the relatives she had locally, and then she was gone and he still had the house in a down market where selling it wasn't easy.

A neighbor told Raveneau, 'He was about as alone as a man can get. He could not accept that she died. My wife tried to get him to take Christ into his heart and she got him to church, but when she went to pick him up the next Sunday he told her it just wasn't for him. That's the last time he ever talked to us. He stopped talking to any of the neighbors and I heard he didn't even talk to his wife's people.'

Raveneau sat with Jennie in her patrol car. This wasn't her only problem this morning and she wanted to be near her radio. She talked about John Royer between fielding radio and cell calls.

'You learned about the wife,' she said.

'Yes.'

'And you saw the car in the garage.'

Raveneau did. The Feds checked for booby traps then activated the garage door opener with a gadget they had. Nothing exploded, the radiation readings were typical background, and there weren't any skulls, but there was a green Subaru that could be what the young couple had seen.

'Pretty good chance he's the one who took them,' she said. 'They tell me he was already a loner but became more so, up late at night and secretive, that kind of thing. We ran the vehicle registration and came up with his name, and the description fits what our second witness and her soldier boyfriend saw. Something in there will tie him to the grave robbing.'

Raveneau pointed at the house directly across the street. 'Is that where the elderly fellow died?'

'It is. The detective at the time was here earlier.'

'I'd like to talk with him.'

'We can make that happen. His name is Abe Burtle, as in turtle with a B, and don't ask me where the name comes from. He and I never got along and he's about as crotchety a human being as I've ever met, but today he's on good behavior. One other thing, and you'll be interested in this: the neighbors right over there said that Royer spoke about finding the line between the living and the dead so he would be able to talk with his dead wife again. After that they didn't want their children around him.'

'New ideas are hard.'

'Here comes Agent Coe. He looks like he's getting ready to hike up a mountain.'

Raveneau tried to balance the taciturn man at Grate's Place with a young, married ambitious man who lived here and whose life had spiraled down after his wife's death. Royer was vulnerable and probably drawn in and at some point drank the Kool-Aid, but it was a long way from here to a mountain bike on Mt. Tamalpais and placing incendiary devices. Raveneau got out as Coe arrived and the sheriff answered a radio call.

Coe offered his hand and said, 'I hope this is worth your time.'

'It's worth my time. The skulls were taken not far from here and there may be more information inside.'

'We would have copied you on everything.'

In about two weeks you would have, he thought and then watched the FBI robot go in through the front door. Two hours passed as they tried to figure out a higher radiation reading inside the house before concluding it was naturally occurring radon. Then in a bedroom closet an FBI agent found a carrying case built to hold two vertical lead cylinders each with the international symbol for radioactivity stamped into the gray lead. They were moved out to a van.

After lunch Raveneau was inside the house with three agents and Coe. Raveneau wanted to sit at the computer but an agent much more agile and computer literate than him was rapidly searching files with keywords. When she finished he knew their next move would be to walk the computer out and he wanted a few minutes in front of it first so listened for her fingers on the keyboard as he and Coe sorted through papers and notebooks in the kitchen. This room seemed to be where John Royer lived his life.

On a short desk-high wooden countertop in the kitchen were three spiral notebooks, each with a pale brown cover and lined sheets and pages upon pages of printed notes in fine black ink. The letters were very small. The notebooks were each titled, again in small letters on the upper right-hand corner on the outside jacket. One had the title *Reported*, one *Actual*, and one *WK*. Coe was at his shoulder as he picked up *WK*.

'What have you got?'

'Notebooks with a lot of writing in them. This was his space. I'll bet he built this counter and chair. It's the same wood.'

Raveneau spread the three notebooks so Coe could read their titles. He read them aloud and then opened the one titled *Actual*. When he turned the pages they were perforated in places where Royer pushed with too much force as he put a period at the end of a sentence.

'Why not use a computer?' Coe asked. 'He didn't grow up with a pen in his hand. What's this *Actual* about?' After a few moments he said,

'I get it. These are events that he was present at.' He flipped more pages then opened the one titled *Reported* and started comparing the two. 'He's writing about what the press reported versus what he saw. Maybe I should start doing that. This one is a parade for returning Iraq vets in St Louis last winter.'

Raveneau pulled the chair out and sat down. He reached for the lamp on the counter, pulled it over and turned it on.

'I saw you went for that one first,' Coe said. 'What's "WK" mean to you?'

'It's about her writings,' Raveneau said. 'WK, Wounded Knee.'

Raveneau opened the first page and read about bright-colored ghost shirts with images of eagles and buffalo that the Sioux wore as they danced in the frigid winter wind and blowing snow. They believed these ghost shirts would stop bluecoat bullets and believed in the prophesy of a Paiute shaman, Wovoka, who saw the dead rising and the white man buried under a sea of new soil that would cover the land and bring back the prairies and the buffalo. Then the Sioux would leave the reservations and return to live life again in the old ways. Raveneau showed the phrase 'the dead rising' to Coe.

Coe read and didn't respond immediately. He returned to the other notebooks and then turned back. 'This is why you flew out. Does this go back to her death?'

'I think so. Alan Siles is a charismatic proselytizer who sees himself as a visionary, but she was a thinker and her thoughts are the glue that holds these guys together. She was a historian first. She imagined the ghost dances. She saw the fires and snow blowing through the rising smoke into a bitter cold night. She saw the Sioux in ghost shirts dancing and the frightened American Indian Agent assigned to the tribe calling for troops. She understood the death of Sitting Bull. I think her gift was she could feel across generations. She felt the anguish of the Sioux tribe, the desperation in the ghost dance and the reaching for what was gone.'

'And your theory is they all talked themselves into believing this?'

Raveneau looked up from the notebook. 'Talked themselves into what?'

'Into believing the dead can rise.'

'I don't know what they believe as a group. Royer is dead. Lindsley stands off. He's not quite inside, so that leaves a group of two as far as we know, Siles and Latkos. Latkos worked as a hacker for the US government, Russian mobsters, and herself. I don't know how spiritual she is, but I know something about the other two. Siles is the true believer. He's the one we've got to find.'

But what did these notebooks add up to but laborious handwritten thoughts vanished into a death ride down a mountain as he torched open country and watershed? Raveneau read and took it in. He asked for a scanned copy of each notebook and was promised he'd get them.

A dead man doesn't care what you take from his house and the Feds took everything they could carry. The neighbors watched all this, as well as watching the guy in the lead suit walking around in the yard with the Geiger counter. He wasn't surfing the sand for dropped change, but Raveneau doubted he would find anything.

He followed Sheriff Jenny to the house of Abe Burtle, the retired detective, and Burtle acted like they were late. It was also clear he didn't like Jennie Crawford much and didn't want to hear her talk. He helped that by finishing the sheriff's sentences for her. He waved at his couch.

'Sit down. You want to know about John Royer and McCabe his neighbor? You want to know what I think happened?'

'Yes.'

'I don't think McCabe was disoriented or confused. He was just old and weak. He tried to get back in his front door and then worked his way around the house. Without his glasses he was nearly blind and it was snowing hard and forecast to snow until two or three in the morning. He tried the garage door and his back doors and had trouble getting through his gate and came back around to his driveway and went a hundred paces down to the street before going back to his house and trying to break a window. Or that's what it looked like.'

'Were there tracks for all that?'

'Of course there were tracks. He was walking in snow. But he wasn't dressed for the cold and his glasses were found on the floor near the front door. Now, would he go outside without his glasses? Would you? Of course you wouldn't, and if Royer killed him it was by taking away his glasses before carrying him outside in his robe. They say McCabe slept in front of the TV every night. He was a widower. Wife died in a car accident in 1991. He didn't weigh much more than a hundred pounds. He was a little fella who had shrunk.'

'Like you,' the sheriff said.

'That's right, Jennie, and I miss you just as much.' He turned back to Raveneau. 'The storm blew through and the dawn was cold and clear and Royer told me he was leaving for work when he saw McCabe's front door open and the lights on. He stopped in front of McCabe's driveway and walked to the door and knocked, and then saw tracks and McCabe's body down along the side of the front of the house.

'I called an old friend of mine, a tracker, and he came out and looked it over. He spent a couple of hours sorting it out. I promised we'd take care of his time, but I couldn't get him paid later. In this county we only pay for law enforcement work if you're sitting down. You can sit in your car or sit in the station, but if you get out and actually do something you don't get paid.'

'I'm not going to say anything,' Jennie said. 'I'll just sit here.'

Burtle continued as if he hadn't heard her. 'The paramedics and the rest of the fools trampled through all the tracks in the driveway and around the front door. So did Royer. It looked to me like he went out of his way to erase them. Still, Bob found pieces of frozen older ones that weren't the old man's bare feet.'

'Barefoot.'

‘Yes, sir, which fits with the idea he was disoriented. I thought I explained that.’

‘It also fits with the idea he was lifted out of his chair and carried outside.’

‘That’s right, and McCabe was so weak he couldn’t fight him off. I suspect Royer. I have no right to and Royer is dead now himself, so we’re never going to know. I suspect him of creeping through McCabe’s house locking the doors and then carrying McCabe outside and turning the lock on the front door.’

‘Why would he?’

‘Why would he? You ask the neighbors and they’ll tell you Royer didn’t like McCabe. Royer kept odd hours and was up to something and now this proves it. I think McCabe saw something and Royer knew it. Maybe he asked Royer about it and Royer started thinking he had to kill the old man. When I came back to re-interview Royer he was gone and then I couldn’t find him. I should have known he’d go to California.’

‘Why is that?’

Burtle never answered, and Raveneau followed Sheriff Crawford to Cagdill and her office. He read through everything she had on the river flooding and the caskets washed out into the field and along the road. He read her notes and sat and talked with her over dinner and then drove back to St Louis in the late night. He flew home early the next morning.

Forty-Five

When Raveneau's cell screen lit up with the words Unknown Caller his gut said it was Lindsley. An hour later he drove into the Presidio graveyard. The road climbed in a slow loop and Lindsley was parked at the upper end and standing outside his car watching Raveneau approach. He wore a dark-brown hoodie that shadowed the sides of his face and moved away from his car and started climbing the grassy slope before Raveneau parked. Rows of gravestones rose through the grass toward trees and Lindsley was well above him when Raveneau started up, calling out as he did, 'Wait there. I'm not going to chase you.' When he caught up, he asked, 'What are we doing here? What are you going to show me?'

'A place Lash took me to up there. We have to get above the grass and the graves. It's up there in the trees if I can find it again. I haven't been here in a long time.'

'How far into the trees?'

'Maybe fifty yards.' He leered. 'Nobody watching will be able to see us. If that scares you we don't have to go. I look like I scare you.'

'You'd scare anybody.'

But the truth was that the color was gone from

Lindsley's face. He was sweating and that could be the hood over his head and the mild exertion of starting up this slope, but Raveneau didn't think so.

'Is this the way you came with Lash? I want to know when and how you got here the first time.'

'We came here in his car and parked where I'm parked.'

'When?'

'I don't remember the year yet. I may never remember it.'

'But it was when you and he were still going to collaborate on writing books.'

'You got it, Inspector, you brought your A game today.'

'How many more surprises have you got, Brandon?'

'Not many. But I learned a long time ago to keep something to negotiate with.'

'What did you have then?'

'I didn't have anything and they kept me awake for forty-eight hours as they questioned me. They lied and did everything they could to get me to confess including showing me a faked statement that my best friend supposedly made. They tried to mimic his handwriting, the whole thing.'

'How did you know it wasn't him?'

Lindsley turned, eyes fever bright and meeting Raveneau's gaze only momentarily. 'I knew his handwriting. You know, right now, I'm getting some of that same good old feeling of having a target on my back. No matter what I say or do the plan is to charge me with whatever they charge Siles and Latkos with. I'll get wrapped in and then they'll offer me a much shorter sentence as long as I testify against them. I'll still get eight years.'

'It'll give you time to finish that book.'

'There you go. It's an opportunity.'

They reached the edge of the grass and started into the trees and there was the pungent eucalyptus smell and the memory of walking the grove below the cottage with Ann Corycll. He followed Lindsley, marking the route in his head, pushing Lindsley again, saying, 'You came here before her remains were found.'

'Like I said, you're on your A game today. I never asked what was buried up here. He just showed me where to find what is buried. He either knew I wouldn't go to the police or he didn't care if I did. I've thought about it ten thousand times since and still wonder. It's stupid to bring you here because somehow it'll get turned against me. I'm going to say it again: I don't know what, if anything, is buried up here. He could have just been messing with me, testing to see what I would do with it. But tell me I'm doing the right thing. I love it when you tell me that.'

'Why do you think he brought you here?'

'He must have known I wouldn't tell anybody until it benefited me. He knew I would keep it like money in a wallet. The professor is a risk taker and I was an ambitious failed grad student. The day before Professor Lash showed me this he told me we would collaborate on three books. The next morning he brought me up here. I could have called the police an hour later, but I didn't. I have to go slower now and look for slash marks on the trees.' He turned and smiled. 'I'm like you when you were trying to find your way back to where she was found on Mount Tam.

'Lash knew I was susceptible, that I would listen and then try to think of a way I could use it to my advantage. I even thought of blackmailing him, and I don't need any more money. Later, when he got sick and had drugs he took at night, I would help him to bed and he would fall asleep and then I would go through all of his things. How's that for a house guest?

'But I convinced myself I had the right. I was helping him and he was getting sicker and realizing he was going to have to sell the house and move somewhere he could get twenty-four-hour care. That's what he worried about and I worried he would die before we got a chance to collaborate on a book. The drugs helped him sleep when he started to get anxious about dying. That was always at night and the caregiver and I got in the habit of slipping him Valium. We learned how to drug him without him knowing and it worked. It calmed him right down and pretty soon it was like slipping the pill your dog needs into its food.

'The caregiver had a boyfriend and I gave her a way to leave early and feel OK about not coming back. When she was gone I went through everything looking for his secrets. Those diaries you talk about, I've read them all. There's no confession anywhere in them but there were plenty of entries in there about me and I had to cut some of those out.'

Lindsley stopped and looked around for a long minute before saying, 'Over here; we go this way and around the side of that bigger tree. I think I lost one or two of his notebooks. They're not really diaries. He wrote about sex with Ann and that was good reading. I read what he wrote about that almost every night for around six months. I know I'm talking a lot. It's sort of a confession, isn't it? Only not the one you want. Man, I wonder if I can find this spot again.'

He turned and looked at trees behind him and then did a full circle, his shoes crunching a dry strip of eucalyptus bark. 'I've got to tell you, I hate to give this spot up. I was saving this for a book about Lash. I figured its discovery just as my book came out would make a great promotion.'

Raveneau pointed out a slash, small but distinct, on a large eucalyptus.

'There you go, Inspector, what an eye you've got. We're pirates looking for the buried treasure. It's all a game, isn't it, getting people to talk and finding all the clues you need to solve the case. Are you excited right now? I would be. Can you find the next tree?' Lindsley waited a moment then pointed at a tree and then at two more with small slashes in the bark as though in each someone had started to carve their name. 'He said string diagonal lines and dig where they intersect.' He turned to Raveneau. 'I'm not kidding. Can you believe that?'

'How deep?'

'Deep. As deep as he is tall.'

'Did Lash bury what's here?'

'He never said it was him. He showed me this and said I could do what I wanted with it.'

'That doesn't make any sense.'

'Ask him.'

Raveneau took photos before they walked down. He made phone calls out of earshot of Lindsley and they set up a perimeter and dug in the late afternoon. It was ten at night when they found the wrapped parcel, a soft leather case with a bloodstained eighteen-inch serrated knife buried a little over five feet down and wrapped in several layers of plastic to protect it from water, though water got in. With it was a small surgical saw. There was dried blood. There would be DNA, and Raveneau didn't think he'd have any problem getting that testing moved to the top of the list.

Forty-Six

The next morning Raveneau sat down alongside Lash's bed. Lash shook his head. He wouldn't answer any questions and the nurse watching him got aggressive about leaving him alone. Raveneau left soon after. Later in the morning he got a call from an attorney representing Lash.

'Professor Lash would like to meet with you this afternoon at five o'clock.'

'Is he feeling well enough to talk?'

'Take what you can get, Inspector. If you don't want the meeting we'll cancel it. He's better but he's still weak. You won't be able to question him for long and he asked me to ask you what this is about. He believes he has told you everything he knows.'

'Tell him I'm going to bring some things I want him to take a look at.'

'What things?'

'Are you going to be there?'

'Yes.'

'Then you'll see them. What kind of lawyer are you?'

'I handle his finances and I'm surprised he called me about this. He's also asked that you come alone. Are you aware that he's moved to a new facility?'

'When did he do that?'

'A couple of days ago and I'll give you the address, but you have to come alone. Professor Lash was very specific about your partner not being there.'

Lash's new facility was near the ocean, close enough for management to promise clean air off the water. Two security guards were intense and careful but friendly. Lash's lawyer, Gordon Meech, frowned at la Rosa's presence and, knowing that Meech was unfamiliar with criminal investigations, Raveneau said, 'I tried, but it's the rule. There have to be two of us when a confession is possible.'

'Who said anything about a confession? He's not confessing to anything.'

'I'm going to give him a chance to.'

'I don't think you understand how sick he is and your partner should wait out here. If something does happen we can bring her in, or not, I really don't know. But he was very specific and I don't think he'll even talk to you if she's in the room.'

'You're making it sound like it's something personal. He doesn't even know her.'

Meech shrugged. That wasn't his problem. He was just following instructions.

'How long have you worked for him?'

'Five years but I was a fan of his books long before that. I wrote him about a book. That's how we met.'

Raveneau left it there and they went in to see Lash, la Rosa hanging back in the lobby on the first floor. The building was like a small boutique hotel with none of the smells of assisted living and with the security detail of an embassy. Lash's room had a leather sofa, armchair, and a view of a garden below and ocean in the distance. Lash didn't look good. His world was closing in and Raveneau realized he wasn't going to make it back to where he had been before he was poisoned.

A crisply dressed young woman in clothes that suggested nursing, but didn't exactly define it, coaxed Lash with a fruit drink that she described as having all the things that would make him well. He sucked awkwardly through a straw and exhaled a few words at her and she leaned over. She nodded and straightened and rolled his wheelchair over next to where Raveneau sat in the black leather armchair. Meech, the lawyer, took the couch and let the young woman know that she should leave now.

Lash's face was quite pale. A large open canker sore was crusted and oozing on the right corner of his lips. His eyes were bloodshot and he must have bled through the nose earlier today. He looked anemic but his eyes were thoughtful, evaluating, not glistening, not drugged.

Lash couldn't smile easily but the sardonic professor who worked to make his reputation greater than himself was still there, studying the homicide inspector insect, the city employee, a tool for social order, a policeman, for God's sakes, a cop, and a glorified one at that. Raveneau had a pretty good idea of what Lash thought of him and his role, but he knew Lash was curious about him. He was glad Raveneau didn't forget Ann Coryell and he liked the attention now. They both knew that. Lash liked the intellectual challenge and even within his wreck of a body and propped in a chair, he wanted it to continue.

'I'd like to get my partner in here. She's waiting on the first floor. She'll be in the room only as a witness.'

Lash shook his head.

'Then I've got to go let her know she can leave. I'll be back in a few minutes.'

Raveneau found la Rosa at the front desk. 'He doesn't want you in the room, but why don't you wait at least half an hour. Text me if you leave.'

'He's got something to say?'

'He's acting like it.'

'Maybe he wants you to collaborate on a

book.'

When Raveneau came back into the room Meech offered up a little preamble about protecting Professor Lash's legacy.

'His legacy?'

'Yes.'

What legacy was that? Was it a successful career as a university professor and a writer whose pop history books sold in the hundreds of thousands a year? Why would they remember Lash? Stop a twenty-one year old and ask them who James Michener was. There was no legacy.

Raveneau stood and walked over to the window as Meech talked. The ocean was dark blue at horizon, the dusk calm, the winds quieting and the fires nearly a hundred percent contained. This was a peaceful room. Raveneau looked out at the water long enough to make Meech uncomfortable and then walked around behind Lash knowing that Lash couldn't turn to watch him talk with the lawyer.

'His legacy is nothing any of us control and I don't think it's something we should spend time on.'

'Inspector, I think you understand what I'm saying.'

'You know what, I really don't, and I hope this isn't the start of some sort of negotiation. Either Albert can help us or he can't, and I appreciate that he is sick and this is an effort for him. But I'm sure he has wondered all these years, the same as I have, whether we would ever find her killer.'

'He does want to talk.'

'Then let us talk.'

Before returning to his chair Raveneau opened photos on his phone and brought his phone to the lawyer, saying, 'This will give you some idea of the places we're talking about. These were taken in a bomb shelter that was underneath a garden shed on the property. The new owners say it wasn't disclosed when the house was sold and the home inspection service they hired couldn't access it during escrow due to dangerous pesticides stored in the shed. Those weren't removed until just before Albert moved out. They're talking about suing your client.'

Raveneau gambled on Meech's natural curiosity. He left Meech scrolling photos and Lash in his armchair facing the windows couldn't see his lawyer bent over, lips pressed together as he stared at the skulls leaned against a dank concrete wall and hollowed out by klieg lights and the photos of the skeletons on the floor and the photos he had uploaded taken where Coryell's remains were found.

Meanwhile, Raveneau leaned forward. He opened a brown paper evidence bag and removed a clear plastic bag with the surgical saw and a second bag with the knife. He pressed the plastic against the tools and that's what they were. He turned them over so Lash could see them in every way.

'Do you recognize either?'

Of course not, and Lash shook his head.

'We'll have DNA results on both within days. Brandon Lindsley met me in the Presidio graveyard and showed me where they were buried. He said you showed him the slashes you made on the trees to mark the location and that you wouldn't tell him what was buried. You were coy, his word, about what was hidden there, challenging him in some way or implicating him if he didn't act. Again, those are his words.'

'Sho–o–wed you?'

'Yes.'

Meech made a point now of bringing Raveneau's phone back. He did it in a way that interrupted what Raveneau was starting and yet couldn't hide his shock at what he'd just been looking at. He was a numbers guy thrust into an awkward role, probably did tax shelters and living wills and kept the relatives at bay.

Lash started to talk again but the words didn't form, only gurgled sounds. That upset him and it took awhile for him to calm down, and Meech brought over a table and laptop, explaining that Professor Lash would use a mouse to type and do that with his forehead. Raveneau waited and when it was all set up they started again. But now Lash's answers would come very slowly.

'Lindsley took me to a place he said you showed him.'

Lash typed: *'lying.'*

'How did he know to go there?'

'don't know.'

'What's buried?'

Lash just shook his head to that question.

'I want to be very sure I understand you. You are saying you never showed Brandon Lindsley this location?'

'*yes.'* He started typing again. *'trying to save*

himself.'

'So maybe he buried these and knows we're not going to get his DNA from them and thinks we'll get yours. Does he believe you've handled this knife and saw?'

Lash shook his head. He denied any knowledge of the knife or saw, or of ever being in the Presidio graveyard with Lindsley or anyone else. He typed: *'hate graves.'* He slurred words Raveneau couldn't make out. Raveneau doubted the wire he was wearing even with the microphone set as high as it was would pick up the broken whispers.

Meech got into the conversation as Lash tired. He explained that Lash agreed to this meeting to warn of an impending attack on the city of San Francisco. The fires were the signal it was coming.

'An impending attack?'

'Yes.'

'That Albert has information about?'

It took Raveneau a moment to register that Lash wanted to cast himself as a hero warning the citizenry ahead of the attack and that he was referring to conversations at his house years ago that included Siles and were hypothetical events conjured over drinks but too similar to what was happening now not to have come from then. When he saw Siles on TV it all came back to him and the great man wanted to make a deal now where he would get credit.

'Watching TV you've recognized Siles as Lindsley's friend.'

Lash nodded.

'Was he another student you were mentoring?'
Another nod.
'Lindsley says he didn't know Siles except in passing and that he was a visiting student studying under you, and that you knew him well but he didn't. Is that true?'
'He did reee–searrch for meee.'
'Did Lindsley ever work with him?'
Lash shook his head.
'But he knew him. It was more than just in passing?'
'Yesss. Frienndsss.'
Raveneau worked the Lindsley/Siles connection for awhile and didn't learn much more. He knew the meeting hadn't gone as Lash expected either. He was disappointed and disturbed. He wanted to talk about the attempt on his life and communicated that he didn't know John Royer and Royer posed as a former student to get to him and as they were alone Royer must have tampered with his medicine. He and Royer hadn't talked about anything. Royer's pretense of being a former student had led to an awkward moment.
Lash typed: *'remember all my students.'*
Raveneau got it now. Lash believed Royer was sent to kill him because Lash would recognize their faces and the ideas bandied about years ago. He remembered drunken debates about how to provoke social change on a large scale. Fires were talked about as economical and viable. Fires were just the start.
'You're still alive, so you're still in danger.'
He typed: *'yes.'*

'OK, now we're somewhere.' And Raveneau leaned back, thinking about Lindsley showing him where to dig, Lindsley trying to extricate himself and Lash talking now again. Raveneau leaned over. Lash tried several times to say the word philosophical. He couldn't do it and Raveneau said it for him, and when he struggled with the next word, Raveneau filled that one in too.

'Philosophical discussions.'

He typed. *'Yes.'*

'You, Lindsley, and Siles.'

'yes.'

'Ike Latkos wasn't there?'

'no.'

Maybe it was a fantasy they all shared and maybe they really got into the details, the mechanics of how to make it work. Lash communicated now that targeting the San Francisco water supply was possible, and Meech explained that Professor Lash wanted police protection. He wanted acknowledgement. Then as Lash faltered and the conversation ended he offered another proposal. Raveneau turned that one back to Lash as a question.

'You have proof that Brandon Lindsley murdered Ann Coryell and if you're granted complete immunity you'll testify against him?'

Lash gave the slightest nod and then closed his eyes.

'I'll get back to you soon.' He turned to the lawyer, Meech. 'Let's you and I go talk.'

Forty-Seven

Outside Lash's room Raveneau turned and said, 'We can sit in my car or we can stand in the street, but I don't want to talk in the building. There's too much video and sound equipment in here.'

They sat in Raveneau's car, and Meech, who was tall, slowly stretched his legs out and tried to get comfortable with a situation he had no experience with and was unprepared for. He was doing his best but when he tried to take the offensive Raveneau cut him off.

'Get him to reveal what he knows and do it now. I know you were thrown into this, but it couldn't be more serious. He's alluding to knowing things the FBI needs to know and if the knife or surgical saw comes back with his DNA or even her blood type we may charge him with Ann Coryell's murder. He can't ignore this. He can't talk his way around it or out of it.'

'He could die from the stress.'

He's dying anyway, Raveneau thought and leaned back against the door so he could see Meech better. He waited a beat before speaking again. 'The FBI is on their way here. They'll ask the same questions but with more urgency. They'll want to know what he can tell them about the evolution of this plot and you'll probably ask for the same conditions. Why does he need immunity? If he didn't kill Ann Coryell or take part in a plot to kill indiscriminately what's the risk?'

Meech struggled with his role. He was confused and didn't understand why his client wasn't more forthcoming. But he also doggedly tried to make his client's case. 'If my client is going to ask for something he has to do it now before he gets encumbered in the process. He's too weak to defend himself and his remaining time shouldn't go to it. I don't have any question about cooperating with the FBI and I'm sure Albert wants to help. He's not asking for any favors or to escape justice. He's asking to be afforded the dignity to die in peace. You know this far better than I do, but I don't believe investigators will release him from the possibility of criminal charges until they're confident they've gotten everything they can from him.'

'You're setting conditions for revealing something he should have volunteered days ago.'

'I'm representing my client's point of view.' He paused. 'But there is another way we can do this.'

'What's that?'

'He does everything he can to help you charge this Lindsley and the others behind these fires and you back off on the old case. You let it go. The house is sold. People have forgotten, and as you said, he'll die sooner than not. You let it go. Close the file and work on something else. Professor Lash wrote a number of good books that have helped the American people better understand themselves. He was a popular professor and well respected. Let him depart with that intact.'

'Put away the murder file?'

Meech turned slightly to face him and adjusted his glasses. 'You looked at him closely once before and cleared him. Yes, put it away.'

'Let it be and forget about her?'

'I'm not saying that.'

'She was young, brilliant, full of promise, emotionally unstable, but maybe that's about genius. I don't really know, and I'm not sure I've ever known a genius. I've known two people who belong to that organization, what's it called, MENSA, and are very proud of their high IQs. I guess technically they're geniuses, but I've never found them to be much different than the rest of us. I think the word is meant for something else and shouldn't be used very often. She may have been that. Or maybe she was just one of us, but either way what you're saying is close the file and forget about her because continuing to investigate could affect what Albert calls his legacy.'

'That's not what I'm saying.'

'I think you need to be very frank with the emperor about his clothes. He's facing death and he'll appreciate candor. He doesn't have any legacy. Why don't you go in there and tell him what everyone else already knows? It might come as a big relief to him to not have to worry about it anymore.'

'Inspector, he has only weeks left. Don't you

have any compassion? You don't seem to want to acknowledge that truth. Why is that?'

'Ann Coryell's life ended ten years ago when it was taken from her. She'd be thirty-nine now. Maybe she would have written the book of her ideas that Lash plagiarized and there's a very good chance this little group of social engineers never would have formed.' Raveneau paused. He was getting lost here and not getting anywhere, but he asked Meech, 'Do you have a legacy?'

'You bet I do. I have two divorced wives who hate me and will always remember and talk about me. I also have three adult children who would like me more if I died tomorrow and left them what I have in assets. I had a tumor removed five years ago so they always ask about my health. I know the younger one has studied every Internet article he could find trying to determine the odds of recurrence. I know that because I've read the same articles and he's right to hope because the odds are it will come back. My ex-wives have taught my children to hate me.'

'I don't have a legacy either.'

'Inspector, he would like to go quietly. If you determine he participated in something terrible, whether with her or others, is there really a need to charge him? He's never going to stand for trial or go to prison.' Now Meech's pale blue eyes found the windshield.

'Albert told you something. What did he tell you about the bomb shelter?'

'I can't answer that, as I'm sure you know.'

'Did he confess to you?'

Meech was silent. He adjusted his glasses again and in the rear view mirror Raveneau saw vehicles approaching. One pulled in just in front of them and two behind.

Raveneau opened his door and said to Meech, 'Tell me before they get here.'

Meech was silent.

'You'll love the FBI,' Raveneau said. 'Come on, I'll introduce you.'

Forty-Eight

When Raveneau walked back in Coe was sitting close to Lash who despite the tubes and wheelchair was in control. He had something to trade and the full attention of the FBI. Coe went along. He read the signals and deferred to Lash, but Raveneau's presence was distracting. It broke the happy cooperative mood and Raveneau soon left. Later that night he picked up a voicemail from Coe. He listened and then called him back.

'Lash wants to trade six months for the rest of what he knows,' Coe said. 'It's not at all clear what that is, but we're rolling with it. He faded on us about eight o'clock and we're back in the morning.'

'You're rolling with it, but you're not sure what he's talking about yet?'

Coe sighed and then apologized, 'Sorry, long day, and yeah, the murder investigation is in the mix. He wants to be left out of your investigation for six months. Obviously, this is your decision not ours, but as his lawyer keeps saying, he's never going to trial. Innocent or guilty, he won't be here. He isn't going to be around and I was knocking on wood when I walked out of that room hoping nothing like that ever happens to me. He got his lawyer to call one of his doctors and then put her on speakerphone and asked her to be frank about the progression of the disease. He asked her to make her best guess on life expectancy and to be detailed about the end. She balked a little and then did it.'

'How long?'

'On the outside four months max. He wants six. He wants a buffer and wants it in writing. He wants it in writing but he also wants your word. He believes you'll keep your word.'

'Translate that for me.'

'If you solve the murder in the next six weeks and he's the killer, you still wait the full six months. He doesn't get charged.'

'Why would he? He's innocent.'

'He's ready to make that agreement now, but it takes you. He'll do it tomorrow morning if you agree. He says he's up before dawn every day and if you want to talk again that's when he feels best. He says he has some things that he'll say only to you.'

'I'll meet you there at five tomorrow morning.'

'You're on.'

Raveneau was up at four thirty the next morning and out the door with coffee fifteen minutes later. He arrived ahead of Coe but not before an ambulance. He parked and hurried inside and knew as he saw the face of one of the security guys that it was Lash.

'What happened?'

'They're saying heart attack. They're trying to figure out how to move him.'

Coe arrived and he and Coe followed the ambulance to UCSF Medical Center. They watched him wheeled in and waited around and talked eventually to a doctor. They asked about talking to Lash and didn't get a verbal answer, just a shake of the head. They were like two ghouls, Raveneau thought, hanging around to make sure Lash wouldn't die on them.

Raveneau turned to Coe as they walked out into the early cool. 'Let's get breakfast and talk. I'll buy. You need some food.'

'What I need is sleep and what I don't understand is why we haven't caught up to these assholes yet. We should have them by now. We've got over a hundred agents here and at headquarters working on this. We've got nine teams and round the clock surveillance on Brandon Lindsley. We're considering every sabotage scenario we can think of, but if you think of anything you call me, OK?'

Raveneau was ready to head to his car when Coe asked, 'What happened at Wounded Knee? I mean, from the perspective of a homicide inspector, was it genocide or a series of misunderstandings and mistakes on both sides that led to an overreaction? I want to know what you think as a career homicide investigator.'

Raveneau stopped. It was an off-the-wall question this morning but it was also something he had thought about. 'On one side you've got people being herded on to reservations and fearful there's a plan to exterminate them, and on the other side people so frightened of an Indian uprising they sent the Seventh Cavalry. One hundred twenty men and two hundred thirty women and children being led by Chief Bigfoot were apprehended by the Seventh Cavalry who then set up a camp for the night. Two Hotchkiss guns were placed on a ridge above and trained on the Sioux tents. Those guns could put out a shell a second. They got used the next morning when an attempt to collect all of the Sioux firearms turned into a firefight after a Sioux brave resisted giving up a rifle he'd paid a lot of money for.

'In a homicide investigation we start with the dead. Almost three hundred Sioux died, one hundred fifty or more in the initial shooting and the rest from wounds. The Seventh Cavalry lost thirty-seven. Almost all of those thirty-seven were killed by friendly fire. I think when the Seventh started firing they didn't stop until they had shot every Indian they could find. They quit when there was no one left to shoot at. They weren't looking for prisoners and the evidence suggest they weren't in danger. It all happened fast, but it wasn't an accident. I'd charge the shooters with murder.'

'Was it a significant enough event to reach down all these years?'

'It's not reaching down. It's still here. That was her point. I'll talk to you in a couple of hours.'

Forty-Nine

Hugh Neilley grew up in a family of five boys who fought with each other for anything and everything, their violence an extension of a father whose frustration with life and marriage usually showed itself at or around the third or fourth drink. That was the story Hugh wove and one that Raveneau believed. Hugh had little contact with any of his brothers. He didn't return their calls, and his sister, Matt Baylor's mother, was the only one in his family who could talk to him. Raveneau's friendship with Hugh had survived other hard times, but he didn't think it would this one. No matter how this investigation turned out, Hugh was going to wall him off. He picked up the phone now and called him.

'You've got about ten seconds to explain what you want.'

'I can do it in less. We've recovered a blood-stained knife and a surgical saw and we're on our way to DNA results. Lindsley led us to a site up above the Presidio graveyard. He said Lash took him there and told him where to dig.'

'Bullshit.'

'What do you know about Lash's diaries or notebooks?'

'What's in the files about them?'

'Nothing.'

'Then I don't know anything. Is there anything else before I hang up?'

'Lash's sister called and left a message this morning. She mentioned your name, said I should talk to you because you contacted her recently. Is that true?'

'She talks to people who aren't there. I thought you knew that about her. She probably heard her brother's name on TV and remembered mine.'

'You didn't call her?'

'When did she tell you this?'

'This morning.'

'You're lying.'

'Lying?' Hugh was silent and Raveneau was ready for him to hang up. 'Lash is talking to us. He knows Alan Siles and called to warn us. You played poker with Lindsley at Lash's when he was working on the book about San Francisco officers. Lash says Siles was there too. You've seen his face. Are you sure you don't remember him? Lash says he started research on that book well before Coryell disappeared and that Siles worked for him. He came up with the backyard barbecues and the poker games as a way to meet SFPD officers and get their stories in a casual way. You may have seen him at one of those get-togethers. If Lash is telling the truth both Siles and Lindsley were at those.'

'Something is wrong with you. There were three homicide inspectors, three out of the sixteen we had at the Detail at the time, who were at those poker games. Don't you think with these fires and the Feds manic to find these guys that someone would have come forward and said, hey, I remember that guy from Lash's parties? No one has done that. Why wouldn't they? I think you're fishing again. You're trying to get to me.'

'I want to meet with you.'

'We played cards once a week and not everybody made it every time but Professor Lash got what he needed. He wanted stories about what it felt like to be a career cop inside the department. There's no secret in any of that, and I didn't meet any of these firebugs. I knew Lindsley because he was like a butler to Lash. Are you implying I know this Siles and I'm not coming forward? If so, fuck you.'

Hugh hung up and Raveneau called Lindsley. An hour later he picked him up at a bus stop and bought him lunch in the Presidio.

'Lash's lawyer contacted us and we've been talking to him about a deal for Lash. His version contradicts yours.'

'Of course it does.'

Raveneau held up a hand. 'I hear you but he says he's only going to live another four months and he wants to leave with a clear conscience.'

'Thanks for the sandwich, but get real, Inspector. Would I lead you to something that I hid that's going to implicate me?'

'Maybe it's going to implicate Siles. Lash wanted to talk about Siles and you, and the three of you, and says you and Siles both did research for him and knew each other. He says you socialized together all the time.'

'Not true.'

'It's his word against yours. He says you all sat around drinking bourbon and talked about a spiritual cleansing. This was after Coryell was dead. The conversation ran toward shocking society and changing the collective unconscious. A spiritual cleansing in San Francisco that meant sacrificing significant numbers of people was to start with fires and then continue with other acts of violence. Lash has written you right into a lead role dead center.'

'Everything I told you about Siles was true.'

'Your problem is Lash says you were at meetings where setting wildfires was discussed as a means to an end by Siles, you and him. He thought of it as a philosophical exercise and had forgotten about it until he saw Siles' face on TV. He wants to trade testimony for immunity for all things for six months. He's already got one foot out the back door and he'd like to go out a hero. Here's my best advice to you: save yourself, and do it now while you still can. After our next interview with Lash, I don't think the offer to you will stand anymore. Either you beat him to it or he takes you down.'

'I didn't have anything to do with the fires and it's not illegal to talk about ideas, at least not yet. I get that it's headed that way.'

'We're going to talk to Lash again this afternoon and this time we'll be taping him.'

'Go for it, and I'm done helping you. I'm lawyering up.' He stared at Raveneau. 'Did you ever see the movie where the guy is in the stone cell with the walls that keep closing in on him and just a little at a time? He goes to sleep at night and in the morning the walls are a little closer together. He starts marking the floor to make sure he's not crazy, and he's right – they're moving a tiny bit every day. He figures out how many days it's going to take before he gets crushed. That's where I'm at and that's after leading you to what may be the murder weapon. It's as if there's nothing I can do. The walls just keep closing in. I'm surrounded. I feel like the man in the movie.'

'It's not working,' Raveneau said. 'It's not going to go down the way you want.'

Lindsley laughed. He held up his phone so Raveneau could read the screen. 'Something is,' he said, then explained. 'If there's any news with Albert Lash's name in it I get an alert. Looks like the professor made the news.' He laughed again, a giddy lightness in it. 'Check this out. What's this do to your investigation?'

He held his phone up so Raveneau could read the screen.

'Author Lash Dead of Heart Attack.'

Fifty

When Coe called Raveneau he was quietly upbeat, yet at the same time uncomfortable with misleading the media. It would come back to haunt him. But Lindsley did swallow the hook and that's what mattered. Lindsley gloated over Lash's death and Lash was now hidden away on an upper floor of the hospital cooperating with the FBI.

'All things considered, he's doing OK,' Coe said. 'I saw him an hour ago. He's hooked up to everything they own but they say his heart has very little damage and they're questioning whether it really was a heart attack. May have been a reaction to the drugs he usually takes and whatever treatment he's had for the radiation poisoning. He called his sister and she's turned over those notebooks to us, and yeah I know you want copies. That's being done. I'll get them to you tomorrow.

'There's something else, Ben. We got a tip we're acting on and you may want to be there. A hiker saw a man along the shoreline at Crystal Springs Reservoir that he thought might be Alan Siles. He was dressed in running clothes, a baseball cap and sunglasses. We have Siles sightings every five minutes now and I'm sure you're getting them too, but this is credible enough to where we're checking it out early tomorrow morning. We need daylight for this lead. The individual that called this in tried to follow the man and the man made it hard for him. He picked up his speed and jogged away. When our tipster first saw him he was down by the water, right down at the edge of the reservoir leaning over looking at something in the water. He was holding a small device in his right hand.'

'Holding his cellphone?'

'No, and it gets more interesting. Our hiker watched him get into a late model Toyota, possibly a Camry, with tinted windows, gray colored. They got a partial plate and then went back and located where he had been along the shoreline. They found the spot because they found some sort of transponder. He sent us photos he took and left the transponder or whatever it is in place. We didn't talk with the individual who reported it until about an hour ago, but we're going down very early to check it out. You've been talking city water supply—'

'I'll meet you there.'

At dawn Raveneau exited 280 forty-five minutes south of San Francisco. He wasn't far from the Pulgas Water Temple and remembered his way to the intersection of Edgewood and the other road. He found a place to park, killed his lights, and got out. The Feds were here already and they hadn't waited on him. He wouldn't have waited either. He found the trail following the water district's fence, avoiding poison oak as he worked his way along.

The water of the reservoir reflected the sunrise and was crimson and Raveneau turned in his head the idea of poisoning the water. It was the damming of the Hetch Hetchy that brought water from the Sierras and allowed San Francisco to grow and fulfill the dream of western expansion. The Pulgas Temple that marked the place where the Hetch Hetchy Aqueduct terminated one hundred sixty miles from its source was close by.

He studied the hole in the chain-link fence. After 9/11 the water district was more careful about allowing public access, but with the acreage of a watershed how could you stop anybody? It would take an army posted and on guard every day all day. But if poisoning the water was the goal it wouldn't be the storage water they'd want to empty radioactive material into. They would want water already in the distribution system, and that was harder to do.

Raveneau found Coe, and the citizen who had reported it was there and still getting thanked every few minutes. No one knew what the transponder was for other than sending a signal marking its location, but you would have thought this guy had brought home a gold medal from the Olympics.

Raveneau left Coe and drove north with a map of the pipe distribution system the Bay Area Water Supply and Conservation Agency emailed him. He stopped at the last major distribution point and studied the layout of the plant, walking the perimeter before continuing on to the Hall.

Now he was with la Rosa crossing Seventh to

get to Café Roma where she would order a double cappuccino and a croissant and Raveneau a medium coffee with an inch of milk foam on top. It was a ritual and a way to get out and talk things through, often bouncing from one idea to the next. It had worked for them before. La Rosa usually took point, asking the questions, as she did now.

'So what do you think about both things?'

'The water threat and Hugh?'

'Yes, but first the water.'

'I think the water is a bluff and they don't have a way of making it happen. My guess is John Royer got a hold of a little bit of nuclear waste from the medical equipment maker he worked for. He knew the combinations. He was cleared. He was able to get in and out and all this about him having trouble getting a lead-lined vessel is nonsense. It's not hard. You can buy them online. He got enough to poison Lash and there was some left over and that's what he swallowed.

'But enough waste to poison a city water supply, I doubt it, though that doesn't mean that's not what they have in mind. They may well. Throwing radioactive waste into the water supply is similar to setting the fires. I doubt the fires were started to kill people. They were more about creating panic and fear and leaving a mark, and radioactive water would get a pretty good reaction, especially if some got sick before the cause was discovered.'

'It would shut the city down.'

Raveneau agreed and she asked, 'Are you

saying Royer drank his own brew?'

'I'm guessing yes.'

'Does Lindsley have access to the radioactive material?'

'No.'

'Why?'

'He's using Siles, and Siles is very aware. I think Lindsley is close to giving us Siles, but he's also afraid Siles might come for him or has enough dirt on him to take him down with him.'

'Siles will be apprehended in the next twenty-four hours.'

'You're on, I'll take that bet. I think they planned ahead and did it well. That's why we can't find them. I also think they're taking a page from the jihadis. They've decided to give up their lives. It's a suicide pact, but that doesn't say everybody is on-board with it. Maybe Royer was or maybe he was helped along after he committed to placing the incendiary devices. Maybe Siles wanted to eliminate the risk of him confessing later. My guess is Royer drank his own brew and missed a little with his timing.' Raveneau paused before throwing his idea at her. 'It's Latkos who's making me think it's a suicide pact.'

'Why?'

'Coe told me she did do cyber work for an unnamed agency and in a loose way they protect her. But she also has enemies. His sources back up the idea she ripped off Russian mob money and then got the hell out of Berlin. That was before the sex reassignment operation. That's when she was still male. Lindsley told me the gender change wasn't anything Latkos wanted to do. It was about hiding and staying alive.'

'I don't believe that. No one switches sex because they're being hunted.'

'That's why it might be true. No one does it. So maybe it would work. It's a lot different than cross dressing. At any rate her face has gone national so it's gone international and she let that happen. If there's someone out there seriously looking for her, they'll put it together.'

Raveneau held the door of Café Roma for her but she hesitated.

'I've got one last question before we go in,' la Rosa said, and Raveneau let the door fall shut. He stepped back from the entrance and she asked, 'Are the Feds being straight with us?'

Raveneau let a gust of wind blow through before answering, 'Not completely.'

'That's what I think too. So what do we do about it?'

'Nothing.'

'I want to get in Coe's face.'

'It's coming from above him.'

'I don't care where it's coming from. He's the one standing in our office talking about sharing everything. If radioactive material gets in the water system it's never going to be the same here. We need everything they have.' Her voice got louder. 'This is home. This is ours. Some goofus sitting in FBI headquarters back east can't know what that means. We need to know everything.'

She glared at Raveneau. Then her eyes softened and as the wind gusted again, she pulled open the door to Café Roma and they went in. There, she said quietly, 'We live here. We have everything at stake. We need everything they have.'

Fifty-One

In the late afternoon a dry north-east wind rose. Gusts straightened flags and rattled the dry leaves of the plane trees along the sidewalk in front of the Hall of Justice. Forecasters predicted strong winds that would peak in the next twenty-four to thirty-six hours and not reach the strength of those that drove the fires. That did little to reassure people. Two of the three suspected arsonists were still at large.

In San Francisco winds of twenty-five to thirty miles an hour were predicted, and as Raveneau walked to his car the wind felt that strong already. He drove toward a meeting with Lash at the hospital. When he got there Lash was sitting up and wearing a device around his neck that was studded with tiny microphones. The microphones Bluetoothed to the computer on a chair in the corner and anything he said ran through software trained to his speech patterns. Fragments became words. Words sentences. The software program corrected, completed, and amplified. It wasn't perfect, but it was good. As Lash exhaled his answers in a whisper his voice came out of two speakers alongside the computer. His voice sounded normal and that was strange.

'Easier to leave some words out,' Lash said. 'Straight to point.'

'OK.'

'Knew Brandon well, never trusted him. Knew his past.'

'He told you?'

'Yes.'

'Did it attract or repel you? I'm asking because I want us to speak truth to each other.'

'Understand.' Lash closed his eyes as he debated how he wanted to answer.

It was a hard-edged question but Raveneau didn't want to hide anything. He waited and thought about what the doctor told him before he walked in here. Lash's breathing problems had worsened and he needed oxygen to sleep. A tracheal intubation was scheduled pending his white cell count coming back up. The doctor added, 'His count is never coming back up. Your announcement of his death isn't false it's just a few weeks premature, nothing like four months. He'll never have the tracheal intubation.'

Raveneau glanced down at the bed a moment and when he looked up Lash was staring at him, his eyes a startling blue.

'Saw I could use him.'

'You could use his past to control him.'

'Yes.'

'Lindsley told me he combed through everything you owned looking for your secrets. He did that when you were asleep. He and the caregiver colluded and slipped you Valium after you were first diagnosed. Were you aware of that?'

'Yes.'

Of course he was. People like Lash didn't miss anything. He was hypersensitive, hyper-aware.

'Despondent.'

'You stopped caring what happened?'

'Yes.'

'Is it possible he found the key to the bomb shelter lock?'

'Yes.'

The software missed a follow up word there, and as Lash frowned, Raveneau tried a couple of phrases to get at what he meant.

'His ambition was transparent. He wanted to co-author the three books you talked about doing with him and after you died step into your shoes.'

'Yes. Strange man.'

'And unrealistic in thinking you would ever write a book with him.'

'Yes.' Lash smiled a sad smile. 'Never going to write a book with him. My legacy. Standalone. Pride.'

'Did you ever tell him that?'

'No.'

'But he figured it out at some point.'

'Became very angry.'

'Then what happened?'

'Started writing book with him.'

'Why didn't you tell him you weren't going to be able to write any more books and ask him to leave? Tell him the collaboration idea was mistake.'

'Needed him. Useful. Good researcher. Liked talking with him.'

Raveneau wasn't sure he believed that. 'You kept him for that or because he was in on some of your secrets and you couldn't risk alienating him.'

'No.'

'Then what?'

'I – was – afraid – of – him.'

'Afraid he might do bodily harm to you?'

'Became vulnerable. Look at me.'

'As your physical condition declined you felt vulnerable and you were afraid he might harm you even if he was locked out of the house.'

'Yes.'

'Did he ever physically threaten you?'

'Yes.'

Lash's software stopped working as well as he described Lindsley leaving his wheelchair too near the stairs and then edging it closer and closer one night after an argument. It didn't ring true to Raveneau. It might be true. It might well be true but underneath was something else and who knew if there would be another chance with Lash. He hesitated a moment and then decided to just put it out there.

'You probably know when he first got into the bomb shelter. I don't. We've got DNA matches with items of Ann Coryell's we removed from the shelter. We also have other blood of varying types that soaked through a mattress on a steel cot that is old enough to rule out Lindsley, Siles, or anyone we've discussed. Some of that blood may be twenty years old. I think when Lindsley got in there he found that and he left it just as he found it. He didn't move anything. He didn't touch anything, and they were careful when they brought the Missouri skulls in. Why was that?'

'Don't know.'

'You don't have an answer, Albert, but I think I've got one. Lindsley was thinking about DNA and evidence and what he had over you. We know that John Royer took skulls from caskets the Mississippi floods uncovered and that those skulls made their way to the bomb shelter, and once they got there they were carefully moved in and leaned against a wall and no one went near the cot. We could tell that from the dust and some other things. Maybe it was just Lindsley or maybe it was all four of them, but I'm betting it was Lindsley who said, "Stay away from the cot. Don't walk in that area."

'A good defense attorney would still argue that's a contaminated scene, but the blood on the cot, the age of the blood, the suspicion of you a decade ago, it would all work against you. So I'm guessing he let you know what he found and at that point you were tied to him. Is that what happened?'

Lash didn't answer.

'I'm not saying Ann Coryell died in there. There's less of her blood than the other blood types. She may have been in there awhile but may have been alive when she was moved. When her remains were found and before she was IDed the Marin coroner examining her torso concluded she was shot through the heart before she was beheaded. That may have happened up on the mountain, but it's our conclusion that she was in the bomb shelter. I know we interviewed your gardener and some other employees and maybe we missed something, but does that throw suspicion on your gardener, your cook, or the handyman who worked for you for years? It could but I'd say at this point it's not likely, and if the cot got used and used again at least four times, and at least two victims lost in excess of a quart of blood, there's a pattern.'

'Gave Brandon a key.'

'You gave him a key? That's different than what you said earlier.'

'Gave him key after conversation about Cold War.'

'You were talking about the Cold War and you remembered, hey, I've got a Cold War era bomb shelter right here in my backyard. Brandon missed that whole era because his mother hadn't given birth to her killer yet, so he'd probably never been inside an old fallout shelter, so what did you do? Did you point at a key on a peg on the back of a door and say, "Grab that key and go get yourself a look at a real one. You'll have to dig around on the floor a little before you figure out how we disguised the hatch cover, but don't give up. It's down there in the garden shed. Make sure you bring a flashlight because it's spooky dark in there and there are things in there too, so don't touch anything the police can tie to you later." Is that what happened? Give me some help here, I'm having trouble understanding why you would give him a key. When was this?'

'2002. Didn't know.'

'You didn't know what was in there. Right, I get the idea. I'm just not seeing it, and it's not only 2002, but before Ann disappeared.'

'Yes.'

'Then later you learned he was using the bomb shelter. You put it together.'

Lash claimed that one night years later just before he put the house up for sale he was looking out the window toward the Presidio and the ocean and saw a flashlight come on near the garden shed door. Lindsley was staying at the house and he believed it was Lindsley he saw going into the shed. The next day when he asked him, Lindsley denied it. Later, Lindsley said he'd found tracks leading up from the Presidio.

Lash's eyes closed and for several moments Raveneau was unsure whether this was the end of the conversation. He was back briefly and then gone again for close to twenty minutes as Raveneau sat thinking it through.

When Lash opened his eyes he said, 'I changed nothing. Not insightful, took ideas of others, but good teacher. I – made – students see. Ann was brilliant.'

'Was Brandon Lindsley jealous of Ann?'

'Envious.'

'And you're telling me he knew about the bomb shelter before she disappeared?'

'Yes.'

'You want me to believe it was Lindsley who killed her, but you're not really giving me what I need, and there's the cot and what happened before Brandon. We're not quite getting there.

Let me ask a different question. Were you in love with Ann Coryell?'
'Yes.'
The answer and the speed of it surprised Raveneau. That was new. Many questions about their relationship were asked in 2003 but Lash never admitted to being in love with her. He told Hugh Neilley and Alcott that he and Ann slept together a couple of times and then it became uncomfortable and she avoided him. It was unresolved at the point she disappeared. It was another reason why he thought she had fled.
'You were in love but she wasn't?'
Lash nodded and said, 'Told others.'
'You did or she did?'
'She.'
It continued like this and Raveneau learned that Brandon left on a trip a week before she disappeared and it's why he was never interviewed. That wasn't new news, and Hugh and Alcott had checked on the trip.
Lash made another claim now. The last time he was in the bomb shelter was 1984, the year his father died. He was inside it only for a moment and didn't look around. That was the day he locked the hatch cover and the key sat in a locked compartment in his desk after that.
Raveneau summarized, ticking off what Lash had said. 'You were in love with Ann. Lindsley was envious of her. Siles and Lindsley were both at your house often and much earlier than we had realised. You gave Lindsley a key to the bomb shelter before Ann disappeared. That's what I've gotten so far, though I'm not sure yet

how it helps.'

Lash talked now about himself. He couldn't accept the disease when it was first diagnosed. He drank too much and tried to ignore the onset. The onset came with some good and some bad days, but mostly bad days. There were times in the beginning when the cramping in his legs was such that he couldn't walk, and Lindsley helped him get around. Lindsley gradually took advantage of his illness, inserting himself more and more. That was all long after Ann Coryell became an unsolved cold case, but Lindsley did have complete access to the house and grounds.

The caregiver would help him get out of bed in the morning but he was awake in the middle of the night and saw lights flickering outside more than once. He guessed there were others that Lindsley invited over as recently as a week before the house sold. He talked and then threw a twist in just as it was clear he was exhausted and couldn't talk anymore. He said when Lindsley first went into the bomb shelter he found the bloody mattress and skeletons on blankets on the floor. He took photos and asked Lash what had happened and Lash told him he didn't know, told him he hadn't been inside since his father had died.

'Did he believe you?'

'Said he should go to police.'

'But he didn't.'

'Thought he would.'

'Why didn't he?'

'We traded. Why I agreed to co-author. Worried – every – day.'

‘About the Coryell investigation activating and you back in the news?’

‘Yes.’

‘Why didn’t you contact police before you moved out?’

After he moved out Lash didn’t expect to live long enough for it to matter. He knew the odds and expected to die soon and it was questionable whether plans would get approved and construction started before he died.

‘You gambled.’

‘Yes.’

He stopped thinking he could do anything about it. He stopped caring. He had no explanation for the bloody cot or the partial skeletons and offered now that maybe it really was the long-time handyman. Raveneau wrote the man’s name down, but it was gratuitous. Neither he nor Lash believed it. Now Lash’s eyes closed and then he spoke one last time, though he didn’t open his eyes again.

‘Brandon killed her,’ he said. ‘I – am – sure – now – it – was – him.’

Fifty-Two

When the main municipal water pumping stations went offline Coe called and said, 'They did it. We didn't think it through well enough. They hacked into the computers at the two main pumping stations and cut the water supply to San Francisco.'

'When?'

'Forty minutes ago. Latkos. Hackers she knows and they're outside the US. From the size of the attack there are probably a dozen of them and probably getting paid.'

'And I'm guessing you know where she is.'

'Nothing we're doing is getting us closer to Siles. We should have caught up to him by now. We were watching the reservoir and pipe system and they came in through the Internet. We're getting beaten here.'

'They'll get the pumps restarted.'

'They're trying. The Water Department restarted one ten minutes ago and it went down again right away. Now they're trying to bypass their computer systems to get the pumps running again. They don't know if that'll work. And you may not know this yet, but your police and fire 911 system is under a denial of service attack as we speak. They're trying to shut it down. What do you think, Ben? You know your city. Where is this going?'

'It's still about fire. The city burned seven times in the first fifty years. It's probably not that hard to shut a pump down and I doubt the city has had the money to harden their computer systems. Latkos would know that. Whatever she did for us elsewhere in the world she can do here just as easily.'

'That's what's going on. Where are you right now?'

'In the Presidio.'

'I'm going to come meet you. Tell me where exactly and give me fifteen minutes to get there.'

Raveneau parked between two cars in a big lot in the Presidio. He should call la Rosa but didn't call anyone yet. He looked at old barracks refurbished now and the officer's houses remodeled, clean, and leased and could not help but think about what a different country it was when World War II was fought. 9/11 changed us, he thought. We got scared and we let these different government agencies and the military create secret units in the name of fighting terrorism. Coe is not even allowed to name who Latkos worked for. How can that be? Is that of the people, by the people, and for the people? Not at all, he thought.

Coe's car slid in two slots away and Coe walked over and got into Raveneau's car. 'This could cost me my career,' he said. 'It probably will.' He held up his cellphone. 'I can call my ASAC and Brian will agree with me on everything and then he'll say we can't do anything until we get approval and not from our SAC or even from headquarters. They'll have to ask and the answer will filter back.'

'Latkos is that protected?'

'She did something for our government that we owed her for. She's going to pay for what she's doing now, but it's got to come all the way down the line and that doesn't work very well. We were told right away where she was living but I haven't been allowed to share that with SFPD. We've had help monitoring her computer and the reason she hasn't been spotted on the street is she hasn't been on the street. We've been waiting for her to lead us electronically to Siles. She hasn't done that and we're having trouble learning about her network because she's encrypting what she has sent out to eastern Europe and about ten other places. She's way ahead of us.'

'Way ahead of you.'

Coe sighed. 'The next war will be in cyber-space. The people paid to study these things say the early phases will be targeted skirmishes like our going after Iran's centrifuges, but sooner or later, airport control towers will go dark. We're cultivating an army of spies and enablers. She was one of those. Almost nothing is hardened and I'm telling you now that she's coordinating an attack on the nine one one system, and even if they get those pumps up a few hours, she and her friends shut them down.'

'Call your SAC.'

'I can't. He'll say wait.'

'For how long?'
'It could be until tomorrow, could be longer. She was a very valuable asset and before she's arrested here they want to weigh their other options.'
'Has anyone told you that?'
'No, and it would get denied anyway. She's part of the forever war effort. I know that much.'
Raveneau didn't pick up that thread. He thought about waiting for an answer on arresting her until tomorrow or later, if it was even allowed, and then said, 'That's too long.'
'I know that.'
'We could find her. We could get lucky. Does she have someone she is going to call if that happened and we arrested her?'
'Possibly, but once she's arrested I think they'll disappear into their agencies. They'll write her off. She's a big talent but they'll let her go. They won't want the blowback that will come with trying to shelter her. I'm going to leave now.' As he said that he pulled out a folded piece of paper and laid it on the seat as he got out. He leaned back just long enough to say, '412 and 414. They're corner condos joined together in a remodel.'
Raveneau picked up la Rosa at the corner of Franklin and Pierce. The building was out toward the Sunset but not deep in the fog belt. It was well-maintained and nondescript with almost no landscaping, a few hedged junipers and a secure entrance with a video camera and a stout metal-framed door with wire glass. Not a place you'd associate with a person who had a

lot of money, but if the money wasn't their own maybe it made sense, and if you lived your life online what difference did the building you slept in make?

A local fire captain had a key to the stairwell and let them in. When they came out into the corridor on the fourth floor and walked down to 412, Raveneau saw the door was slightly ajar. He touched la Rosa's arm and pointed at the door. Backup units were on their way so they didn't have to approach yet and he knew it was likely Latkos was tapped into the video cameras that were not only outside the building but in the corridors and the fire stairwell they had climbed.

They didn't have to approach but they were going to and it turned out he was right about the video cameras. Latkos had a set-up like a security office and the screens showed all approaches to her condo. She was in a chair with a view of nine monitor screens. On her head was a set of Bose earphones and faintly Raveneau heard Mahler's Fifth Symphony. On the screen in front of her was a panorama of a beach and clear water and what looked like a perfect day somewhere in the North Aegean.

Not a perfect day for her though. She had two entry wounds in the back of her skull and a piece of forehead missing where one exited. The shooter came in the door and she had to know, must have seen her killer coming for her. She put on the earphones so the last sounds would be Mahler not gunshots and she put this image on the screen.

'I'll call it in,' la Rosa said, because Raveneau hadn't moved or said anything. 'I'll get one of the uniform officers to take charge of the front door.'

Raveneau backed away from the body. They needed to start knocking on doors to ask if anyone had seen or heard anything. He looked around the room, expensively furnished, immaculate, and checked out something floating in a jar on the mantle above a fireplace. He stared and then checked out the rest of the space. Everything about the combined apartments said she lived alone. Nothing looked disturbed. Two of the bedrooms looked as if no one had ever walked in there after the decorator left.

He returned to her body in the chair and the array of screens. Did she leave the door open and unlocked for her killer? His guess was she did. He walked out into the corridor, called Coe and listened to sirens as he waited for Coe to answer.

Fifty-Three

Raveneau was still on the phone with Coe when the dull whumph of an explosion crumpled the air. It was close but not that close. Still, it was somewhere in the city and two more blasts followed within seconds, and then a third, fourth, and Raveneau counted three more after that. With the last he saw a fireball. Coe heard them too. Coe said, 'Fuck. I'll call you back after I know what this is.' He hung up.

Now the air filled with sirens and black smoke rose from the direction of the Upper Haight. He and la Rosa heard a report over the radio that they were car bombs. Then a uniform officer approached a silver Toyota Prius where an initiating explosion had failed to ignite a gas-filled plastic water storage bladder lying on its side in the back. The seats were folded down, the bladder under a blanket; the officer, a little more foolhardy than brave, walked up after the windows blew out and the smoke from the initiator cleared.

Seven cars exploded, all of them in the upper Haight, each adjacent and upwind of historic wood frame Victorian houses. A report of a seventh explosion came in just a little later and for a moment its location was confusing, then

Raveneau recognized it as one of the storage lots of a towing company that contracted with the city. The car must have been parked illegally and ticketed and towed.

Intense heat from the car bombs caused nearby cars to catch fire. Houses were burning along several blocks in the Haight and a general evacuation was under way in a ten block area. The Water Department did manage to bypass their computer system and jury-rigged a way to get the pumps running, so that was good news. But the pumps were running slowly and erratically and the water pressure was way down. Tanker trunks rolled toward the Haight. A Coast Guard helicopter ferried water from the bay though wind gusts were making that problematic and Raveneau heard they were going to give up on it.

At Latkos' apartment they waited for the medical examiner and as la Rosa interviewed residents Raveneau went back through the videotape. From the body and the still wet blood he knew he didn't need to go back more than six hours. He looked at the time on the tape first and wrote it down as he saw a figure with their face fully masked approach the same fire door he and la Rosa entered the building through. It looked like a man. They watched him enter with a key.

The apartment manager and the security subcontractor were with Raveneau as the man entered the stairwell. The security guy switched to the stairwell videotape. That took a few minutes and then the man was climbing the stairs with his head down. On the fourth floor he opened the door to the corridor and there was another pause to switch video feeds. As he waited Raveneau thought about Latkos. If she was watching she would have seen that someone was on the fourth floor coming up the fire stairs with a mask on and now in the corridor.

The tape started to play again and there was no hesitation as the man turned left coming out of the stairwell and headed toward her condo. He knew the building or the layout of the building. It could be either.

'Freeze the next frame,' Raveneau said, and then studied the man's build. It could be him. 'OK, start it again.'

They watched him slowly slide a key into her lock and bring out a gun, and then turn the key and open the door. He stepped in with the gun ready. The door shut and Raveneau wrote down the time on the videotape. Now they waited and minutes went by as he thought about it. At the ten minute mark they started forward again with the videotape. Less than sixty seconds later, the door opened. The gunman left it ajar, slipped into the stairwell and although Raveneau thought he would exit the building as fast as he could they still switched cameras. They watched him go down the stairs. He didn't peel the mask off until he left the building and must have known that if he didn't turn his head his face would never show. He pulled a sweatshirt hood up to cover the back of his head as he peeled the mask off and even with the frame frozen Raveneau couldn't make out his hair color.

From behind him la Rosa asked, 'Was it Lindsley?'

'No.'

'The medical examiner is here.'

'OK.' He stood and when he was sure there would be no misunderstanding about the video-tape, that it was police evidence, he followed la Rosa. He asked her, 'How's it going?'

'They've given up on one row of houses and are having trouble with another block.'

'How about here?'

'CSI is minutes away.'

They talked with the ME and when the CSI crew arrived Raveneau took the elevator down and stepped outside. Black smoke spiraled up from the Haight and a report was coming in over one of the police radios that an armored car was knocking over fire hydrants not far from the fires. There wasn't a count of how many, but a new report came as he stood there listening, of a man abandoning the armored car and running to another car. Police units were now in pursuit.

Raveneau learned it was a middle-aged Caucasian male and that he had turned into a parking lot behind a two-story commercial building in the Richmond then ran up a flight of stairs to what appeared to be a second story office. The blinds were down so the officers couldn't see into the street facing windows and no one had approached the back steps.

Raveneau listened to this and then called la Rosa and said, 'I've got to get over there. I'll call you.'

The office building was two offices overhead and retail below, a nail parlor and a florist. The florist fled leaving the door open and the wind carried the scent of newly cut flowers across the street. Both offices had street faces of glass and were accessed by a stairwell between the florist and the nail shop and by wooden stairs in the back that led to a small wooden deck. Both exits were covered and Coe and the Feds were on their way. The suspect had not shown himself since lowering the blinds. An officer used a bullhorn to order him out, but so far there was no response. Raveneau talked with the pursuit officers who got the best look and now he was around to believing it was Alan Siles.

Maybe this was a pre-arranged rendezvous point, and lacking anywhere else to go and knowing he had a couple of radio cars following he came here thinking he could get inside the office before they had enough vehicles to shut-down his escape.

'What do you think?' Coe asked as he arrived.

'That if it's really him, and it looks like it is, then he didn't expect to get away but he wanted to get here. He had the armored vehicle and car after he abandoned that. He drove here at high speed. The officers hung back. They kept their distance until he turned into the lot and they came in with sirens and lights. By then he was already taking the stairs two at a time. They got a good look at him and ordered him to stop, and he ignored them and they made the decision not to use force. He's locked himself in the apartment.'

'They're sure it's Siles?'

'One of them is. The fires in the Haight are the grand finale. After the 1906 earthquake the big mansions along Van Ness were dynamited to stop the fire. Otherwise, the Victorians burning now would have burned then. Van Ness was wide enough that the fire didn't cross. Lindsley studied that period and he worked it again when he was researching for Lash on the SFPD book. It's Siles and it was probably a rendezvous point, and I'll bet this hydrant bit was never in the original game plan. But this is it. There's no dirty bomb, no Fourth of July finish. It's over and we need to talk him out.'

'We've a sniper setting up two blocks away and let's hope he's not needed, but we don't know what he's doing in there. He may be turning that office into a bomb.'

'I don't think so.'

'All right, as reigning expert on these psychos what do you recommend?'

'That I go up the stairs in the back and tell him it's over.'

Coe smiled.

'I'm not kidding. I'll put on body armor; I'll knock on the door. He knows it's over and I'll let him know he can surrender without getting shot.'

'You really are a full service shop. What are you going to say when he opens the door with a shotgun blast?'

'I've got a thread with him no one else has. I've read Coryell.'

'What if he has decided there's nothing left to live for and plans to take as many people with him as he can? That's a likely scenario. It's a believable one and may sound a lot better to him than a prison sentence of one hundred fifty years. This guy just set off car bombs and knocked over hydrants so he could avenge the American Indian. What kind of rational conversation do you think you're going to have with him?'

'Any other way he's going to end up dead. There'll be a SWAT team at three in the morning and he'll be dead when it's over. Smoke bombs and flash bang and still somehow he'll end up dead. I think me trying to talk to him is worth a try.'

'We can just as easily wait him out. We can cut off the water and power. We can wear him down without risking anyone.'

'I'll wear a flak jacket and he'll recognize me. He'll get I'm there to talk to him and there's still a chance there is more to come, so maybe we can prevent that.'

Two hours later, Raveneau drove slowly on to the lot in a vehicle with tinted windows. He paused, pulled forward, parked and climbed the stairs, his shoes a quiet tapping on the wood treads. He called to Siles as he climbed and knew snipers' scopes were trained on the door. He called for Siles again. He stood to the side and rapped hard on the door. He called again and tried the door handle and finding it unlocked he pushed it open. He told Siles he was here only to talk and his heart pounded as he exposed himself enough to take a look.

Fifty-Four

Wind from behind Raveneau slapped the door against the wall. Blinds rattled. An oil lamp from another age threw flickering light from a low table. Alan Siles lay motionless on the floor nearby, head resting on a small rounded pillow, arms close in along his body and legs, straight as though the position was somehow chosen.

Raveneau pressed the mike. 'Call paramedics and come on up.'

His eyes were closed but his mouth open, head canted to the left, and now Raveneau saw the left hand was clenched, the right open. Raveneau felt for a pulse along his neck and didn't find anything. He saw a glass of water and a small dark glass jar that looked as old as the oil lamp. The lid of the jar was off. Inside were small white pills. Next to the pill jar was a notebook with a strip of leather that tied it shut. He wanted to but didn't touch it yet and just stood and tried to put it together.

Siles was a suicide. John Royer may have killed himself, and Ike Latkos let herself get killed. He turned at the voices behind him at the footfall on the loose wood stairs, but not before taking in the small office, its one desk, the books, the dated furniture and look of disuse, and then at Siles's hands again. How was one hand clenched, one open?

'I guess he's out on the Boundary now with her,' Coe said as he looked at the hands. 'I'll bet you the clenched one is glued in that position.'

Raveneau pointed at the hand-bound book. 'That'll be their story. I know the writer.'

'Whose office is this?'

'It's going to turn out to be Lindsley's.'

Raveneau moved away and called la Rosa.

'Are you sticking there?' she asked.

'For now, I am. We don't want to lose control of what Siles left behind. And it looks to me like Lindsley was supposed to be here and head to the Boundary with him. There's a second pillow and mat. I'll take a photo and send it to you.'

Coe called it the quiet end to an unlikely terror attack. After Siles's body was removed, but before they left, word came that the fires, including the block that burned, were on their way to being controlled. No one had died or been injured, and Raveneau moved down to the lot and stood talking with an animated, upbeat, and assertive Coe.

'No matter what he wrote in that book or pamphlet there isn't anyone who'll ever understand these guys,' Coe said.

'In some ways I do.'

'What do you really understand about them? I know, Coryell, but what made them do all this? That's what I'm talking about. Who did Siles die for? Or Royer? Or should I ask Lindsley? Where are you going now?'

'To check on the fires then I'm back to Latkos'

apartment.'

Along a block of Lyon Street where it runs into Haight nearly all of the buildings burned, as had some of the commercial buildings on Haight Street. A fire captain told him, 'Those helicopter pilots saved us. I don't know how they did it with the wind, but they somehow did.'

Raveneau was standing with la Rosa when Ike Latkos's body was removed. The computers were already gone. When they left there they got word that Lindsley was temporarily at large. His general whereabouts were known and he was on foot.

La Rosa shook her head. 'I had a dog named Mac who was like this. He was always figuring out how to get out of the house. I'd be gone an hour and a neighbor would call and say, "Your dog is in our backyard. Come get him." How does Lindsley walk away from surveillance?'

'They're not that close to him. They're tracking him electronically through the throwaway phones he thought were safe to carry. Now it's looking like he knew that.'

Raveneau also tried calling Hugh Neilley. He didn't expect Hugh to answer, and when he didn't, Raveneau called the Southern Precinct captain and was told Hugh, like others, was out looking for Lindsley. Everyone was out on the street either helping with the fires or hunting for Lindsley.

'Can you try to get Neilley for me on the radio?'

'Why is that?'

'He's got some information for me.'

'I don't think he really wants to talk to you, Inspector.'

'Just do it, OK?'

'I'm going to put my captain on.'

When the captain picked up with Raveneau again, he said, 'Neilley will call you when he's on a break.'

'When is that going to be?'

'I have no idea.'

In the Homicide office Raveneau called Hugh from his cell and then sat through the recording and left a message. He opened one of the two Coryell murder files and went slowly page by page, his mind moving between the files and the events of the past week. When he finished the first file he lifted it aside and opened the second. But he wasn't looking for an answer in the files as much as in his head. He was closing on something that he could feel but not see yet.

An hour later, Lindsley phoned a Channel Five reporter and told her he was innocent of any responsibility in all of the fires and that his mistake was trying to help SFPD and the FBI. Neither had kept their word to him and both were hunting him now to lock him up and blame him for their failure to apprehend Siles, Royer, and Latkos. He asked for the public's help in keeping law enforcement officers from killing him.

'Why would they do that?' the reporter asked.

Lindsley answered, 'Because they ignored my warnings and people died. The fires, the deaths, all of this could have been prevented. I approached Homicide Inspector Benjamin Raveneau over a week ago and warned him.'

The station put up a tape of the call on their website and tape went viral. Raveneau's reaction was to go home and sleep for four hours on the couch. When he woke it was dark and Celeste was there. He made coffee and called Coe from his car. Coe was back in the FBI Field Office and impatient with the harassment he was getting for Lindsley out there walking around and talking to reporters.

'Where is Siles's phone?' Raveneau asked.

'It's in the lab.'

'Text Lindsley from it.'

'Why? Siles is dead and Lindsley switched phones again. The phone he was using is in his apartment and he's not going upstairs to his apartment before we talk to him. I can promise you that.'

'I listened to the YouTube the TV station put up of their interview with Lindsley. He's stressed. You can hear it, and I know he believes in the Boundary. You could let him go home. That's where he's going to head eventually if you don't find him first. He'll expect to get arrested. He believes in the Boundary. He told me it's possible to communicate back to the living in the same way the Native Americans called to the spirits of their ancestors. He'll either believe it's us or Siles is still alive and we faked his death, or he'll believe the thing we have trouble even imagining, that Siles is communicating from beyond death. I think that's what Siles's hands were about. It's worth a try, and I'll come to your office. I'll do it.'

'It's a complete waste of time and you don't need to come here. What do you want me to type? "Weather is perfect, wish you were here. Missed seeing you yesterday, Brandon, did you fuck me over and talk to the police?" What's the message you want, Raveneau, and you know if this works you can quit the police and make a mint with a phone commercial where you text dead people.'

'Just type, "I'm here."'

'That's it, just those two words? That's a missed opportunity. Shouldn't I ask how crowded it is and whether he's heard any scuttlebutt around the Boundary about a heaven or a hell? But, OK, you're the boss on this. I'm typing, I'm here. Talk about anticlimactic, but OK I've done it and am pressing Send. I know I never caught up on my Coryell reading, but someone, namely you, should have told me you can call home from the Boundary. That's a game changer. It takes a lot of the stress out of passing on. You still there?'

'I'm here.'

'The message sent. It's probably pinging for Lindsley in his apartment right now.'

'Good work. I'll talk to you later.'

Raveneau sat down at his desk, untied the leather string and opened the leather-bound book that was found with Siles. It was two hundred eighty-six pages and in the foreword its author, Brandon Lindsley, described his spiritual journey as one the country needed to make. Raveneau read the start of the first chapter then flipped though, stopping occasionally, stopping on a passage he recognized from Dee Brown's *Bury*

My Heart At Wounded Knee, telling of a meeting in 1851 with four of the great tribes of the plains and a treaty signed at Fort Laramie with the US government that promised good faith and friendship and allowed white men to establish roads and cross Indian land. The tribes granted access but relinquished nothing, but like all the treaties before and after it didn't stand. Gold was discovered at Pike's Peak in 1858 and a gold rush ensued. The city of Denver rose on Indian land, and in the mountains of the Rockies mining towns.

There were also quotes from generals, soldiers, settlers, Congressmen, and chiefs of tribes. Near the end of Lindsley's book he found an entry with a notation saying it was written by a *'Mrs Z. A. Parker, at that time a teacher on the Pine Ridge reservation, writing of a Ghost dance observed by her on White Clay creek on June 20, 1890.'* In smaller letters he read: *'Segment of Parker's account quoted in James Mooney's book* The Ghost Dance Religion and Wounded Knee.' In detail Parker described *'the ghost shirt or dress'* the women wore and the ghost shirt the men wore.

A line caught Raveneau's eye as he read the description of what the women wore, a *'dress cut like their ordinary dress, a loose robe with handkerchief, with moon, stars, birds, etc, interspersed with real feathers, painted on the waists and sleeves. While dancing they wound their shawls about their waists, letting them fall to within three inches of the ground, the fringe at the bottom. In the hair, near the crown, a feather was tied. I noticed an absence of bead ornaments, and, as I knew their vanity and fondness for them, wondered why it was. Upon making inquiries I found they discarded everything they could that was made by white men.'*

That was at Pine Ridge in 1890 six months before Wounded Knee and Raveneau flipped to the last page. No surprise that again it was Dee Brown's *Bury My Heart At Wounded Knee* that Lindlsey mimicked. Though Dee Brown's book was attacked by academic historians who viewed it as pop history, it sold millions. It was the very thing Lindsley aspired to and that Lash earned his wealth with.

The book was also written from the viewpoint of the Native American and touched the unseen thing Ann Coryell wrote about. On the last page of Brown's book was a quote from Black Elk forty-two years after the massacre at Wounded Knee. The quote was taken from Black Elk Speaks, a collaboration between John Neihardt and Black Elk in 1932. It read,

'I did not know then how much was ended. When I look back now from this high hill of my old age, I can still see the butchered women and children lying heaped and scattered all along the crooked gulch as plain as when I saw them with eyes still young. And I can see that something else died there in the bloody mud, and was buried in the blizzard. A people's dream died there. It was a beautiful dream ... the nation's hoop is broken and scattered. There is no center any longer, and the sacred tree is dead.'

Raveneau shut Lindsley's book. He waited.

Then a text came. The text could be Neilley. It could la Rosa or his lieutenant or Celeste, but it had to be Lindsley. It read: '*where are u?*'

He wrote back, *'Let's meet.'*

'tonight. late. will call u.'

Fifty-Five

Raveneau called Ferranti the general contractor five times in quick succession, hanging up each time it rolled to voicemail. On the fifth try Ferranti picked up.

'Tell me again, what was Hugh Neilley's price for the demolition on the house?'

'About twenty thousand.'

'More than twenty thousand dollars or less?'

'Less.'

'What was the next highest bidder's price and how many bids did you get?'

'Three bids and I don't remember the numbers. I see a lot of bids. I'd have to check, but does it really matter?'

'It does and we can meet at your office if you need to look them up.'

'I can tell you roughly. One was fifteen thousand higher and the other was double Hugh's.'

'Double?'

'People shoot from the hip. Sometimes they just throw a number at it and hope they get the job.'

'Did you tell Hugh he was too low?'

'I don't know if I did. I think I just asked him if he had everything covered. He said he was good.'

'OK. Now I've a different question and I've asked this one before. How did you find out Hugh's nephew was dumping off the side of the road?'

'One of his laborers told one of mine—'

'My partner talked to all the laborers and Hugh never took them on any dump runs. When they got in the truck with him at the end of the day he dropped them close to where they live.' Raveneau let a beat go by. He gave him a chance to deny it. When he didn't Raveneau said, 'I'm going to give you a free pass on that and let's try the question again. How did you figure it out?'

Now there was a long silence.

'Nothing is going to happen to you. I'm about the murder investigation.'

'I always go to my jobs early in the morning. That's when I walk them without having to answer any questions. Hugh's nephew was always there in the early morning before anything was open. He'd be sitting in his truck drinking coffee and one morning he was there with an empty truck though I knew he'd left too late the day before to get to one of the transfer stations. So I knew he got rid of the load somewhere and I started keeping track. I mean, it could have been legit. He could have dropped it on another job and someone else picked it up from there, but no one likes to move stuff twice so I knew it probably wasn't that. I had one carpenter on the job and I had him start writing down the time of day Matt left with the truck. The next time it happened I followed him.'

'And then you reported it and came up with the story about one of their laborers telling your laborer.'

'It wasn't exactly a lie.'

'Did you report the illegal dumping to the police?'

'Yeah, I guess so.'

'Were both loads there?'

'Yes, and maybe more.'

'Did he do it again?'

'No.'

'Why did you do the thing about the fraudulent tags? Why didn't you confront him?'

'You want the truth?'

'Sure, why not?'

'The truth is I didn't want to get into it with Hugh. I thought he would freak out.'

'OK, here's the last thing, I need to know exactly where that load got dumped.'

'The county people know where it is. I showed them the area. I didn't have the exact area because I couldn't get too close, but they found it. It's not like it was that hard.'

'Good because I'm going to want you to show me. What are you doing right now?'

'Really? They cleaned it up. There's not going to be anything to see.'

'There'll be something and I can't wait for the county.'

'But what's the point?'

'I can't tell you right now.'

Raveneau met him forty minutes later and they drove the winding road into the hills in Ferranti's new Ford pickup, which was like a rolling office. It had everything a contractor could want except good gas mileage, and he was driving Raveneau who wasn't a prospect or client or a way to make any money. Ferranti found the general area on the second try but it didn't make any sense that Baylor upended the dump load off this main road, so they tried a side road and then a dirt driveway to a site where it looked like a house was started and then abandoned. They backtracked from there and found it, and it clicked for Ferranti once he saw the site. He remembered watching Baylor turn on to the dirt road. There were white-painted pieces of stucco from Lash's house way down the slope and a few chunks of broken concrete they probably figured weren't worth moving.

'I want to be sure,' Raveneau said, and got out and half slid, half walked down the steep slope as Ferranti watched. Raveneau brought back a piece of stucco about the size of his hand. It was cement gray on one side and white-painted with a sand texture on the other face. Wire mesh lath poked through and he held on to it with the wire lath as he scrambled back up.

'Is that house color? Does this look right?'

'It's definitely it.'

'Half the time people say definitely to me they change their minds later. How certain are you?'

'I'm certain.'

'OK, drop me back at my car.'

He called la Rosa first and walked through his

idea with her. When she couldn't pick it apart he called Coe figuring the Feds were still in as long as Lindsley was a person of interest. Coe pushed back a little, asking, 'Why don't you use your own K-Nine unit?'

'We will but it's a big area and we'll need help.'

'How again does this connect to Brandon Lindsley?'

'I didn't say it did. I said it might.'

'I'll have to call you back.'

That was the Fed way and that was good enough for Raveneau. Coe was in. Coe would get approval and they could get dogs out there tomorrow.

Fifty-Six

Raveneau struggled with the idea then sat with his commander and talked with him before calling the Special Operations Unit and asking for surveillance on Hugh Neilley. It was difficult to do and depressing. That night he got a call from the two officer team tracking Hugh. Hugh left his house half an hour ago and now was in San Francisco in China Basin close to where Raveneau lived.

'He's headed toward you, Inspector. What's this about?'

'I don't know yet.'

A few minutes later one of the undercover officers reported that Hugh had slowed not far from where Raveneau lived, but did not stop and drove past. He skirted the water in China Basin, passing the ball park and continuing along the Embarcadero past the Ferry Building and on to Bay Street and beyond Fisherman's Wharf before doubling back to North Beach, parking down the street from a bar and walking. He probably just wanted to talk to me, Raveneau thought. He felt a strong sense of relief, a feeling like a wave passing through his chest.

The next call from the undercover unit came with a question. 'Is he a drinker?'

'He is.'

'He's still at the bar. He's been in there since before midnight, almost an hour and a half, and he's been drinking sparkling water. Does that sound like him to you?'

'Not the guy I know.'

'OK, it looks like he just got a text message. He's picked up his phone and now he's waving the bartender over and he's got his wallet out. He's paying. It looks like we're rolling again.'

Hugh drove toward the Marina and up to Chestnut Street and right on Chestnut. After four blocks they guessed he might be heading to the Presidio or the bridge, but then he backtracked. Before he reached Lombard he went right and then drifted down several blocks and parked.

'He's on foot.'

Hearing that Raveneau hurried to his car. He cut across town listening to them report Hugh walking three blocks then making a cell call from a street corner. The phone went back in his coat pocket, and he continued on another block and a half then turned and went up a flight of steps of a house. The front door opened quickly and he was inside.

'Girlfriend?' one of the team asked and Raveneau didn't have an answer, but it was on him to decide what to do next. That Hugh had walked three blocks without looking for parking closer to the house didn't make sense to Raveneau. He was here now. He saw places to park. He eased and told himself his imagination had run too far too fast. It probably was a girlfriend and parking farther away had to do with street permits and avoiding a parking ticket. He played everything back through his head again and one of the surveillance team, a young woman officer, took a walk past the house. As she did, she heard one then a second sound from inside the house and said, 'Gunshots. Three.'

Now Raveneau was out of his car and hurrying toward the house steps. He took them two at a time with the surveillance team close behind. He pounded on the door and the door opened and Hugh without a word moved aside to let him in. As Raveneau stared at Lindsley he knew Lindsley was dead.

'Ben, he pulled a gun on me. I had no choice. He called me and said he wanted to surrender himself and had always trusted me. He told me he wanted me to bring him in. He knew me from Lash's poker games. I knew it was risky but I was already in North Beach at a bar and he said he was close to killing himself. He said he would if I didn't come alone. I almost called you but with the way it's gotten between us I just couldn't do that. I drove here, parked three blocks away and called 911 just before I went up. That's what the sirens you're hearing outside are about. I figured they would get here as he surrendered, but he didn't want to surrender. What he wanted to do was kill me. I think he was afraid I would remember something that happened way back when and maybe that's because of something you've uncovered with your cold case investigation. I don't know what it was but he had a gun. It's still there on the couch.'

'What would that be?'

'I have no idea but he may have been getting ready to tell me as he eased that gun out from between those sofa cushions. Fortunately, I saw the gun before he started to raise it. I aimed at his chest and hit him on his left side. He got one shot off that went into the wall behind me. I could have easily missed him. I could be dead.'

'Hugh,' Raveneau started and then stopped. The on-call inspectors would handle this. They would get Hugh's statement and his.

Raveneau made sure Hugh was moved out of the building. Two uniform officers led him down to a car and he waited in the back until the on-call inspectors showed. Raveneau waited too, but on the sidewalk. He called la Rosa. He called Coe, told him Lindsley was dead, and Coe said quietly, 'We suspected he had a place in San Francisco. I'll be there inside an hour.'

'I won't be here when you get here, but I want to know we're still on for tomorrow.'

‘Skyline Boulevard, seven a.m., bring our dogs though they don’t scent well to construction debris. Why aren’t you staying there at the Lindsley scene?’

‘Because the on-call inspectors just got here. I’ll see you in the morning.’

Fifty-Seven

At dawn the next morning Raveneau parked so the K-9 units would see his car as they drove up the road. That way no one would miss the turn-off on to the dirt road. He carried his coffee as he walked out the dirt road and the chill air felt like the start of the true fall. Fog had come in with the night and strands of fog moved through the trees in the ravines below; the trees dripped and the bay leaves were pungent with the damp and the road dark with moisture though it would dry with the first sunlight. He had fifteen to twenty minutes before the K-9 units would arrive and wanted to walk it alone first.

He stopped where Baylor had backed up and the rear tires of the heavy truck sank along the edge of the road as the dump bed lifted. Baylor took a pretty good risk as the bed rose and more weight transferred to the rear axle before the heavy debris slid out. He could have ended up down in the ravine. The construction debris tore through the brush leaving what looked like an avalanche scar. Looking at it more closely today, he understood why Hugh's bill for the clean-up was so big.

He walked out to where the road ended at the abandoned house site. Before construction started it must have been a rounded knoll that got bulldozed into a flat dirt pad. The builder got part-way through the foundation before the financial system seized up and the bank called his loan. Rebar cages rose out of piers drilled in the ground and filled with concrete. Along one side, the builder had stacked form boards to pour a retaining wall. On the rest of the site the dirt was damp and dark like the road in, but also cracked and hard from the long hot summer and dry fall.

The new house would have looked out down through the treed ravines and out across to coastal mountains. He walked through, touched rusty rebar and sun-hardened wood, now twisted and gray. He finished his coffee and walked the perimeter of the shaved-off knoll. He looked down into the trees and kept his mind off Hugh and the clothes in two bags in his trunk. He found a deer trail and walked a ways down it and then climbed back up and walked out to the main road as the first SFPD K-9 Unit showed up.

After a phone call and a little mix-up on directions, the FBI dog handler arrived. Raveneau's idea was to search both sides of the dirt road, keeping the dog teams separated with one team on either side working along the steep embankments toward the knoll with abandoned construction. He put the coffee mug back in the car and the bags with the clothes out of the trunk then watched how the handlers let their dogs scent the clothes. He showed them the tire tracks and pointed out debris from the two loads dumped here.

'He either backed in or drove in to the construction site and turned around, and that's what I think he did. He drove in and turned around because with the trees overhanging it would have been hard to back in.'

No one said anything. If they had, they probably would have said, so what? They didn't care how Baylor drove the truck. Neither did they like the steep terrain, poison oak and brush. The Fed dog handler asked how far down they needed to go and Raveneau, imagining Baylor pointed down at a big oak, said, 'At least that far, and both sides of the road and all the way around the construction site.'

'That's going to take hours.'

'That's why we're here early.'

That was the end of conversation before the handlers started their dogs. Now they were well down the steep sides and he heard the dogs barking and the handlers' voices in fragments carrying up through the fog. He listened for a while and then walked out to the house site with a knot in his stomach and an image of Hugh making the phone call from the sidewalk a block and a half from where Lindsley sat waiting. He could easily be wrong about this search today.

A couple of hours passed and the early cool warmed and sunlight dried the road. Both handlers hiked up at different times to give their dogs water. Neither was to the knoll yet and then both were and neither dog had scented anything yet. They worked their way around the knoll and met up. When that happened they climbed back up to the construction site together.

The Fed handler said, 'My girl here is about done.'

'Can she go another half hour?'

'She's pretty well done.'

'I want to get one of you to go lower. There's a deer trail off the back of the site. I want to move the perimeter out another fifty yards just at the knoll here.'

Harrison with the SFPD German shepherd said, 'That should just be one of us. I'll do it.'

He went down with BP, the dog named after the Gulf oil spill, and Raveneau, like the handlers, didn't hold out a lot of hope of still finding something, but the deer trail was the obvious way to get farther down. The deer were probably here before the house and from the tracks they were here after it. He saw Baylor emptying the bed and then coming in here to turn around, but after doing that, and before leaving, shutting the engine off and getting out. From here you couldn't see Skyline Boulevard. The trees hid it and no one driving by would see the truck, and the truck once turned around would block the entrance to the site.

Baylor would have checked it out. He would have found the deer trail and figured out it was the easy way to get down where no one would ever go. He took a call from la Rosa now, and then heard the dog, BP, barking louder. 'I've got to call you back. Is Baylor willing to talk to us?'

'Only if we offer him something. Any luck out there?'

'Not yet.'

But now Harrison was calling to him and Raveneau hurried down the trail, nearly tripping on a root. As he got there, Harrison, the handler, asked, 'How did you know?'

'I didn't. I just figured the timing worked. It was his opportunity.'

Raveneau stopped talking as he saw what the dog had found.

'Why here when those other dump loads of debris were bound to get found?'

'Timing. It was on a day when he had a full load to dump. He was here to do the illegal dumping and he figured that off this end of the construction site was far enough away from what slid out of the bed.'

The skull and the clothing were together. That was another mistake. He could have lost the clothing anywhere, absolutely anywhere. Dropped them on a street corner, dropped them in a garbage, donated the clothes to Salvation Army or left them on a bus station bench and no one would have been the wiser. The skull he should have broken into pieces, but maybe there was a reason he did it this way, Raveneau thought, leaving the plastic bag he carried the skull and clothes in as well. Maybe he wanted them together and maybe that was driven by anger.

Raveneau waited hours for a photographer. He asked the Chief Medical Examiner to drive down, and he was at the site until mid afternoon.

But now he was with la Rosa across the table from Matt Baylor in an interview room. They had brought Baylor up the fire escape to the Fifth Floor and Baylor didn't complain about climbing the stairs in manacles. He was in an upbeat mood. Maybe he thought he was being offered a deal because his Uncle Hugh 'had nailed one of the guys who set the fires last night and the cops didn't want to be going after a hero officer's nephew.'

Baylor might have believed that but Raveneau didn't think so. Still, neither Raveneau nor la Rosa did anything to alter his mood yet. They talked up the risk Hugh took to confront Lindsley alone and liked the idea of Baylor feeling that he was basking in Hugh's halo. The media ran the story that way: career officer lured to a late night meeting kills the fourth arsonist in a shoot out. Inside the Homicide Detail was a different view but if they were correct Hugh did it the right way. He contaminated the scene in a way that would make it difficult to solve.

La Rosa set up her laptop and Baylor asked, 'What's up with the laptop?'

Raveneau answered for her. 'We've got some photos to show you.'

'You're wondering if I've ever seen the guy that Hugh wasted?'

'If you have we'd be interested, but this is different. We're going to come around to your side of the table. We've got this set up as a slide show. We're not really high enough up in the brass to do PowerPoint and there's no intro music, so we're going to be right into the opening shots right away. I'm guessing you'll recognize where they were taken and I should tell you they were all taken today.'

'What is this about?'

'You're going to have to tell us that. You're the man with the answers.'

The first photo could have been from someone's vacation somewhere looking down a dirt road with the oak and bay branches overhanging it and out toward a foggy vista.

'I took that,' Raveneau said. 'Do you recognize the road?'

'No.'

'It runs out to the secret prison.'

'Why are you fucking with me?'

La Rosa was wondering the same thing.

'I'm not really. I'm just slowly getting into a good mood. You probably haven't ever seen me in a good mood, so it seems strange.'

La Rosa gave him another look and he nodded and moved to the second photo. This showed the dirt pad leveled and the foundation construction, pier rebar poking up, twisted form wood of the retaining wall.

Baylor frowned. He looked down at the photo again and he looked up he said, 'OK.'

'OK, what?'

'I recognize this. It's where I dumped those loads.'

'That's right, and we were out there with dogs today. I've got a question as we get to these next photos.'

Baylor didn't respond. He just watched the screen and waited for the next one and that was the deer trail leading down off the back of the site. The fourth showed the skull and clothes.

'My question is why didn't you bury it deep or at least lose the clothes? The dogs might still have found it, but I doubt it.'

Now there was a long silence as Baylor stared at the screen and Raveneau and la Rosa sat quiet. They could only imagine what must be tumbling through his head. Raveneau was banking on the fight Baylor had with his uncle.

'He wanted me to lose them.'

There we go.

'Who did?'

Another long silence. It was hard for him and then his anger returned and he spit out the words, 'Uncle Fucking Hugh, and I don't know why I did it for him. Because he said he'd deal with some other problems I had going, I guess. It was weird and I felt strange doing it but he said not to worry about it, that it didn't matter. He said it was old news and over with. Those were his exact words.'

'Did he ever say whose skull it was?'

'He told me where it was in the bomb shelter and it was pretty obvious it was hers. He said he didn't kill her and he didn't find out about the skull until later. I got it out the day I went down there the first time. He said I owed him and that's when he said it was old news and over with and didn't matter anymore. It was just something that needed to be done so he didn't get questioned about what kind of job he did on an investigation.' Baylor looked at Raveneau. 'Hugh didn't trust you. He's retiring at the end of the year and he didn't want some asshole asking questions about the case.'

'Asking him or asking someone else?'

'I don't really know, but, yeah, maybe he didn't want you finding it and then talking to other people.'

'He told you where to find it. Did he say he had been in the shelter and seen it?'

'I don't think he ever went down there. Someone else told him it was there. Something like that, and I don't know if you know but Hugh was getting paid by the professor. He was getting ten grand a month as a consultant when the professor was writing his book. That was after his divorce and it went on for years. He didn't want to fuck that up.'

'He told you that?'

Baylor nodded and this was a thing about Baylor he'd learned. You couldn't really know with him. Raveneau doubted Hugh did anything more than tell his nephew that he worked as a consultant for Lash on a book and probably told him how much he made. For years he had wanted his nephew to like and respect him.

'He was getting the money in cash and he told me it saved him.'

'When did he tell you that?'

'We were drinking at the house one night. It's all fucked up, I know, but that's what happened. So if I testify or whatever, what do I get? One thing I want is out of jail right now.'

'How did you get back in?'

'Hugh backed out of the bail deal.'

But even then there wasn't enough to take on

Hugh Neilley. Hugh wouldn't say a word. He'd lawyer-up, and the one who told him about a skull and some clothes in a bomb shelter, the one 'hanging around the professor's house', as Baylor put it, Raveneau guessed was Lindsley. Hugh could answer that if they could get him to talk.

They held off interviewing Hugh. They waited on DNA confirmation on the skull and then re-interviewed Albert Lash. Raveneau told Lash, 'Ann Coryell's skull was recovered from the bomb shelter. We believe Brandon Lindsley killed her and if you can help prove that we'll clear you. We'll put out a statement and hold a press conference and tell the world how you got framed.'

Lash looked suspicious but interested. Not a bad place to start. He answered quickly and the voice software worked well. 'What do you need?'

'It's complicated because Lindsley made an effort to frame you. He told Inspector Neilley in 2006 that you had killed her and her skull was in the bomb shelter. He told Neilley about the shelter and how to access it. Similar to how he tried to frame you with the knife and surgical saw. We're going to need Neilley to cooperate, and to get some leverage on him we want you on tape saying you were paying Hugh Neilley ten grand a month in cash as a consultant.'

'What does that do for you?'

'Hugh Neilley had his nephew remove and try to dispose of the skull and some clothes of Ann's before calling 911.'

'Have to think.'

That took another four days and then he gave them the video-taped statement they needed. Raveneau started off by telling Hugh he would need a lawyer, but that they were going to give him some information first.

'I'm not going answer any questions.'

'We don't expect you to and may not need you to. We have Ann Coryell's skull and a statement from Matt Baylor about what you asked him to do. He also told us about the ten grand payment you got each month from Lash. We took that to Lash and he gave us a statement. We'll play that for you now.'

They did that, and Hugh folded his arms over his chest and said, 'He's lying.'

'We get it, Hugh. We understand you didn't want to stop that ten grand a month from coming in. You needed the money.'

'I earned that money.'

'You were still getting it years after the book came out. Lash got sick. He didn't write anymore. What did you do to earn the money in 2010?'

'We were working on new stuff.'

'Were you? Like what? We need to know who told you about the skull and how you verified it was there.'

Two days later through his attorney Hugh relented and admitted to having been told by Brandon Lindsley about the presence of a lone skull with clothes neatly folded next to it. He was told the location of the bomb shelter and that there were two partial skeletons in there as well. He claimed he didn't believe Lindsley, so he never checked. But Hugh would have checked. He checked and then weighed having Lash arrested versus collecting ten grand in cash a month, and maybe that's why the consulting fee got paid up until Lash was moved into assisted living.

'We're going to charge you with her murder,' Raveneau told Lash and knew as he did they would never really learn what happened on the cot in the bomb shelter to Ann before she was taken out and killed. 'Lindsley helped you move her up on Mount Tamalpais. Was she too weak to walk or resist? Did you shoot her there or was it Lindsley who shot her and cut her head off? Was that to make it harder to identify her? You knew animals would deal with the rest. We'll name Lindsley as your accomplice and we know he tried to frame you later. Who shot her? Who killed her?'

'He – did.' Lash exhaled two more words. 'Sitting Bull.'

Raveneau couldn't make any sense of that, at least not then and Lash wouldn't say another word. Raveneau knew some considered Sitting Bull the last true Indian, but it was a couple more days before he figured it out and did that by reading accounts of Sitting Bull's death. That was in the weeks before the Wounded Knee massacre when Sitting Bull was vilified as the one leading the Indian 'Messiah Craze'. Raveneau read excerpts from the *New York Times* and other newspapers that described Sitting Bull as a venal and evil man shot down in a failed arrest. He was struck by two rifle balls and there were conflicting reports on the first shot. The second shot struck him in the head, but Raveneau knew it was the first that Lindsley and Lash had focused on. That bullet struck Sitting Bull on the left side in the ribs and may have passed through his heart and with it came the end of a way of being and of a people.

He saw Lash only once more and Lash kept his eyes closed and wouldn't acknowledge Raveneau's presence in the room. He died five days later before charges were brought. Raveneau knew from the doctors that Lash was going and could have asked a favor of the District Attorney to get Lash charged before he died, but he didn't. He did make sure the media knew the truth though, and Lash didn't get the obituary the press had ready. They wrote another and that one noted that Albert Lash was charged posthumously for the murder of Ann Coryell.

She was owed that. Lash and Lindsley escaped any penalty for taking her life, but her death was answered, the truth not lost. She of all would understand that.